THE LEGACY OF ANGER

As PA to successful banker Richard Lorival, Margaret Gates is the envy of her colleagues in the typing-pool. When Richard's wife dies in a tragic accident, the relationship between Richard and Margaret is put to the test. But this is the 1950s, and women like Margaret put duty before passion. Many years will pass before Margaret finds the love and happiness that she has sought for so long...

THE LEGACY OF ANGER

Sara Hylton

Severn House Large Print
London & New York

This first large print edition published 2010
in Great Britain and the USA by
SEVERN HOUSE PUBLISHERS LTD of
9-15 High Street, Sutton, Surrey, SM1 1DF.
First world regular print edition published 2008 by
Severn House Publishers Ltd., London and New York.

British Library Cataloguing in Publication Data

Hylton, Sara.
  The legacy of anger.
  1. Private secretaries--Fiction. 2. Love stories. 3. Large
  type books.
  I. Title
  823.9'14-dc22

ISBN-13: 978-0-7278-7824-3

DEAD DREAMS

Lie still in the heart
lost dream that is dead,
for new dreams will come
and tears that are shed
put sorrow to flight.
Go forward with gladness,
your troubles are sped,
better things lie ahead
than a dream that is dead.

                              Anon

Part One

One

Margaret Gates left her car on the sloping driveway in front of the house, aware that her mother
was standing impatiently at the open door. She
was late home and her mother hated to be late
for her WI meeting.

'You're late,' her mother complained as soon
as Margaret was within earshot. 'You know I
hate being late and I promised we'd pick Mrs
Jarvis up on the way.'

'Get in the car, Mother. I'm sorry I'm late but
my boss is home now and we're very busy.'

Her mother plonked herself into the front seat
with a huff and Margaret wished she'd keep
quiet about her employer and her job, but not to
be deterred her mother said, 'Doesn't he realize
you have a home to go to and a life outside your
job?'

'Well, of course he does. He's a very considerate employer.'

Margaret Gates had worked for Richard
Lorival for twelve years and she'd been in love
with him for almost all of that time. He liked her
– she was efficient and loyal – but that was as
far as his feelings for her went. She knew he
could never love her, but the pleasure she got

from serving him was sufficient.

'I liked it much better when you worked for him at the bank. That was normal.'

'Well, I like it now, working for him at home. I don't have to drive in the evening traffic or rely on the train and there are girls at the bank who envy what I'm doing and wish they were in my place. Where exactly does Mrs Jarvis live?'

'There, the second house. She's waiting at the door, probably thinking we've forgotten her.'

Margaret opened the door and ushered Mrs Jarvis into the back seat while her mother turned around to say, 'Did you think we'd forgotten you?'

'Well, I was beginning to wonder.'

'It's Margaret and that job of hers.'

For the rest of the journey Mrs Gates complained to Mrs Jarvis that Margaret had been late arriving home, then explained a little more about the job she did and her employer until Mrs Jarvis said, 'How unusual to work privately for a banker, Margaret. I always thought you worked in the City.'

'I did at one time, but things are just easier this way,' Margaret explained, trying to hide her irritation. 'Here we are, it looks like being a busy meeting. What time shall I pick you and Mrs Jarvis up, Mother?'

'Oh, I'm sure you don't need to bother, dear, somebody will run us home.'

'You're sure?'

'Quite sure. I imagine you've brought work home, you invariably do.'

10

Margaret was looking forward to having the house to herself for a short while. Her mother was always curious about the work she brought home but on this occasion she would be doubly so.

It was not often her employer's wife visited Margaret in her office but this afternoon she had surprised her by entering the room just as Margaret was about to eat her lunch. She was smiling, holding a sheaf of papers in her hand when she began apologizing profusely for inter-rupting Margaret's lunch.

'It's the dinner party at the beginning of December, Miss Gates, my husband says the usual people will be invited but I can't exactly remember all of them. I was wondering if you could help me out?'

'Yes, Mrs Lorival, I'm sure I can.'

'Well, here are the invitation cards and a partial list from last year. I expect you'll be familiar with all of them, and I'm sure Richard intends you to join us as usual.'

'Thank you, Mrs Lorival, I shall be delighted.'

'I'll leave them with you then. I hadn't realized how quickly the Christmas festivities were upon us, it's probably because we've spent more time abroad this year. Thank you once again.'

With a bright smile she was gone, and Mar-garet was looking down at the papers and the invitation cards. She read through the list care-fully, realizing that she knew all the guests from her time at the bank and thinking that this was the one real perk that she had above the other girls. She made a mental note of those names missing from the list as she sat down in front of the fire with the invitation cards at her feet. She thought whimsically about the four dresses hanging in her wardrobe, one bought for each dinner party she'd attended since she'd come to work at the Lorivals' house, all of them more expensive than she could really afford, and all of them worn only once.

When her mother saw the dresses she'd asked how much they'd cost and Margaret had halved the price she'd paid for them. Her mother thought the few shops in the High Street were too expensive and she never ever shopped in the city.

Nobody would notice if she wore one of them again; they'd all been designed to be smart but discreet, not to be remembered for their threat to outdo anything any of the other women would be wearing. Her only real remembrance of the previous parties was Mr Lorival's smile and his quick words of praise for her work and the fact that she looked charming.

Laying aside her work, Margaret went up to her bedroom and flung open her wardrobe door to look at the four dresses hung side by side in shades of beige, black, navy and magenta. The magenta had been a mistake, she'd felt the colour didn't really suit her, and blonde Mrs Carling was wearing exactly the same shade.

Some of the women might remember if she wore one of them again, but they wouldn't really care. After all, they were the wives of the high-flyers, and she was merely Mr Lorival's secretary. All the same, some punishing sense of pride made her feel she owed it to herself to buy something new.

Most of the girls working at the bank envied her. They glamorized her job, fancied her boss and were happy to read more into it than there was. It suited Margaret for them to think that way. It gave her a sort of boost and there was no harm in it.

She went back downstairs and started to address the cards.

Mrs Lorival employed outside caterers who prepared the food and waited at the table. Everything was always beautifully done and Olivia Lorival accepted her guests' words of praise with her usual beautiful smile and shy depreciation.

After the meal they invariably drifted into the drawing room and Olivia was asked to play the piano for them. Later they wandered around the house looking at the pictures she had painted and then soon after midnight they left. Margaret was always the last one to leave after reassuring herself that nobody had left anything behind, that the house was back to its pristine condition and that she'd done her best.

She'd leave with her boss's warm thanks ringing in her ears, although Mrs Lorival by this time had wished her goodnight and retired to her room.

Mr Lorival would smile gently, saying, 'She's

really quite exhausted. An evening like this isn't really Olivia's scene. She'd much prefer there to be just the two of us or a quiet table in some discreet restaurant.'

She looked at the clock when she heard her mother's key in the door. The meeting was over early and looking down in some dismay Margaret attempted to gather the envelopes and cards together but she was too late. Her mother stood in the doorway eyeing the clutter, then said sharply, 'I can see you've brought plenty of work home.'

'Nothing much, Mother, just invitation cards for the Christmas dinner party.'

'Why do you have to do them, she's the hostess surely?'

'And I'm Mr Lorival's secretary, it's part of my job.'

'It's got nothing to do with banking.'

'Oh, Mother, I'm his PA. I'm expected to do all sorts of things outside banking, like calling to bring his daughter home from boarding school and booking his plane tickets.'

'Are you invited to this dinner party?'

'Yes, of course.'

'By him?'

'Mrs Lorival invited me.'

'There are some dresses upstairs that you've worn only once. I suppose you'll be adding to them?'

'Well, what else do I spend my money on? And I have to look right for every event.'

Her mother sat down wearily on the nearest

chair. 'Oh, Margaret, I don't care about your spending your own money, but I was happier when you worked in the City, mixed with a lot of women of your own age and worked civilized, ordinary hours. Now I don't like what's happening to you.'

'What exactly is happening to me, Mother?' she asked, trying to hide her irritation at what she knew was coming next.

'You're besotted with him and he's besotted with her. You're a nice-looking girl with a good brain, you could find some nice man who's unattached instead of working for a man who doesn't really know you're there.'

'But he does know I'm there, Mother, he relies on me, I'm always there when he wants me and I'm doing what I want to do. Now can we drop the subject, Mother? How did the meeting go?'

'Like every other meeting. I'm going to make myself a cup of tea and go to bed, I can see it's no use my trying to drum some sense into your head.'

'No, Mother, it isn't. Goodnight.'

Two

Richard Lorival was already at his desk when Margaret arrived at his house the next morning, and after a smiling good morning he said, 'My wife tells me you took home the invitation cards for the dinner party?'

'Yes, I attended to them and I've posted them off this morning.'

'Good, my wife has invited you of course?'

'Yes thank you, Mr Lorival.'

'She was feeling rather guilty that she'd handed them over to you but she's really very anxious at the moment to finish a painting she's promised. I hope you didn't mind.'

'Of course not, it's part of my job.'

'But is it?'

'I think so, since I came to work for you privately.'

He smiled, the charming appreciative smile that made a slave of her heart, then he said cheerfully, 'What would I do without you?'

Get another secretary, thought Margaret angrily. Some other woman who would think that he was wonderful and that she was incredibly lucky to be working for him. Some other foolish woman like herself.

In her studio at the top of the house Olivia surveyed the picture she was painting of an old manor house set high up on the Cumbria fells. The painting was going well. She had captured the beauty of the gentle fell country and its backdrop of Lakeland mountain. She had no doubt that the family would be pleased with it.

She turned with a smile at the opening of the studio door and then Richard was there, smiling his delight as he regarded her work.

'It's going well, Richard, don't you think?' she asked softly.

'It's beautiful, darling. All your work is beautiful.'

She smiled, knowing full well that if it had been less than perfect Richard wouldn't have said so.

'Margaret got the invitation cards done and she's posted them off this morning. Do you want her to help with anything else?'

'Not really, darling. I've asked the same caterers as last year since we couldn't fault them, and the same people will be coming.'

'It's good of you to bother, darling, I know something like this is not really your scene ... We'll be picking Vanessa up from school in a few weeks. I suppose she'll enjoy decorating the house.'

'A few weeks, Richard, so soon!'

'Christmas holidays, Olivia.'

'Yes, of course, but I doubt if the painting will be finished. I remember that last year it took the entire day – wasn't there the school concert and

17

tea afterwards?'

'Well yes, but the parents are expected to be there, dear.'

'Oh, Richard, I'm hopeless I know, but couldn't you go, couldn't you invite Miss Gates to go with you? Vanessa won't mind and you can see how I'm fixed. I did promise this painting for Christmas and I can't let them down. They're paying an awful lot of money for it, Richard.'

'Well, it looks almost finished to me.'

'Darling, of course it isn't finished. I know what still needs to be done. Can't you mention it to Miss Gates? She might enjoy it, having lunch on the way, listening to the concert. It was quite good last year.'

'Well, I don't know, I'm sure she has other things to do...'

'What about your sister then? Surely she would go with you.'

'Definitely not Mina, Olivia. She's already accused me of being unfair to Vanessa, I don't want any more arguments with Mina.'

'I'm sure she doesn't mean it. She was probably a little envious about our cruise and the villa in Amalfi.'

Richard was well aware that he had already lost the argument but when he returned to his office he was reluctant to ask his secretary to take his wife's place at the school concert. He knew that his sister despaired of them as parents; he didn't know how his secretary assessed them.

He'd talk to Olivia again, they'd get the dinner party over first then when it was the success he knew it would be they'd talk about Vanessa again.

On the day of the dinner party Margaret was told that she could get off home after lunch to get ready and that Richard would expect to see her again around seven o'clock.

That was when she decided to take a look in Marcello's, a new and very expensive shop in the next town. It was the sort of shop where only one dress adorned the window, several pairs of dressy shoes and a large hat, a confection of tulle and gently shaded flowers.

She sneaked round the large room while the assistants chatted to another woman and a younger girl, evidently with a wedding in mind, which gave Margaret time to realize that everything would be expensive and probably far too ornate.

Eventually one of the assistants approached her to ask if she could help and Margaret said with as much indifference as she could muster that she was attending a dinner party, in the evening, a low-key affair, but she wondered if they had anything that might be suitable.

The woman was quick to produce chiffons and lamé, luxuriously beaded evening gowns, but Margaret shook her head at each and every one of them. Then another assistant appeared, an older woman, who declared, 'No no, these are not suitable for madam. I know exactly what she is looking for, something discreet, something exclusive and dignified.'

Then came a dress which Margaret knew was right for her, but the price took her breath away and she said hastily, 'The dress is lovely, but far too expensive. I'm sorry to have wasted your time.'

'We've nothing else to do, madam, it's what we're here for,' the assistant said. 'But why not try it on just to convince yourself that you are right to turn away?'

Margaret tried half-heartedly to resist, but allowed them to remove her dress and help her into the gown, which felt smooth and elegant against her skin. When she looked in the mirror she felt immediately that she had been transformed into another being, glamorous and remote, so that in the next half-hour she bought shoes to match and saw four months' salary disappear into thin air.

She knew she would have to dig deep into her savings and her immediate worry was how to smuggle the dress into the house without her mother seeing the name on the exclusive wrappings. Marcello's was the shop young brides were eager to bankrupt their parents for. The women who would be attending the dinner party could afford to shop there, but not Margaret Gates, whose father had worked in the Transport Office and whose mother had worked as a clerk in the doctor's surgery. Good, respectable people, honest as the day was long, but not rich enough to open Marcello's door to look at what was inside.

She could hear her mother tinkering about in the kitchen when she got home, so she darted upstairs without a backward glance, until in the next moment her mother called out, 'Is that you, Margaret? You're early. I don't suppose you want much to eat with that party going on later?'

'No, Mother, I don't.'

She could hear her mother climbing the stairs so she hastily thrust her purchases in the wardrobe and closed the door sharply behind them, then she took off her coat and laid it on the bed just as her mother entered the room.

'I thought he'd let you off home early today. Did you come straight home?'

'No, I had one or two things to get in the village and I saw one or two people I chatted to.'

'So, what are you wearing this evening, did you get something new or are you being sensible and wearing one of the others?'

'I'll come and show you how I look when I'm ready. Mother.'

'That can only mean you've been spending money.'

As they drank their tea Margaret was aware of her mother's eyes constantly upon her, but she made herself read the morning paper, occasionally commenting on something or other until her mother said, 'I suppose you'll be late home?'

'I don't know, Mother. Obviously I wait to see if there's anything for me to do before I leave.'

'I thought they had outside help?'

'They do, but they don't know the house,

21

where things go, and they invariably disturb something.'

'Why doesn't she do the catering? She has a housekeeper and that young girl, do either of them do anything?'

'Yes, I'm sure they do.'

'But not as much as you.'

'I don't do very much. I arrive with the other guests, and come home soon after they leave.'

'What do you talk about? You don't know them well.'

'The men talk business; the women chat about their clothes, their holidays, Christmas and their families.'

'Well, you don't go to shows, there was that holiday we spent in Torquay and we're not exactly pushing the boat out for Christmas so you have to admit your conversation's going to be very limited.'

'Yes, Mother, it is, but I get by. They don't expect me to hog the conversation, I leave it to the others, and when I do talk I hope I sound intelligent and reasonably educated.'

'You did very well at school.'

Margaret didn't answer. The fact that she'd done well at school was irrelevant. She'd probably done better than many of the women the Lorivals would be entertaining but they'd all married well. For most of them education had been a doorway to a lucrative marriage rather than a means of earning a living. She couldn't expect her mother to understand.

'Are you going out this evening, Mother?' she

asked, hoping to change the subject.

'No. What time do you expect to be home?'

'I'm not sure, but you mustn't wait up for me.'

The dress was beautiful, she thought, surveying herself in the long Cheval mirror. Dark brown hair and hazel eyes were hardly out of the ordinary, but the warm beige of the dress somehow or other brought a warmer glow into her hair and she did have a good figure. The snakeskin shoes were the exact colour of the dress and the handbag was another exact match. She shuddered to think how much they had cost her; if she told her mother only half she would be horrified.

Mrs Gates stood in the hall watching her walk down the stairs and after sniffing derisively she went into the living room, closing the door sharply behind her.

Snatching up her best coat from the hall wardrobe Margaret opened the door and stood for a few minutes looking at her mother, whose head was buried in the evening paper.

'Well, Mother, do you like my dress?' she asked softly.

For a long moment her mother stared at her, then she said resignedly, 'I've never seen you looking prettier, but for what, I ask myself. How much did that lot cost you?'

'It doesn't matter, Mother. It's the money I work for; I shouldn't be asked to account for it. I see that you go nothing short.'

'It's not the clothes, Margaret, nor the money, it's what it's all for. Tomorrow they'll go back in the wardrobe with the others and I don't suppose he'll even remember what you wore tonight.'

'Mother, if you knew Mr Lorival you'd like him. I don't feel like an employee, I feel like a friend, I never felt like that in the big office at the bank.'

'And how does his wife treat you?'

'Well, I hardly ever see her. She's very nice, but she's busy painting her pictures, we really don't need to come into contact with each other.'

Her mother sighed. It was really no use their arguing about it; she'd never win. At the same time, however, she felt increasingly unhappy with the situation.

Margaret was the first to arrive, in case her help was needed. The caterers' large white van stood at the side of the house and already the place was a hive of activity with pristinely-attired waiters dashing here there and everywhere, while others set out cutlery and glasses on the long table already decorated with holly and Christmas roses.

She went into her office to hang up her coat and it was only a few minutes later when Richard Lorival stuck his head round the door and smiled at her across the room.

'I thought you'd be the first to arrive, Margaret,' he said. 'I told Olivia if she needed any help you'd be here. You're looking very nice, extremely elegant.'

Margaret blushed but in the next minute he

said, 'Perhaps I'd better go upstairs to see if she needs any help, she's only just come out of her studio.'

Studio or no studio, Olivia would appear radiant and beautiful in whatever she had chosen to wear. Throughout the evening she would shine like a beacon, accepting praise and flattery with charming diffidence, and Richard would stand beside her, worshipping and grateful.

The guests were beginning to arrive now, she could hear their voices as the butler from the catering firm greeted them in the hall. He would usher them into the drawing room and waiters would ask their preferences for drinks, then Richard and Olivia would arrive and the evening would begin.

Margaret felt no urgency to join the others, but minutes later the door opened and Richard was entering the room with a man Margaret already knew from the bank. He shook her warmly by the hand, saying, 'I thought you'd be joining us Miss Gates, and looking extremely elegant, if I may say so.'

Richard smiled. 'Join the others, Margaret, I just want to show Mr Carnaby one or two things I've been working on before he decides he simply wants to enjoy himself.'

They were the same people she'd met before, who greeted her graciously, and from across the room she saw that Olivia was wearing lilac, and looking like some celestial being from another planet.

One of the younger wives approached her, saying, 'I thought it would be unusual if you weren't invited, Miss Gates – or may I call you Margaret?'

'Oh, Margaret please, I remember you from last year. Mrs Simpkin, isn't it?'

'Sophie, darling. This is only my second visit, we've just crawled on to the band wagon.' Margaret smiled politely, and Sophie went on, 'I ask myself sometimes if we'll ever be in the position to throw a "do" like this for the High-Ups, will Kevin ever be able to filch one of the secretaries from the bank.'

'I'm sure he will, he's highly thought of.'

'Nice of you to say so, dear. Olivia's looking super as usual, do you see much of her working here?'

'Very little actually. She has her studio up-stairs and we work in the office on the ground floor. She is looking very beautiful, isn't she? That colour would do very little for me.'

'Or me. They have a daughter don't they?'

'Yes, Vanessa. She's away at school.'

'Is she like her mother?'

'No, not at all. She's tall with auburn hair, but she's pretty. At the moment she's a schoolgirl without make-up, in school uniform and little else.'

'I'm sure Richard would like her to be like her mother.'

'I don't know. He doesn't discuss her with me.'

'I must say I like your dress, that's another

colour that does nothing for me.'

That was the moment another woman joined them and this time, greeting Margaret, she said, 'Everything is so perfectly arranged. Do you have any hand in it, Miss Gates?'

'Actually no. Mrs Lorival sees to the caterers and all that.'

'Well, my husband and I always enjoy it. Olivia always looks so beautiful, puts me in the shade completely. Some friends of ours met them on a cruise liner, she was the envy of everybody on board, and yet they said she hadn't been very well.'

Margaret smiled briefly. 'She's fully recovered now, Mrs Eastman. Please excuse me, I have to see if there is anything I can do to help.'

She knew that Mrs Eastman was an inveterate gossip and the proof came much later when she overheard a remark made by her to another lady about Margaret's own attire. She shouldn't have stayed to listen but the words were too tempting to walk away from them.

In something resembling a stage whisper, Mrs Eastman was saying, 'If I wasn't entirely convinced that Richard Lorival wasn't completely besotted with his wife I'd say there was something going on there.'

'Whatever do you mean?'

'His secretary. That dress she's wearing, I can hardly think a secretary's salary would stretch to something like that.'

'She's probably very well paid.'

'Oh, I've no doubt, but that dress. I know how

27

much it cost because I looked at it myself.'

Mrs Turnbull smiled and moved away. No doubt she knew Mrs Eastman's reputation but Margaret didn't really know whether to be incensed or flattered.

The dinner party had been its usual success and now the guests were departing while Olivia and Richard stood together to receive their praise. In the dining room the caterers were clearing up ready for departure and Richard made it his business to thank them for what he called a most splendid evening.

Having collected her coat from the office, Margaret came back into the hall to find Olivia standing at the door looking strangely absent and Margaret asked if there was anything she could do before she went home.

She was met with Olivia's sweet, faraway smile before she said, 'No thank you, Miss Gates, everything is being taken care of. Have a safe journey home.'

'Thank you, Mrs Lorival, the evening has been wonderful.'

She received another charming smile then Olivia's husband was shaking her hand and saying, 'You can have a lie-in tomorrow, Margaret, it's Saturday. I'll see you on Monday morning.'

It had taken him months to call her Margaret but from his wife it was still Miss Gates.

She hoped her mother was asleep; time enough tomorrow to tell her about the evening, and no doubt to receive her usual criticisms.

Three

From the office window Richard watched Margaret's arrival on Monday morning and he smiled as he met her eyes. She was always punctual. He really was very lucky to have her at his house – that she already lived in the village had been a bonus – but now he was unsure how she would receive another task he was presenting her with.

As she took her place at her desk he walked over to stand looking down on her, his expression cautious before he said, 'Margaret, if all this is inconvenient please say so, but I have a very big favour to ask of you.'

She looked at him questioningly and he went on, 'You know Vanessa will be coming home for Christmas and we normally collect her at the school and stay for the closing concert. Unfortunately, this year things are rather different. Olivia has promised to finish the picture she's painting and we were rather wondering if you might come to our rescue.'

'You want me to go for Vanessa, Mr Lorival? Of course I will.'

'No, I was wondering if you will accompany me. Vanessa knows you and they know you at the school. We could have lunch at a very nice hotel Olivia and I like on the way, and you will enjoy the school concert. They have their own orchestra and some of the girls are very talented – not, I'm afraid, Vanessa – but am I asking too much?'

'Oh no, Mr Lorival, I shall be delighted to go.'

'Well, it's on Wednesday, we'll get away around ten in the morning as it is some distance away, and we'll probably get home around eight in the evening. The school lays on afternoon tea and then everybody tries to get away soon afterwards.'

Margaret's first thoughts were what she should tell her mother. Doing her job was one thing; too much involvement in a purely private matter was another. Her mother would picture all sorts of things, the long drive to the school and lunch where they would be seen together, then there would be the school, the teachers and the talk among the staff about Vanessa's father and his secretary. No amount of reassurance on her part would convince her mother that that was all there would ever be to their relationship.

She didn't care. She wanted to go with him to Vanessa's school, just the two of them like a couple, picking their daughter up from school, and then the day would be over. Richard and Vanessa would come home to Olivia and she would be greeted with her mother's woeful lecture on her stupidity.

'Don't look so worried,' Richard said with a smile. 'You have my wife's blessing. Actually it was Olivia's suggestion.'

30

'In that case, Mr Lorival, I shall be pleased to come.'

With a smile of relief, he said, 'Why do you never call me Richard? We've worked together for a long time, Margaret.'

'I would never have called you Richard in the office.'

'No, but that was a long time ago. We're in rather a different situation here, don't you think?'

She smiled. 'Perhaps. Will you want me to drive here on Wednesday morning or will you pick me up at home?'

'Oh, I'll pick you up at home, I've never actually met your mother, you can introduce us, let her see that I'm quite respectable.'

'I'm sure she's never doubted it.'

'Well, that's all fixed up then.' He smiled and left the room, leaving Margaret to try and ignore the butterflies in her stomach and get back to work.

Richard shook hands with Mrs Gates, favoured her with his most charming smile and enquired after her health in quite dreadful weather. He hoped she was looking forward to Christmas and wished her all the very best, then he was holding the car door open for Margaret and they were driving away.

Margaret heaved a sigh of relief. Their conversation had been brief, giving no time at all for her mother to show her disapproval, and now she could look forward to her day alone with

Richard. She thought to herself, This is what it would be like if I was his wife, driving off to pick up our daughter from school, bring her home to spend Christmas together in a beautiful house where there would be laughter and Christmas festivities.

For today at least she could dream, and indeed it seemed that everything was going right. A pale wintry sun shone down on rain-soaked fields and leafless trees and the morning traffic was light.

Over an excellent lunch Richard talked about his work, his schooldays but most of all he talked about Olivia, their meeting in their early twenties, their marriage, and how much he loved her. After a while he said regretfully, 'I'm boring you, Margaret. Why don't we talk about you for a change?'

'I'm sure your life has been far more interesting.'

'Have you ever travelled abroad?'

'I went to Paris when I was nineteen, since then all my holidays have been spent with my mother in England, after my father died.'

'Next summer we'll invite you to spend time at our villa in Italy, we can work from there just as well as from home. Will you be able to come?'

'It would be wonderful if I could.'

'Well, we'll talk about it some more nearer the time. Vanessa will be there and perhaps we'll ask her to bring one of her school friends.'

He was in a high good humour. They had

enjoyed a bottle of Riesling and what yesterday might have seemed an impossible pipe dream today became a reality.

Their arrival at the school caused no raised eyebrows. The staff had met her before, knew that she was his secretary, and he'd been quick to explain that Olivia was busy finishing her picture. Vanessa greeted them with a smile, her father hugged her and after a few moments she said, 'Why isn't Mummy with you?'

He explained about the picture and Margaret didn't miss the deprecating smile on his daughter's face. It seemed to her then that Vanessa had heard it all before.

They took their places in the hall to hear the school's orchestra, the choir and the usual selection of Christmas carols. Richard whispered, 'Vanessa is not a performer, although her mother always hoped she would be. She's more like me, likes tennis and horses. I'm sure we both feel we've let her mother down rather badly.'

Stung to retort Margaret said, 'It would be a very dull world if we were all alike and thought alike.'

He smiled. 'I'm sure you're right, but I really do wish Vanessa had some of her mother's talent.'

Later in the afternoon they enjoyed the excellent tea the school had laid on and they were being introduced to Sally Fielding, Vanessa's friend, and her family.

The Fieldings were friendly and were quick to ask if Vanessa would be able to visit them during the long school holidays, enabling Richard to issue his invitation for Sally to spend time in Italy, causing both Sally and Vanessa to enthuse about it ecstatically.

After good wishes had been exchanged all round they were heading for the car and Margaret said, 'Sit in front with your father, Vanessa. I'm quite happy in the back.'

But Vanessa was already opening the rear door and with a little smile she said, 'I always sit in the back, I don't mind.'

Somehow or other the journey home seemed to lack the relaxed atmosphere of their journey out. Vanessa sat in silence and Richard seemed indisposed to talk. At last, almost by way of apology, he said, 'The frost has come down early this evening, Margaret. I need to concentrate on my driving.'

'Of course,' she murmured, and indeed the fields were now white with frost and a thin mist hovered ominously over distant views.

Richard deposited her safely at her front door just before nine o'clock and after thanking him for what she termed a most delightful day she turned to Vanessa, still sitting rigidly in the rear seat, and said, 'I might want some help in the office one afternoon, Vanessa. You seemed to enjoy it the last time.'

Vanessa smiled without saying whether she would help out or not, and it would seem Margaret had to be content with that.

Her mother had heard the car and was in the kitchen making tea when she let herself into the house.

'Well,' she demanded, 'I suppose you've enjoyed your day. What had the daughter to say when her mother wasn't with you?'

'I'm sure she understood, Mother. The school concert was excellent, everybody enjoyed it.'

'Aye, well, with the school fees he'll be paying, you can expect the best.'

'Now that you've met Mr Lorival, Mother, what have you to say about him?'

'That he's charming. I expected that, it's the effect his charm has on you that's worrying me.'

'You'd have the same thing to say about any man I happened to be working for.'

'But it's different, Margaret, like I've said many times, if you were working in a big office with other girls and other men it wouldn't worry me. It's all too intimate, in his house, it's too cosy.'

'With his wife there and now his daughter too. Come on, Mother be honest. Surely you liked him?'

'Like I've said, he had all the charm I expected, and the looks. This is where I want it to stop.'

It was no use. She'd never make her mother change her mind so she took hold of the tea trolley and pushed it into the living room. She wanted an end to the conversation so picking up the morning newspaper she buried her head in it while her mother sat morosely in front of the fire occasionally looking up to stare at her with a worried frown.

Margaret was not reading the paper, she was thinking about the days leading up to Christmas. She would hear people visiting, the sound of their voices and laughter and Olivia would be there, gracious and beautiful, and Vanessa would come into her office with that resigned, cynical smile that was far too old for her years. Margaret had a mother who was too involved; Vanessa had a mother who was too distant.

Work in the office was hectic leading up to Christmas and Vanessa seemed happy to help with folding letters and sealing an avalanche of envelopes, then two days before Christmas Olivia appeared in Margaret's office with a large bunch of carnations and a beautifully wrapped gift.

'My husband had to go into the City this morning, Miss Gates,' she explained, 'but he asked me to give you these. The flowers are for your mother, the gift is for you in acknowledgement of your work for him. He's told me to tell you to take a week off and he'll see you in the New Year. Christmas is so hectic, isn't it, and Vanessa is demanding to go shopping and other things.'

'Thank you, Mrs Lorival. I bought you and Mr Lorival this and another for Vanessa. Shall I leave them here or give them to you now?'

'Oh, that's very kind of you, we'll put them under the tree. Vanessa insisted she must have a tree so we've brought one in from the garden. I expect all the needles will cover the carpet but decorating it has given her something to do.'

After she had gone Margaret went to the table where Olivia had left the flowers and the small parcel, and picking it up she looked down at it idly. It was wrapped in gold foil, adorned with a delicate gardenia, and even though it was small Margaret assumed that it would be expensive. Last year it had been a Royal Doulton figurine which took pride of place on her dressing table. This year she could only guess at the parcel's contents.

She was putting her coat on later that afternoon when Vanessa appeared and after thanking her for her present she sat down in her father's chair and with a bright smile said, 'Do you have a Christmas tree, Miss Gates?'

'Not for many years. Will you please call me Margaret? Miss Gates makes me feel like your granny.'

'Do you think he meant it when my father said he'd invite Sally to spend time with us in Italy?'

'If he said so, I'm sure he meant it.'

'You like him, don't you?'

'He's very nice and very easy to work for. I've worked for men I haven't liked nearly as much.'

'I suppose my mother's lucky really to be working for herself. I'm no good at art and I'm not a musician either, I sometimes wonder what I'll be good for.'

'Well, I can't paint for toffee and I'm no musician, but I can earn my own living and you will too one day.'

'In the meantime they don't really know what

to do with me, do they?'

'Vanessa, you really mustn't think like that. They love you very much and are very proud of you.'

'Not really. You're just cheering me up.'

'Well, of course I'm not! We can't all be alike or think alike.'

'I suppose not.'

'What do you want to do when you leave school?'

'I don't really know. Marry a rich man perhaps, and travel the world.' She laughed. 'I've shocked you, haven't I?'

'Are you trying to shock me?'

She laughed. 'When I say things like that to my aunt Mina she laughs and calls me a minx. If I said them to Mother she'd say I was being silly.'

'What's happening here over Christmas?'

'Oh, we're invited out to dinner with friends and one or two of them are coming here. It's all going to be frightfully boring because there's nobody of my age. Sally Fielding told me they were going to the circus and to a pantomime. I've never been to either of those. Mother would hate it.'

'Does your friend have brothers and sisters?'

'Yes, lots of them.'

'That does make a difference, Vanessa.'

'Yes, I suppose it does.'

Idling to the desk, Vanessa picked up the gold-wrapped gift. 'Is this what Dad's bought you?'

'Yes, the flowers are for my mother, the

smaller one is for me.'

'And I'll bet that's some sort of jewellery. It couldn't be anything else in such a small package.'

'Well, I'm not going to open it until Christmas morning, so I'll have to wait and see.'

'You'll tell me if I'm right though, won't you?'

'Of course.'

'Will you be going with Father to take me back to school? Mother'll find some excuse not to go, I'm sure.'

'Your father hasn't discussed it with me, Vanessa, I'm sure your mother will want to go.'

'Can't you find me something to do?' Vanessa asked plaintively, and Margaret said, 'Well, I'm going home now, Vanessa, all work suspended until the New Year. Why don't you ask Mrs Peterson if there's something you can do for her?'

'Oh, she likes the kitchen to herself. I always feel I'm being a nuisance when I go in there.'

'I'm sure your mother'll think of something.'

'Oh sure, I can sit and watch her paint or listen to her play the piano. I wish I liked the things she does but I don't. Do you like the things your mother likes?'

'We don't really have much in common either, but we get along, we live in the same house so we have to.'

'When I'm older I don't intend to live with my parents. I'll get a job and live on my own or with some other girls in some flat or other!'

'Have you talked to your father about it?'

'No, it's too soon, but I will.'

It was a holiday Margaret could have done without. A week when she would get under her mother's feet and when her mother would constantly bemoan the fact that she didn't need help to prepare Christmas festivities for the two of them and that it was all a waste of time anyway. So Margaret went to the shops and to the library and it was on such a morning she met Vanessa strolling along the village street with her eyes on the ground and looking totally dejected.

'Why don't we have coffee and scones in the café?' she asked with a smile. 'Anything to get us out of this cold wind.'

Vanessa accepted and Margaret got the distinct impression that the girl was feeling as superfluous as she felt herself.

After a long silence she asked, 'Well, are you ready for Christmas, Vanessa? I suppose there'll be lots of parties?'

'Parties?'

'Well yes, you'll have visitors and didn't you say your cousin Alex might come?'

'He's not coming, he's going to Austria. His parents are coming on Christmas Day and going home on Boxing Day.'

'Did your mother finish her picture?'

'Yes, they came for it yesterday, they thought it was wonderful.'

'I'm so glad.'

'Mummy's talking about going to Italy in the

New Year, she says she hates January and I'll be back at school.'

'What has your father got to say about it?'

'Oh, he'll go along with whatever Mummy wants.'

'What about work?'

'Perhaps he'll ask you to go with them, he can work there just as well as here I suppose.'

Margaret was taken aback. Vanessa must have listened to her parents' conversation but she couldn't visualize spending January in Italy. Her mother would think she was insane.

'Please don't tell Daddy I've told you all this,' Vanessa said plaintively. 'Perhaps they won't go, perhaps they'll wait for the spring.'

'Yes, that would be better.'

Four

The subject surfaced on Christmas afternoon and immediately Aunt Mina said, 'Italy isn't guaranteed to be warm in January. We spent some time in Rome in the winter and we might as well have been here.' Her husband gave her a warning glance, but undeterred she went on: 'Can you really afford to spend so much time out of the country, Richard? What about your job?'

'I work from home; I can work there equally as well as here.'

'And what about your secretary, surely it's not going to work for her?'

'Margaret is very adaptable.'

'All the same, Italy in January sounds silly to me. Italy isn't Egypt, surely you can see that Olivia?'

'The villa is beautiful, I paint better there than I do here and I have several commissions I need to think about.'

'They're having snow in Austria,' Nigel said to change the subject. 'Alex will be full of it when he gets home.'

'One expects snow in Austria,' his wife said sharply. 'We were talking about Italy, they get it there too.'

'Not perhaps in that part of Italy,' Nigel persisted.

'Well, it won't bother you, will it Vanessa?' her father said with a smile. 'You'll be back at school.'

'If you go to Italy in the summer you said I could invite Sally. Can I?'

'Oh, I'm sure you can, she's a very nice girl. What do you think, darling?' he said, addressing his wife.

Olivia nodded, but looking at her face, Mina had the distinct impression that her thoughts were miles away, probably in Italy, and on the pictures she expected to paint there.

It was so easy for Vanessa to close her ears to the arguments that went on around the dinner table, she was used to them. She didn't want to look at her aunt's accusing expression or her father's exasperation. While they argued she thought about Sally, no doubt enjoying what Vanessa thought of as a real Christmas, not this hotchpotch of conflicting emotions that occurred so frequently.

She had to collect her thoughts when her aunt asked, 'When are you due back at school, Vanessa?'

'Around the fourth of January.'

'And will your parents be taking you as usual?'

'Well of course we shall,' her father answered tetchily.

'Well, you didn't go to bring her here – at least, Olivia didn't go.'

'Does it matter, Mina? Olivia was busy so I went with Miss Gates.'

'Hardly a secretary's job, I wouldn't have thought.'

'Very much a secretary's job to do what is required of her.'

'Oh well, if you say so, Richard,' Mina said with a sneer.

'Can we change the subject? I'm getting rather tired of these frequent inquisitions,' Richard said, exasperated.

'Yes, give it a rest old girl,' Nigel said. 'Why do you two need these arguments? I'm beginning to think that we should have gone abroad for Christmas...'

'Christmas is for families,' Mina said sharply.

'Even this disjointed family,' Richard said dryly.

When Margaret Gates returned to work in early January she found Vanessa in the hall surrounded by her luggage and parcels containing the goodies Mrs Peterson had packed for her. She was wearing her school uniform and had been ready to leave for quite some time.

'I hadn't realized you were leaving today,' Margaret said with a smile.

Vanessa followed her into her office and perched on the edge of her desk. 'Did you have a nice Christmas?' she asked.

'Quite nice, nothing exciting. How about you?'

'Yes, Aunt Mina and Uncle Nigel came, but not Alex, he was abroad. Do you know that my parents are going to Italy? They decided over Christmas.'

'No, Vanessa, when are they going?'

'Oh, soon, you'll be hearing about it.'

At that moment Richard looked at them from the doorway, saying, 'Happy New Year, Margaret. Nice holiday?'

'Yes, thank you. And thank you so much for the beautiful brooch' – she indicated the swirling art nouveau flower pinned discreetly to her lapel – 'it was very generous of you.'

Vanessa raised an eyebrow and Margaret immediately regretted bringing it up.

'Oh, think nothing of it. A reward for all your hard work. I hope you like it? Olivia chose it, of course...'

Margaret's heart sank. Of course Olivia had chosen it. And of course it meant nothing to him.

'We're ready to leave now, Vanessa. I'll see you in the morning, Margaret. I've left a file of instructions and other matters for you to look at, we'll talk about them in the morning.'

Margaret watched them leave from the window, Olivia wrapped in her furs while Richard opened the front door of the car for her, and Vanessa throwing her luggage in the back seat in what could only be termed as a somewhat sulky manner. She absentmindedly removed the brooch from her blouse.

Later in the morning when Mrs Peterson brought her coffee they exchanged New Year greetings and Mrs Peterson said, 'They won't be sorry it's over for another year. Mr Lorival and his sister are hardly good friends.'

'Isn't it all rather good humoured?'

'Hardly. It's Mrs Lorival she doesn't really like, she makes it obvious.'

'But not to Mrs Lorival, surely?'

'Does anything register with her? I doubt it.'

'Vanessa said something about them going to Italy. Do you know anything, Mrs Peterson?'

'Well, only in passin'. At this time of year, I ask you, why are they so restless?'

Margaret shook her head, and Mrs Peterson said, 'How'll it affect you, him there and you here?'

Margaret didn't have the answers; no doubt she'd hear all about it in the morning. In the meantime she opened the file he had left her and settled down to work.

The grey January day deteriorated as they neared the school and Olivia said fretfully, 'We can't stay long, Richard, we have to get back before the day worsens.'

'We'll have a word with the people who matter, darling, then we'll make our excuses. You realize we can't stay long, don't you, Vanessa?'

Vanessa didn't answer; she hadn't expected them to stay long anyway.

'If your friends have arrived we'll introduce them to your mother, dear. If they haven't introductions will have to wait for another time.'

'They're always late, Daddy,' she answered.

He turned around and smiled. 'Well, here we are, some of them are already getting away early.'

Vanessa's eyes scanned the driveway but saw no sign of Sally's father's car and in the next moment they were hurrying up the steps and into the school.

The teachers offered their usual hospitality of tea and buttered scones, but everybody had an eye on the weather.

Vanessa was dismally aware of her mother's anxiety even when she made herself chat to the headmistress, the teachers and several of the parents she had met before, and eventually there was a desperation in her voice until finally Richard said, 'We'll have to get off now, darling. We'll write often, Vanessa, and Easter will soon be here.'

'Can I tell Sally we're going to Italy, Daddy? You promised.'

'Well, I'm not very sure that I did, but we'll talk about it.'

'But you did promise, didn't he Mummy? You heard him.'

'We're not sure that Sally's parents would wish her to go to Italy, dear. Like your father says, we'll talk about it.'

She watched them driving away from the top of the steps, oblivious to the cold wind and the light snow in the air until her headmistress called, 'Come inside, Vanessa, it's too cold to stand out there and your parents have gone.'

All around her girls were exchanging memories of the Christmas they had spent, tinsel and Christmas trees, presents and parties, parties where children played party games and where there was laughter and companionship. She didn't want to hear any of it. She'd had a mountain of presents, most of them expensive, and yet there had only been older people. Perhaps next year she would invite Sally, but Sally would hate it, she'd miss her family and the fun they had.

Conversation was minimal on the way home for Richard and Olivia. She sat huddled in her furs, hating the threatening sky and the whirling snow. Richard gave his full attention to the road, but as they neared their destination the snow turned to rain, and somewhat relieved, Olivia said, 'Oh, I do so hate January in England. However bad it gets in Italy it's never as bad as this.'

'So you really do want to go there, Olivia?'

'I can paint there, I always loved it so, and you can work there, can't you Richard? You've said so many times, you're freelance, you don't need the bank behind you.'

'I have a lot of irons in the fire, Olivia, but I am still working for them, and what about Miss Gates? What is she going to do while I'm in Italy? I got her away from the bank to work for me, what am I going to tell them and her?'

'Can't she come with us? She can work for you in Italy just as well as here, I can't think she'll say no.'

Richard thought about it very hard before he said cautiously, 'There could be talk, Olivia. A secretary invited to spend time in Italy, it's unusual.'

'Oh, darling, you're surely not saying that they're going to talk about you and Miss Gates? I'll be there, I am your wife, darling, that's silly, of course they're not going to talk.'

Richard drove in silence. Olivia lived in her own little world, the world she'd grown up in with a father who had been as faraway as Olivia often was. Suppose Margaret Gates didn't wish to go with them to Italy? Then it would be impossible, and he'd have to see what the bank thought about it, but Olivia interrupted his thoughts.

'Darling, let me talk to Miss Gates, tell her how necessary it is for me to be there and that she'll love it. I don't suppose she's ever been out

48

of the country, she did once tell me that she and her mother holidayed in England.'

He already knew the argument was lost but he was not happy with it.

Nor, the following morning, was Margaret Gates happy with Olivia's pressing persuasions that she should travel to Italy with them in two weeks' time. There was a friendliness about Olivia that had never really been there before and encouragingly she said, 'It won't all be work, and there is so much to see there. You can sail over to Capri, see Vesuvius, even visit the opera in Naples. Richard isn't a slave driver, he'll give you lots of time to yourself, I'm sure. Do say it's possible, Miss Gates.'

'Well, there's my mother, Mrs Lorival, I'll have to see what she thinks about it.'

'Well of course, but a great many daughters work away from home you know, I'm sure your mother will see that. When Vanessa leaves school I doubt if we'll see much of her, that's how children are these days.'

'But not in my days, Mrs Lorival.'

'No, perhaps not, but I'm sure your mother's a nice, reasonable woman who will see all the advantages for you and refuse to look at the problems.'

'I'll talk to her this evening, Mrs Lorival. If I find I can't go to Italy what is the alternative?'

'Oh, Richard will have to discuss that with you. Back to the bank, I suppose, but let's not think about that at the moment. Let's look on the bright side.'

She left the office with a bright smile and Margaret spent the rest of the afternoon worrying about her mother's views on her job and Italy.

To say that her mother was stunned by her news was an understatement, until she had had time to gather her thoughts together, and then with some asperity she said, 'What are you thinking of, Margaret? Think of the talk at the bank, think of your reputation and think about me here on my own.'

'Mother, I don't have to think about my reputation, Mrs Lorival has asked me to go with them, we're going to work, and it won't be for long. You have friends, you have good neighbours and before you know it I'll be back.'

'Who goes to Italy in January? It won't be like a real holiday with sunshine and long summer days.'

'It isn't a holiday, Mother, it's work.'

'You've always wanted to go to Italy but you're not going to see anything at this time of year. You don't go with my blessing.'

'I told Mrs Lorival I'd have words with you and I'd tell them my decision in the morning.'

'And what will happen if you don't go?'

'The worst thing that could happen is that I lose my job with him and I'll have to go back to the bank. He'll have no difficulty in replacing me, most of the secretaries at the bank would give anything to be in my shoes.'

'Have they said as much?'

'Many times.'

'And I don't suppose anything I say will make much difference. You'll go like a grateful puppy and be thankful for any crumbs that fall off the table.'

'I can't think why you're so prejudiced.'

'Because I've got a daughter who's twenty-six years of age and is behaving like a teenager.'

'That isn't true, Mother.'

'Margaret, you're in love with him, if you weren't then I wouldn't mind where you went. You're going to get hurt and neither he nor his wife will care. You're not important to either of them.'

'Outside my work I know I'm not, I don't need you to put it into words.'

'So you're going?'

'It's my job, Mother, it's what I get paid for, it's what we live off.'

'There's nothing much more to be said then, but one day when my words come true you'll wish you'd taken notice of what I've been trying to tell you. When will you go?'

'I don't know, they will tell me, but soon. Mrs Lorival has commissions for several pictures and she paints better there. They'll be home for Easter I'm sure, I'll probably be home before them.'

'But you're travelling with them?'

'I expect so, at the moment, Mother, you know as much as I do.'

The rest of the evening was hardly congenial. Margaret had a book open on her knee but the pages never turned, and her mother's knitting needles were silent. Margaret's thoughts were on mundane things to prevent her worrying too much about her mother's strictures: the clothes she would need, what they would talk about in the evenings and would she see Capri or Vesuvius alone or with her boss. Would Olivia be so sure of Richard that she would allow him to escort her to places of interest she longed to see? But then Italy in January was hardly the Italy she had pictured in her imagination. She looked up to find her mother's eyes on her, and her eyes filled with tears at the sadness she saw in her eyes.

Jumping to her feet, she said, 'I'll make tea, Mother, or would you prefer something else?'

'Tea'll do.'

'I've been thinking of the clothes I'll need,' she said brightly. 'What do you think?'

'You've got plenty, why not take the dresses you've spent a lot of money on and worn only once? I doubt if either of them will remember seeing you in them.'

Margaret gave up.

Five

Margaret walked through the garden on the way to the villa and turned before she entered to look towards the bay almost hidden by the mist that had descended upon it just after midday.

It was cold and she pulled the collar of her coat closer about her shoulders. She had met few people on her walk; sensible Italians were happier inside their villas on such a day, and the lights strung out along the bay had come on early to light up the gloom of the January day.

It was Sunday. In the morning she had witnessed the people in their Sunday best attending the churches dotted about the town, the sound of their bells penetrating through the morning mist. For a few brief hours a thin, watery sun had tried to shine but it was well and truly hidden as she let herself into the house.

Olivia spent most of her time in the room she called her studio, seemingly oblivious to the view outside her windows, and Richard would have his head buried in yesterday's English newspaper or in one of the office portfolios. He hadn't asked where she was going, but simply smiled at her absentmindedly. He didn't care, it had often been left to Olivia to suggest that he show Margaret something of the area and inwardly Margaret had seethed that Olivia should be so sure of her husband, so absolutely certain that come hell or high water, he was hers. That Margaret was a nonentity who posed no threat was obvious; she could almost picture her mother's sardonic smile that proved she'd been right all along.

Maria, the Italian housekeeper, greeted her with a smile, saying, 'The signora is in the studio, she ask for tea, you join her, signorina?'

'I don't want to disturb her, I'll have tea in here, Maria.'

'She alone up there, the signor gone down to the boatyard, she be glad of company.'

Margaret disagreed but allowed herself to be coerced, and Olivia greeted her with a smile so that Margaret went to look at the picture in front of her, surprised to find that it was a picture of a large bowl of flamboyant poppies instead of a view of the Bay of Salerno.

'It's very good,' she said. 'I thought it would be a picture of the scenery here.'

'Oh no. I came here to paint pictures but not necessarily of Italy. I can paint those in the summer when I get about more. Where did you go on your walk?'

'Just along the bay, but the mist came down and it is very cold.'

'Of course, but not so damp as in England. Richard has gone down to the boatyard. We have a boat, you know, but it's hardly the weather to take it out. If it had been better

54

weather I would have asked Richard to take you out in her, across to Capri perhaps, or simply along the coast, it is so beautiful.'

'Yes, I'm sure it is.'

'Oh well, there are other times, spring and summer, when I know he'll be delighted to show off his boat and what we so love about Italy.'

If Margaret didn't love Richard Lorival she would have thought his wife was merely being kind, but she found Olivia's suggestion that she view the scenery with her husband both patronizing and ridiculous. Was she so plain and un-attractive that she could never pose a threat to this woman so engrossed with her painting that all she could do was stand back and eye it with a self-satisfied air?

Turning around, Olivia said, 'Oh well, I can't really do much more at the moment, painting in artificial light is not as good as daylight. Perhaps I'll get changed for dinner and we can listen to Richard going on and on about his boat. Do you have a man friend, Miss Gates?'

'Nobody special.'

'But you'll know how men go on and on about their boats, their cars and their golf.'

Margaret smiled politely, but longed to say, 'And your pictures, always your pictures.'

'We'll meet over dinner,' Olivia said with a smile. 'I'm going to have a long hot bath and change into something that doesn't reek of linseed oil. That's the worst of it, but the results are usually worth the inconvenience.'

They had been at the villa for two weeks and

Richard hadn't indicated when they might be going home. Their work had continued exactly as though they were at home: he spent time on the telephone and a great deal of mail arrived from day to day. He kept her busy, but it was the weekends she dreaded most when he insisted she take time off just as she did at home, and she never really knew how to spend the time.

He was coming in at the front door when she went downstairs and with a smile he said, 'So you got back safely. Go far?'

'No, just along the bay.'

'I've been to look at the boat, it's quiet down there at this time of year, what a pity the weather is so bad, it will be so much more enjoyable in the spring or summer.'

Margaret wanted to say, 'But I won't be here in the summer, I'll be in Bournemouth with my mother and you'll be here with Olivia,' but he had turned away and was halfway up the stairs when he turned to say, 'If it's a decent day before we go back you must drive into Naples with me, take a look at the Opera House and the cathedral, and the journey along the cliff top is one of the most famous in the world.'

What was she supposed to say, that it would be wonderful to drive along the cliff path, see Naples? Didn't people say, 'See Naples and die'? Well, chance would be a fine thing.

The next day was fine and over breakfast she listened to Richard and his wife discussing the weather and Richard's efforts to persuade her that they should take advantage of it.

56

'Darling, you know I have to finish my picture for Easter,' she argued. 'I know this coast, I've seen it so many times and look forward to seeing it in the summer, but not today, Richard, not when I should take advantage of the light in the studio and do some work. Why not ask Miss Gates to go with you? She's been here several weeks and seen nothing of the place.'

'Well, I do really need to go into the city today, would you like to come with me, Margaret? You can't really go home without seeing Naples.'

'Thank you, I'd like that.'

'You really don't mind being left on your own, Olivia?'

'Darling, of course not. I prefer being on my own.'

'Well, we'll get back in the early evening.'

'Darling, why should you? Why don't you take Miss Gates to that sweet little taverna in Positano, the one we both fell in love with?'

All night she'd dreamed about it, it should have been the most perfect day of her life but even on their drive into Naples she was aware of his reticence so that the drive was taken largely in silence, and only occasionally Richard seemed to remind himself that he had a passenger. He said he had business to attend to at one of the banks so he dropped her off at the Opera House, advised her to stroll around and pointed out where he would pick her up at two in the afternoon.

She duly admired the Opera House and the enchanting squares but was rather less captivated by the throngs of poorly-clad children roaming the streets, occasionally accompanied by a priest who had considerable difficulty in controlling them. She sat at one of the tables outside the café Richard had pointed out to her and where he had said he would meet her. It was cold, the sun lit up the square but in February there was little warmth in it and she was relieved to see Richard walking across the square to meet her.

He ordered a bottle of Orvieto and she thought he seemed to have recovered from his earlier depression.

'Well, what do you think of Naples?' he asked her.

'From what little I've seen it's a very beautiful city.'

'Yes, you must see it in the summer, then it really comes alive. What do you suggest we do now, Margaret?'

'I really don't know. All this is new to me, Richard.'

'Well, yes of course. It's not the day to sail over to Capri so I suggest we drive along the coast. Olivia suggested the taverna in the hills there so we could make our way there.'

The drive was enchanting, the meal perfect but what did they talk about? They talked about Olivia, their meeting, their marriage, their love, until in the end Margaret wanted to scream at him to look at her, that she too was a woman.

At last she had to ask him. 'How long are you intending staying in Italy, Richard?'

He frowned. 'Well, that's something that's

been worrying me all morning, Margaret. It was my intention to stay here until the beginning of March, then return home to collect Vanessa, now it would appear Olivia has other plans.'

'What sort of plans?'

'Well, it would seem she's promised two of her pictures for Easter and she wants to stay on here to finish them and then return home for Easter.'

'So would that mean we shall stay here until Easter?'

'Well, actually I need to get back before then and Easter is late this year. Though there's Vanessa, she'll be very disappointed, she'd actually invited her friend to join us.'

'So where does that leave us?'

'We shall return home next week and I shall have to come back just before Easter to collect Olivia with her paintings, and have to break the news to Vanessa. Still, she probably won't mind too much, she can have her friend here in the summer.'

So it all revolved around Olivia, her pictures, her needs, regardless of either her husband or her daughter.

Something in her expression made Richard ask tentatively, 'None of this conflicts with your plans, Margaret, your mother will be pleased to have you home.'

'I suppose so.'

'You could join us here in the summer, Margaret, see the sights. Italy is so much more beautiful in the sunshine and you really haven't seen it at its best.'

Margaret reflected that she really hadn't seen it at all but she was regretting the questions she knew her mother would pose.

Olivia drove them to the airport in Naples. She was gracious with Margaret, extremely tender towards her husband and the flight home was largely taken in silence, with Richard poring over a file of business papers and Margaret dozing fitfully.

It was early evening when the taxi deposited her at her home and she saw that the lights were on behind the curtains in the living room, shutting out the dark chill of the winter's day.

Her mother looked up from her chair in front of the fire and Margaret said swiftly, 'I didn't let you know, Mother, it was all decided rather suddenly.'

'Well, I wish you had let me know, I've nothing prepared for supper.'

'No problem, Mother. I'll get unpacked and probably go to bed early. Do you want me to make us some sandwiches?'

'Did you see anything of Italy?' asked Mrs Gates as half an hour later they ate sandwiches of cold meat by the fire. 'Or were you stuck at your desk all the time you were there?'

'The weather wasn't all that good, Mother, but I did get into Naples and when we did get a good day I strolled around to get a taste of the area.'

'On your own?'

'Well, I am in my twenties, Mother, and nobody looked as though they had ulterior designs on me.'

'What was his wife doing all the time you were there?'

'Painting, that was why she wanted to go there.'

'And has she come home with you?'

'No, he's going back for her before Easter.'

'So there's just you and him until she gets back? Doesn't that strike you as being ridiculous, what sort of marriage do they have?'

'Mother, I don't want to talk about their marriage, my stay in Italy or my job. I'm tired, I intend to go to bed and get on with my job tomorrow.'

'Have they asked you to go back with them at some future date?'

'We haven't discussed it, Mother. Goodnight.'

She had said she was tired but sleep did not come easily that cold late-February night. She thought about Vanessa, who would no doubt have been looking forward to inviting her friend to spend time at the villa. She would be bitterly disappointed, so when would he tell her, and how long would it be before she rebelled?

Six

Richard found himself staring into two pairs of amazed eyes before Vanessa's eyes looked away in some confusion.

It was Sunday afternoon and he had arrived at the school just after lunch to ask the head-mistress's permission to invite the two girls out for afternoon tea.

Caroline's Café in the High Street was a favourite among parents, teachers and scholars, and they had enjoyed the usual array of buttered scones and cream cakes before Richard felt able to drop his bombshell, for such he could see it had been.

There would be no Italy for them in the Easter holidays and the dismay on both their faces told him they had been looking forward to it with some anticipation.

'I'm sorry, girls, I can see you're both very disappointed but there'll be other times – August, for instance, when the weather will be warmer and everything will have come alive.' Neither of them spoke so he hastened to say, 'I'm right, Vanessa, you should know that after last August.'

'Sally goes away with her parents in August. Why can't we be there at Easter?'

'Well I've explained, dear. Your mother has promised to finish her picture and bring it home for Easter. It's a birthday gift, she didn't want to disappoint them. I've left her there to finish it, then I'll go back there to bring her home. Would you like to stay with us in Hartford for Easter, Sally? We live in quite a small village but there's quite a bit to see. Do you ride?'

'No.'

'Well, you could have lessons, there's quite a decent set of stables there, they look after Vanessa's horse for her.'

'We haven't room for a horse,' Sally said with a brief smile. 'In any case, I don't know how to ride.'

'Well, there are other things you could do, isn't that right, Vanessa?'

'No, Daddy, I never know what to do. I've got my horse and I tramp in the woods, but it's not Sally's scene.'

He knew he was floundering, but in desperation he said, 'Well, what about August then?'

'Daddy rents a house in Bournemouth near the coast. He joins us for just over a fortnight and we stay there for a month. I have two brothers and two sisters and we invite lots of other people to join us, I have to help Mummy with the shopping and the cooking.'

'I see, so she'd really want you to be there with the rest of them?'

'Yes.'

'So it's beginning to look like next Easter then?'

Neither of the girls answered so in some desperation he said, 'Well, I am sorry, I really can't apologize enough but it is just something that couldn't be helped. I'd better get you two girls back to school.'

They drove back in silence and as he deposited them in the hall he said regretfully, 'Well, once again, girls, I'm very, very sorry to have disappointed you about Easter. I'll be here to pick you up Vanessa, and I hope to see Sally in the very near future.'

Sally took his outstretched hand with a smile, saying, 'Thank you, Mr Lorival, I'd like that.'

He watched them walk towards the stairs where they both turned to smile, then he left with some degree of relief.

In the hall there was a crowd of girls who invited them to join them on a walk in the hills, but Vanessa said quickly, 'You go, Sally, I don't feel like it.'

Looking at her with some concern, Sally followed Vanessa up the stairs and found her lying on her bed in a flood of tears. She sat on the side of the bed, saying, 'Honestly, Vanessa, it really doesn't matter. Your father said I could come to you – or would you like to come to us? Mother would be delighted.'

'I hate him, Sally, I really do hate him.'

Sally stared at her with wide eyes. 'You don't mean it, Vanessa, you're just disappointed. How can you hate him, he's so nice and so kind.'

'I hate him because he doesn't love me. He doesn't love anybody beside my mother.'

'How can you say that! Your mother's beautiful and nice.'

Vanessa sat up and glared at her furiously. 'You're like everybody else, you only see what she wants you to see. She uses everybody just to suit herself and my father can't see it. It's never going to change. He doesn't love me because I'm not like her, I'll never be like her.'

'But it doesn't matter. You're just as pretty in a different way.'

'Look at me. I'm not blonde and beautiful, I'm not small and dainty and I can't paint pictures or play the piano.'

'I'm not like my mother but my father doesn't mind. My mother's plump and jolly, my dad says I'm skinny but that doesn't make him wish I was like Mother.'

'Your father isn't like my father, he's not besotted with some dream or other.'

'But you love your mother, surely? Don't you love her any more?'

'I *did* love her, I wanted to be like her, but I knew I never would be. I didn't think they would be disappointed about it but they are.'

'Oh, Vanessa, I'm sure you're wrong. You're just very disappointed because we're not going to Italy. You'll see, you'll be so glad to see them both at Easter you'll forget all about this.' Sally looked at her friend's doubtful face but Vanessa's next words dismayed her utterly.

'Miss Gates, my father's secretary, has been in love with him for years and he doesn't even know she exists.'

'How do you know?'

'From the way she looks at him, and the way he treats her.'

'How does he treat her?'

'Like a secretary. Oh, I know that's supposed to be normal but not when she so obviously cares about him.'

'You're imagining it, Vanessa.'

'No I'm not. She came here with him when it was half term, but it was at Mother's suggestion. She's so sure of Daddy, that he'd never ever look at anybody else.'

'He probably wouldn't.'

'But she throws them together, she was invited to Italy. Why, for heaven's sake, except to keep him company so that Mother could paint her wretched pictures.'

Sally didn't know what to say. 'Do you mind about Miss Gates?' she asked softly.

'No, I'm sorry for her like I'm sorry for me. She's quite nice really.'

'But surely you wouldn't want your father to fall in love with her, would you?'

'I don't know. Perhaps it would bring Mother down to earth, make her realize that she's got to change, care more about us.'

'I'd hate to think that my father would have an affair with anybody. I can't believe you want your father to fall for Miss Gates. And I don't suppose he's feeling very happy about this afternoon either.'

Sally was not to know how accurately she had assessed Richard Lorival's feelings. All the way

home he agonized at his daughter's disappointment and the sweet way her friend had tried to
defuse the situation. Sally was a nice girl, he
was glad his daughter had found such a friend.
He really would have to have a word with
Olivia, make her see that they should make the
girl welcome in their home and make sure she
enjoyed a holiday in Italy.

He had other thoughts too, concerning his
secretary.

Richard Lorival was not a fool; he knew that
the woman had feelings for him outside her
work and because he was not a vain man he was
not flattered. Margaret Gates was a nice woman,
a very good secretary committed to her work
and extremely loyal to him. He didn't want to
think that she thought of him as anything else
outside her work.

He had met her mother only once, but in that
brief moment he had been aware of the woman's
jaundiced expression and thinly veiled disapproval. To Mrs Gates, he was taking advantage
of her daughter's feelings for him and it did not
meet with her approval. It was really none of her
business, but at the same time he saw the logic
of it. Why hadn't his wife been going with him
to collect their daughter? Why Margaret?

He felt sorry for himself. For three long weeks
the house would feel empty without Olivia,
three weeks before he could fly out to be with
her, then a couple of weeks to placate Vanessa
before they returned her to her school.

Instead of driving straight home he called at

the village inn where he was immediately hailed by two men standing at the bar.

'We don't often see you in here, Richard,' Roger Markham said with a smile.

'No. I've been over to see Vanessa at the school, I don't fancy an empty house at the moment.'

'Olivia away then?'

'Yes, she's in Italy, and I've given the staff a day off. I suppose I could order some sandwiches?'

'I expect so.'

'I hear you've been in Italy? Hardly the best time of year,' Peter Jarvis said with a smile.

'No. It wasn't very warm and hardly sunny apart from one or two days. Olivia went to paint, she's there to finish a picture.'

'Didn't your secretary go with you?' Roger asked.

'She did. My, how word gets around. She went at Olivia's instigation not mine.'

'A bit touchy, Richard, no innuendoes meant, I'm sure. We all know there's nobody in your life to even approach Olivia in your estimation.'

'No, there isn't.'

'Let me see, how old is Vanessa now?'

'She's fifteen.'

'Is she going to be the beauty her mother is?'

'She's very different, but she's pretty, yes.'

Richard was wishing he hadn't called at the inn, but in the next breath Peter said, 'Aren't you sorry you gave up the hub of the City for the tranquillity of working at home, Richard?'

'No, I'm kept very busy, if I get fed up with it I suppose I could always go back, but that's very much in the future.'

'And it suits Olivia?'

'It suited us both.'

'It wouldn't work for me,' Roger said shortly. 'I like city life, I like the hit and thrust of it, I like people round me and I come home to enjoy the peace and quiet when the day's done.'

'Yes, well, each to his own, I think,' Richard said quietly.

Later that night, sitting in front of the fire with a whisky on the table by his side, Richard reflected on their conversation. He knew that he and Olivia were a topic of conversation for some of the people in the area. The two men had been friendly, not too inquisitive, but some of their suspicions had got through to him.

Since they had come to live in the area they had never involved themselves with local pursuits. They never went to the cricket club and he never seemed to have time to play golf, even when he was a member of the club. They went to church at Christmas and Easter, but that was the extent of it, and it was inevitable that people talked. He would really have to have a talk with Olivia to suggest that they invite a few people round, spend one or two evenings at the golf club.

The house felt so empty. The weather forecast had been vile, there'd been a silly play on the television and the news hadn't been exactly cheering. He was relieved to hear Mrs Peterson's key in the door and more relieved when she opened it to bid him good evening.

'I'd have got back sooner if I'd known you'd be home, Mr Lorival,' she greeted him.

'Well, I got home while it was still light, the girls had to get back to school.'

'But did you have anything to eat, sir?'

'I called at the pub and they made sandwiches for me. I had a decent lunch and I took the girls out for afternoon tea so I wasn't really hungry.'

'Can I get you anything now, sir?'

'No thank you, Mrs Peterson. Is it raining?'

'Pouring down, sleet it is, and that girl's still out. Girls these days, they're not like we were.'

'Tell me about it, Mrs Peterson.'

His thoughts turned again to his secretary. It might not be a bad idea to invite her out for a meal one evening. They'd have plenty to discuss business-wise, she was an intelligent woman, it needn't be anywhere local and she was sensible, hardly likely to read more into it than there was. But then there was her mother; no doubt she'd have something to say. Well, to hell with it, he was lonely with Olivia away, and Margaret would be good company.

Seven

When Margaret appeared at the breakfast table her mother stared at her in amazement. She was wearing the dress she had worn for her boss's dinner party. 'What's all this in aid of? Aren't you going to work this morning?'

'Yes, Mother, but Mr Lorival has invited me to have dinner with him this evening.'

'Just you and him, do you mean?'

'No. I think there are several other people, business colleagues.'

It was a lie. When he had invited her to eat dinner with him he had made no mention of any others being involved; he was simply missing his wife and wanted companionship. She couldn't tell her mother that.

'So, where are you having this meal and what time will you be home?'

'I don't know, Mother, he didn't say.'

'And I suppose you're thinking it's wonderful, better than anything you could have expected at the bank?'

'Well, isn't it?'

'What, with a man missing his wife and you acting like a seventeen-year-old?'

'Mother, why are you going on and on about

71

my job? I keep you in some sort of affluence that even your neighbours envy.'

'No more than if you were still in your old job.'

'Coping with the evening traffic, getting home much later and leaving considerably earlier in the morning. I'm at the other end of the village, Mother, and if you're not well you know where I am.'

'Don't you think I would have preferred it to what you have now?'

'I can't win with you, Mother. You seem to think I'm in some sort of an affair with Richard Lorival but I'm not. He is totally committed to his wife, he adores her. Why would he ever want to jeopardize that?'

'Oh I don't suppose he would, but it doesn't stop you hoping he will.'

'I'm going. Don't wait up for me,' she snapped, but as usual all the way to work her mother's words troubled her because she recognized the truth in them.

Even Richard's housekeeper eyed her with a sour expression which spoke volumes. No doubt her employer had informed her that he would not be in for his evening meal and she had surmised he was dining out with his secretary. Angrily Margaret told herself that it was none of Mrs Peterson's business what they did, but at the same time her attitude rankled.

They worked steadily all morning; then Richard informed her he was eating a sandwich lunch at the village pub, and faced with Margaret's surprise he said, 'I've been down there once or twice, Margaret, met some of the chaps and felt I should have done it sooner. We really have been keeping ourselves to ourselves.'

'I shouldn't think the village inn is Mrs Lorival's scene,' Margaret couldn't resist saying.

'No, perhaps not, but we have to make an effort. I thought we'd try that new place tonight. Have you heard anything about it?'

'No. We don't get out much in the evening.'

He stared at her steadily for several minutes before saying, 'An attractive woman should have some man in her life. Is your mother a problem?'

'Why do you say that?'

'I'm sorry, Margaret, perhaps I'm assuming too much, but on the one occasion I met her I thought she might be quite a demanding woman.'

'Well, she's had to bring me up more or less single-handed, my father died when I was twelve. There are times when I feel she still thinks of me as a child.'

'And that makes it difficult?'

'I cope. Where is this new place you were thinking about?'

'A restaurant in the hills above one of the villages, I've heard it's good. Olivia and I decided we'd try it one day.'

'I really don't mind, wherever you suggest.'

He smiled. 'Then we'll give it a whirl, find out for ourselves.'

Later, sitting at their table near one of the

windows, Margaret looked around her curiously. She didn't recognize any of the other diners but the restaurant was charming, intimate, and the food lived up to its reputation.

Halfway through the evening they were hailed by another couple who had just entered and Margaret's heart sank when she recognized the Simpkins, nor did she miss the speculation in the other woman's eyes.

'We're meeting the Greshams,' her husband said, 'so you don't mind if we don't join you?'

'Of course not,' Richard said. 'We're almost finished anyway. I kept Margaret rather late and suggested we eat out, Olivia is in Italy so she took pity on me.'

'Why not? When will Olivia be back?'

'I'm bringing her back before Easter.'

'So you're not spending Easter in Italy then?'

'No. I rather think your couple have just arrived, I'll be seeing you one of these days at the bank I expect.'

'Oh yes, I'm sure you will.'

They both smiled and joined their friends and Richard said, 'I expect the women will be putting two and two together and making five. Don't women do that sort of thing?'

'Some women, yes.'

'Oh well, it could have been the Eastmans, she has a reputation for being vitriolic.'

Margaret smiled, but she was remembering Mrs Eastman's remarks about her at the Lorivals' Christmas dinner.

They moved into the bar and Margaret was

well aware that four pairs of eyes followed their movements.

'Well, what do you think about the place?' Richard asked.

'It's very good, nice atmosphere and the food was excellent.'

'Yes, I thought so.'

Whether it was the advent of the Simpkins or for some other reason she suddenly felt that he seemed more distant, consulting his watch, and lapsing into silence.

At last she said, 'I'm ready to leave when you are, Richard.'

'Oh, gracious, I am being a rotten host, Margaret. It's nothing to do with you, but I like young Simpkin; I'm not too sure about Gresham though, that's who I've been thinking about.'

'I've never met him.'

'No, he's a new face, ambitious, big-headed. He's already been making enquiries about working overseas.'

'Did you never consider working abroad?'

'Many times. Hong Kong, Singapore, America, but it was not Olivia's scene. She's immersed in her painting, she's known here and that villa in Italy is very precious to her.'

'But not to you?'

He stared at her with a serious face for several minutes, then with a brief smile he said, 'When I knew Olivia wasn't interested I decided I should forget about it.'

'Mr Gresham has a wife.'

'He has and I know nothing about her. Like I

said, he's ambitious and determined. Perhaps Mrs Gresham won't count for much if he gets the opportunity to move on.'

Margaret was thinking that if she'd stayed in the City she'd know more about Gresham, she'd listen to the talk, the cut and thrust of people climbing the ladder towards goals they considered within reach. For the first time she began to ask herself if she'd been wise to consider working for Richard Lorival at his home. He knew what he was doing, now she began to feel unsure, then he smiled and the doubts in her heart melted away. Of course she was happy working for him in whatever capacity he asked of her. None of those other secretaries at the bank would be dining with their boss in an expensive restaurant listening to his views on business.

They left before the other two couples came into the bar, giving Margaret the distinct impression that Richard did not particularly want to talk to the Greshams.

As they neared Margaret's home he said, 'Shall I drop you off at home, Margaret, or would you like to come back to the house for a while, the night's still young?'

She didn't want to go home where her mother would no doubt be ready to ask questions; she had hoped her mother would be in bed by the time she got home and the questions would have to wait.

They sat in comfortable silence on either side of the fireplace but Margaret became increasingly uncertain about what they talked about. Richard was a good conversationalist but her mind began to wander. The scene was too intimate, too dangerous, perhaps not to him, but certainly to her.

Nervously she consulted her watch, and he said quickly, 'It's late, Margaret, I've been talking you to death. Perhaps I should think of taking you home.'

She rose to her feet uncertainly and he said quickly, 'Stay there, I'll get your coat.' He stood holding it for her and then she turned to button it, afraid to look up into his face, then with a little smile he leaned forward, put his arms around her gently and kissed her, the kiss of a friend, a brother.

'Thank you for taking pity on me, Margaret. I hope you've enjoyed it.'

'Yes, very much.'

'Then I'll get you home.'

She followed him out of the room, confused and somehow dazed. It was then she stumbled and slipped in the hall and he was helping her up and they were staring at each other with astonished uncertainty, then she was in his arms and he was kissing her and she was responding with every fibre of her being.

'Don't go, Margaret, stay,' he pleaded.

Suddenly sanity returned to her and tearing herself out of his embrace she said chokingly, 'Richard, I must go, please, this isn't right.'

They stared at each other, then he said softly, 'No, it isn't right, I'm sorry Margaret, I'm so sorry.'

They drove home in silence and it was not until they reached her house and he got out of the car to open her door that he said again, 'I really am sorry, Margaret, do you forgive me?'

'Of course,' she murmured. 'I'll see you in the morning.'

'Yes, and we'll forget tonight ever happened, at least the latter part of it.'

'Yes.'

He waited until she had undone the door and moved inside, then she heard the sound of his car's engine as he drove away. For a long moment she stood with her back to the door, unable to move inside even though the house was in darkness and she knew her mother was in bed.

How would she greet him in the morning? Would she be able to forget it ever happened, and how would it affect their working relation-ship in the years to come?

He would bring Olivia home, his life would return to normal. This evening had simply been a lonely man needing a woman's presence, the warmth of her affection. In the sober light of day he'd be horrified to think she was in love with him. Did she really want to spend her working life with a man who was well aware that she loved him but was totally committed to loving his wife?

Breakfast at the Gates's house was eaten largely in silence, and it was evident Mrs Gates had no intention of breaking the silence so it was left to Margaret to say, 'Did you go out last night, Mother?'

'No. You know I wasn't going out.'

'I thought you might have changed your mind.'

'Well I didn't.'

'Don't you want to know what sort of an evening I had?'

'And have you accuse me of interfering again?'

'I'm sorry, Mother. We had dinner at a nice restaurant in the hills above Halston, a new place. It was very good.'

No word from her mother so Margaret said, 'Aren't you interested, Mother?'

'Just you and him then?'

'Two more couples, Mr and Mrs Simpkin and a Mr and Mrs Gresham, he's new to the bank.'

'Did they know his wife was away?'

'Oh yes, Mother, if she'd been here he wouldn't have been dining with me.'

'No, he wouldn't, would he?'

'The men talked business and we talked shopping.'

'Very civilized.'

Margaret smiled. 'Oh Mother, can't you accept it for what it was? A very pleasant evening, nothing more.'

'I have accepted the nothing more bit, I hope you have too.'

Why do I bother? Margaret thought. She'll not change her attitude so what's the point? She collected her breakfast things and took them into the kitchen.

She was not looking forward to meeting Richard in the office. Would he be furious with himself for indulging in a romantic situation that meant nothing or would he be able to pass it off with a bland smile of indifference? Surely he wouldn't allow it to affect their relationship in the office, she needed her job.

She needn't have worried quite so soon. Mrs Peterson met her in the hallway, saying, 'Mr Lorival's gone into the City, he told me to tell you he's left some notes on your desk and you'll know what to do with them.'

As she leafed through the notes Margaret asked herself if he had felt the need to go into the City to get away from meeting her so early. They had to meet sometime, for herself, she'd rather have got it over and done with.

Mrs Peterson came in with her mid-morning coffee and on Richard's desk the telephone shrilled and Margaret went to answer it.

'Is that you, Miss Gates?' Richard's sister asked shortly. 'Is my brother there?'

'No, I'm sorry, Mrs Belthorn, he's had to go into the City.'

'When do you expect him back?'

'I have no idea, is it something urgent?'

'I don't know. I've had a letter from Vanessa, she wants to come to stay with us over Easter, says she doesn't want to go home. Do you know what it's all about?'

'Only that she's disappointed she and her

friend are not going to Italy for Easter. Mr Lorival is flying out there to bring his wife home and he has told Vanessa they will be here for Easter.'

'Well, the child's obviously upset but if her parents are home they'll hardly want her to come to me. Obviously the poor child's disappointed, that's all.'

'Vanessa is hardly a child, Mrs Belthorn, she's fifteen years old.'

'That doesn't make her a woman, and it doesn't make her parents more considerate.'

The phone went dead, and as Margaret replaced the receiver she could well imagine Mrs Belthorn's frustration.

She had forgotten that Mrs Peterson was still in the room and meeting the other woman's eyes she said, 'Mr Lorival's sister about Vanessa. Didn't he say when he expected to be back?'

'No.' She waited for several seconds to see if there was more but Margaret decided to say nothing else. Mrs Peterson's penchant for gossip was well known to her.

It was late afternoon when Margaret heard the sound of his car on the drive, and then she started to feel nervous. How would he greet her, had he even remembered?

If he had he showed no signs of it as he picked up the letters she had replied to and started to sign them as though he had been at his desk all day, and thankfully she said, 'Your sister's been on the telephone, Richard, I told her you'd telephone her when you got back.'

'I wonder what she wants?'

'If you've finished signing those I'll post them on my way home.'

'Oh yes, thank you. Heavens, is it that time? I got held up in the traffic.'

So matter-of-fact, so ordinary. Kisses that had meant nothing, not even worthy of some vague regret. She put her coat on and was opening the door when he looked up to say, 'I'm flying out to Italy at the end of the week, Margaret. A little earlier than I'd expected but more sensible than travelling at Easter, don't you think?'

'Yes, I'm sure it is.'

He smiled. 'Goodnight, Margaret, I'll telephone my sister. I expect it's something and nothing.'

Eight

Richard stood on the terrace looking out across the Bay of Salerno thinking that he was well blessed. Olivia's father had always maintained that it was the most beautiful view in the world with its white villas nestling on hillsides dominated by tall cypresses, and below the blue sea rolling in gently over the golden sand. Even though it was early, already expensive yachts had begun to arrive to their summer moorings, and some way out he could define the smudge that was Capri.

Olivia came to stand beside him, and putting his arms round her he said, 'It's beautiful, darling, why do we ever go home?'

'You go home Richard, my heart is always here.'

'Then why do you let me?'

'Because I know I can't stop you. The bank, your work, England.'

'England?'

'Well, of course darling. Too many memories, family and schooldays friends, familiar things. I can forget them, you never will.'

'The only family I have now is Mina and you know we argue like mad. As regards the bank, the world is my oyster. There's Vanessa and her education, that does come into it, darling.'

'I know, she won't be at school for ever.'

'That's true. It's also true that we don't know what she will want from life.'

'That would matter, wouldn't it, Richard, more than what I might want from life?'

'It will always be what you want, Olivia. What are we going to do these next few days?'

There was a degree of cynicism in her smile as she left him to climb the steps up to the bungalow. Richard was good at changing the subject but what would he say if she said, 'Richard, I don't want to go back to England, I want to stay here and paint. I want you to leave your stuffy old job and stay here with me'? She knew what he would do: think that she didn't mean it, tell her it was impractical, talk about money and ambition, *his* ambition, talk about Vanessa. But Vanessa was too young to know what she wanted from life.

He joined her, staring down at her doubtfully, and with a smile she said, 'What do you want to do these next few days, Richard?'

'Wander around Capri, perhaps even take a look at old Vesuvius although that's never appealed to you has it?'

'No. It's a monster, I always have this fear that one day it will erupt again, spoiling some of this beautiful country, killing people, leaving some more devastation that people like us will be looking at years from now.'

'All right then, we won't bother with Vesuvius. We'll do something else, go to the opera perhaps or the shops in Naples, you love those.'

'What shall we do over Easter at home?'

'Well, Vanessa will be home. I told her she could invite that friend of hers, they were supposed to be coming here if you remember.'

'I suppose she was disappointed?'

'I'm afraid so.'

'But you explained about my picture, Richard. I did promise it, you know.'

'Yes, I told her, I'm not altogether sure she took it in.'

'And are we having her friend for Easter?' Olivia asked.

'I don't think so. I rather think she's decided to go to her family, quite a big family I believe.'

Olivia managed to hide her relief. One disgruntled schoolgirl was too much; two would be dreadful. She had always felt close to Vanessa when she was a child, but more and more she felt there was a distance between them, a distance neither of them could diminish.

Margaret's mother came into the breakfast room reading the front page of the daily paper, then as she sat down she handed half the paper to Margaret and retained the other half for herself.

'I don't know why we take the paper every day,' she moaned. 'There's never any good news in it.'

'You'd be lost without it, Mother.'

Margaret rose to her feet, handing the paper to Mrs Gates. 'I'll be home at the usual time, Mother, are you going out?'

'I might, I haven't made my mind up. Perhaps I'll walk into the village, call and see Mrs Parsons.'

On her way to the Lorivals' house Margaret reflected somewhat grimly that nothing ever seemed to change at this time in the morning: the same postman delivering his letters; the same boy on his bicycle pedalling away on his way to school after delivering the newspapers; and the busload of children outside the school. Ten years, twenty years, probably the same, only the people would have changed.

Richard's gardener greeted her with a smile, saying, 'I'm mowing the lawn this morning, Miss Gates, the first one of the year so it looks as if spring's on its way.'

Mrs Peterson stood in the doorway, saying,

'Have you seen that girl? It's ages since I sent her down to the house further down, we got their mail this mornin'.'

'I haven't seen her, Mrs Peterson, I'm sure she'll be back soon.'

Mrs Peterson had placed the morning mail on Margaret's desk but there didn't seem to be too much of it, and after she'd dealt with it she'd already decided that she'd tidy up the desks and the filing cabinets.

Richard hadn't said when he and Olivia were returning home, but it had to be the end of the week, surely. Next week was Easter week and arrangements had to be made to collect Vanessa.

Halfway through the morning Mrs Peterson brought in her coffee and sat on one of the office chairs prepared to chat. She was interrupted by the strident ringing of the telephone and Margaret excused herself so that she could answer it, surprised when a man's voice said sharply, 'Miss Gates, this is Arthur Latimer. I'm afraid I have some very bad news for you, Richard Lorival has been in a very bad road accident this morning but I can't as yet tell you any full details.'

'Is he hurt, Mr Latimer?'

'I really don't know how badly or if at all. But I'm afraid to say that Mrs Lorival has been killed.'

She was too shocked at that moment to say anything more and the president of the bank's voice said gently, 'As soon as I have more news, Miss Gates, I will let you know. In the meantime simply try to continue what you were doing.'

Across the room she looked into Mrs Peterson's eyes and the older woman said, 'What's happened? I heard you ask if he'd been hurt, I take it it's Mr Lorival?'

'Yes. Mrs Lorival has been killed. That was the bank's president, it's all he knows at the moment.'

'Gracious me, what will he do? There'll be no consoling him. She was his life, everything in the world to him. What's he going to do?'

'We don't know, Mrs Peterson. As soon as I know something more I'll tell you.'

Margaret went about the rest of the day mechanically, tidying drawers that didn't need tidying, remembering Olivia and her beauty, her talent and her charm, and trying to picture Richard without her. Then suddenly she thought about Vanessa. How would the girl react to her mother's death and who would have to break the news to her? When the telephone rang shortly after two o'clock she rushed to answer it, expecting to hear the president's voice but it was Richard's sister, shocked, tearful, and Margaret asked quickly, 'Did the bank let you know?'

'Yes, but some doctor in Italy phoned. Richard had me down as next of kin, fortunately he spoke perfect English.'

'Do you know anything else?'

'Very little. Olivia's dead, Richard is dazed, shocked but apparently uninjured.'

'Thank God for that!'

'Well yes, but I know Richard, without Olivia

he'll wish he was dead too.'

'There's Vanessa, he has to think about her.'

'I'm not quite sure what I should do about Vanessa, obviously she has to be told but I'm not sure whether Richard will want to do it or if somebody else should. Doubtless it will be in the newspaper tomorrow and I don't want her hearing about it from outside the family.'

'No. I can understand that. Surely Richard will get in touch with you as soon as he is able.'

'I don't know, Miss Gates. I don't seem to be able to think straight and Nigel thinks we should perhaps go there in the morning. That wouldn't alter the problem of Vanessa, though.'

'Perhaps you should have a word with her headmistress, at least if the news does get out in the morning she would know what to do.'

'Well, that's an idea certainly. Thank you, Miss Gates. I'll have a word with my husband now and see what he has to say. We may not have to wait until morning, the media will get wind of it.'

Margaret was wishing she could go home. If the news had already been on the radio or television her mother would know about it and her mother was capable of putting all sorts of interpretations to it about her job, her future and her feelings for Richard Lorival.

She was glad when Mrs Peterson came, bringing a tray of tea, and even more glad when she sat down to drink it with her. It would seem that neither of them wanted to be alone.

'Have you heard anything more?' Mrs Peterson asked.

'No. That was Mr Lorival's sister worrying about Vanessa, how she's got to be told and by whom.'

'Well, I wouldn't like to be the one to do it, I suppose the girl did love her mother.'

Margaret looked at her in surprise. 'That's a strange thing to say, Mrs Peterson.'

'Oh, it's only that recently they've seemed so distant with one another. Vanessa was hardly in the house at Christmas, and although they had people in, there was never the sort of family party atmosphere. When I went to my sister's the difference really struck me.'

'I suppose people do enjoy Christmas in different ways.'

'That they do, but it never seemed right to me somehow.'

'There's nothing more I can do here,' Margaret said, 'but I feel I have to stay on in case the bank telephone again. Surely by this time they've heard more.'

'Well, they'll telephone you at home if they need you, don't they have your number?'

'Yes, but he said he'd ring me here.'

'I can't do any good with young Molly. She's weeping and wailing down there in the kitchen. She keeps on askin' what's to become of us. What do I tell her?'

They both jumped when the telephone rang and Margaret hurried to her desk to answer it. It was Kevin Simpkin, his voice sombre to suit the situation. 'The president has asked me to ring you, Margaret. We know very little more at the moment, we haven't spoken to Richard and the boss suggests you get off home, perhaps in the morning we'll know more.'

'Mr Lorival has my home number if he wants to get in touch with me.'

'Of course. Ghastly business, isn't it? Poor Olivia.' His voice was cautious, uncertain, and Margaret became aware of thoughts that may have been harboured about her relationship with Richard over the years. Now Olivia had gone and he was wary. 'I'm sure Richard will get in touch with you whenever he gets the chance. However, whenever we hear from him we'll be sure to put you in the picture.'

'Thank you. Will you want me to come to the bank, there's very little for me to do here?'

'We'll be in touch, leave things as they are for the moment.'

When she went into the kitchen to tell Mrs Peterson that she intended to go home, she was aware of Molly's tears and the atmosphere of deepest gloom.

'Will you be here as usual in the morning?' Mrs Peterson asked.

'I expect so, unless I hear anything in the meantime.'

'Aye well, your mother'll be waiting to hear what you've got to say, it's already been on the radio. It'll be on television and no doubt in all the newspapers in the morning.'

'I expect so.'

'It's going to be nothing like the Easter we

had planned.'

'No, Mrs Peterson. I feel I should telephone Vanessa's school but I'm sure Mr Lorival's sister will already have done so.'

'Poor child. She'll not be ready for such news, now there'll be the funeral to think about. I wonder where that's to be.'

'I think things will drag on for some time, Mrs Peterson.'

'Like a cloud loomin' over us. Poor Mr Lorival, he'll never get over her.'

It was apparent immediately to Margaret that her mother had heard the news. Her face was doubtful, undecided if it should exhibit gloom, sympathy or anticipation, but Margaret was quick to say, 'You've heard the news, Mother?'

'Yes, on the radio. What will it mean to you?'

'Oh, Mother, how can I know? Mr Lorival is still in Italy, he hasn't contacted me, I heard the news from the bank. He'll be desolate.'

'Isn't he hurt at all?'

'I don't know. Olivia is dead.'

'I know. It will make a difference to you, Margaret, that's what's worrying me.'

'I don't see why. I still have my job, either here with Mr Lorival or at the bank. I can't see why you're so worried.'

For several minutes her mother looked at her in pitying silence before she said, 'I'm worried because you think too much of him, now with his wife gone you might want more than he's prepared to give. You might think he'll turn to you, but will he? That's what's worrying me.'

'Oh, Mother. How can you even think about anything like that at such a time? It will take him a long, long time to get over his wife's death, and I don't come into it. He's got a daughter to think about as well as his job. Really, Mother, I don't want to hear any more about how it might or might not affect me.'

'I won't say another word, but you can't stop me from thinking.'

'What are we having for dinner?' She had to change the subject. She didn't want dinner, at that moment she wanted nothing more than to be left alone, but watching her mother's face throughout the evening that followed she was well aware of the thoughts behind her silence, the fears and worries of a mother who knew her daughter too well.

Mr Simpkin telephoned her the following afternoon but only to tell her he knew nothing further and to enquire if she had heard anything.

'Of course these things drag on a bit,' he said, 'inquests, how soon they'll allow him to bring her body home. I know a bit about it, my mother's brother died in France. Are you coping there at the office, Margaret?'

'There's very little to cope with, I feel that perhaps I'd be more use at the bank.'

'Well yes, why don't you come down? We're busy at the moment, we have two people off sick and one girl on maternity leave. Yes, I'd say it was a good idea for you to come here.'

Her mother thought it was the best idea anybody had ever had. This is what she should have been doing for the last few years, working at the bank, meeting a lot of people, normality, not some silly thing her daughter had thought of as promotion but which to her mother had been anything but.

Two days later the president sent for Margaret, inviting her to sit down and asking his secretary to provide coffee, then saying, 'Richard telephoned this morning, he's back at the villa near Amalfi and things are finally moving. He's decided that Olivia should be buried in her father's grave in Italy. I must say I'm rather surprised at that, he wants it quiet, but he thinks it's what she would have wanted.'

'But what about his daughter? Will he expect her to go there, and what about his sister and her husband?'

'He didn't mention any of them. No doubt he's been in touch with his sister, I don't think it's any concern of ours.'

'No, of course not.'

'I suggest you stay on here with us at the bank until we know what Richard has planned. No doubt he'll wish to carry on working from home; on the other hand he may decide to branch out into something else. One never really knows with Richard.'

'No, that's true.'

'Would it matter, Miss Gates?'

'It's my job, sir, either here or at his house. I need the job, I hope you've always found me satisfactory.'

'More than satisfactory, Miss Gates, that's

why Richard was so insistent that you left to work solely for him.'

'Thank you, sir. I'll try to fit in with whatever he and the bank decide.'

'I was sure you'd say that.'

Even when she returned to her desk she found herself wondering if the president had known more than he was letting on. But surely they wouldn't have talked about business when there were so many more personal things occupying Richard's mind?

She was remembering the little church on the hillside overlooking the Bay of Salerno where Olivia's father had been buried. One day she had wandered through the graveyard looking at the ornate tombstones decorated with cherubs, saints' statues and pictures of the deceased. To her English eyes they had seemed too ornate, too embellished, but she had to remind herself that this was Italy, a place where people were proud of their emotions.

When she told her mother that Olivia's funeral would be in Italy Mrs Gates's only comment was that at least it would all be out of the way when he decided to return home.

When Margaret stared at her mother she said, 'I'm not being insensitive, Margaret, but I do think in some ways he's being sensible. She loved Italy and that villa, she was happier there than anywhere, perhaps he thinks it's right that she should stay there.'

'But Vanessa, Mother?'

'That's up to him isn't it. Nothing to do with

you, Margaret.'

She was right. Nothing in Richard Lorival's life had anything to do with her, she should be brave enough to realize it.

Nine

Only a handful of people stood on the hillside overlooking the sun-kissed Bay of Salerno listening to the final prayers as Olivia Lorival was laid to rest in the tomb her father had been buried in years before. The gardeners and the women who had worked in the villa for her stood with sad expressions clutching their floral tributes while Richard Lorival stood beside his sister and her husband, his stern face betraying none of the agony he was feeling in his heart.

It was over, and as they walked to their car Mina was the one to speak gently to the Italians gathered around her and to thank them for being there.

It seemed to Mina that all Richard's grief was bottled up inside, making it impossible for her to get close to him, and as they walked through the gardens of the villa she thought that Vanessa should have been there. This was the girl's mother they had laid to rest, and it was almost as if her father had forgotten her.

She couldn't help thinking about their meeting

with Vanessa in her headmistress's study when she had been unable to assess how Vanessa had taken the news of her mother's death. She had expected cries of bewildered pain and tears, not the empty stoicism that never changed, not even when they told her she was not expected to travel to Italy for the funeral. After Vanessa had excused herself to return to her room the headmistress had said feelingly, 'The poor child is in shock, I really doubt if it has registered yet.'

Mina didn't think her niece was in shock, the pain had been something that had grown over the years, not something that had happened days before.

Back at the villa, for what seemed an eternity they sat in silence until Richard said, 'Thank you both for coming, I really didn't expect you.'

'How could we not come, Richard? You surely don't think we would let you go through this alone.'

When he didn't answer her husband said, 'Is it too soon to ask what you intend to do about the bank, I don't suppose you've really had much time to think about it?'

Richard looked at him bleakly before saying, 'I haven't even thought about it, but it will all be there waiting for me, I suppose.'

'Perhaps it's not a good idea to work from home.'

'Perhaps not.'

'Have you thought about this place?' Mina asked.

'No,' he said tersely.

'Richard, it's early days, one day I'm sure you and Vanessa will want to come back here, it's very beautiful and you know how much Olivia loved it.'

'As I feel at the moment I don't ever want to come back. This place reeks of her, she's everywhere, to come here and not have her would be a nightmare.'

'So, when are you going home?'

'I'm not sure, there are things to see to.'

'But Vanessa will be home for Easter.'

He stared at her uncomprehendingly for several seconds, then he said wearily, 'Of course, I'd forgotten about Vanessa! I'll ask Margaret Gates to pick her up and take her home, she won't mind.'

'I'll mind, Richard. I'll go for Vanessa and take her to our house; when you make up your mind to come home you'll know where to find her.' She hadn't meant to be sharp with him. He had enough to worry about without her sharp tongue to add to it. Her husband was giving her meaningful glances but how could Richard have forgotten Vanessa? No wonder the child's face had been frozen into apathy over her mother's death.

Sally was having great difficulty in understanding her friend's reaction to her mother's death. No tears, no words of anguish, nor was she to know that while she slept soundly throughout the night, Vanessa lay awake agonizing about her future.

An invitation came from Sally's parents to invite her to spend Easter with them, but she declined on the grounds that she would be spending it with Aunt Mina, but then on the day she expected her aunt to collect her at the school she was aware of her father's long black car coming along the drive and her heart sank. What would Easter be like with a father who was sunk in the depths of despair, a father who would expect her to be at one with him?

He acknowledged the headmistress's expression of condolence with a brief word of thanks, then Vanessa was there, staring at him with wide, doubtful eyes. He was glad that she was not like her mother; if she'd been a copy of Olivia he didn't think he could have borne it, but the tall, distant girl with her pale, unsmiling face seemed like a stranger.

He searched for some sort of conversation but she was unhelpful and largely their journey home was taken in silence. It was when she was getting out of the car that she said, 'Is Miss Gates at the house?'

'No. She's working at the bank for the time being.'

'Will she be coming back?'

'I expect so, Vanessa. Now we'll ask Mrs Peterson to make a cup of tea while you get unpacked. I take it you're home for the usual two weeks?'

'Yes.'

Two weeks! What would they do, where would they go, and left to themselves what would they talk about?

It was over their evening meal when he said tentatively, 'Are you very unhappy that I didn't ask you to come with Aunt Mina to your mother's funeral, Vanessa?'

'I didn't think about it.'

'Well, I didn't really know they were coming, they simply arrived, and it's not the funeral, dear, it's our memories, what she meant to us, how we remember her.'

When she didn't answer he said gently, 'She'll always be here, Vanessa, her pictures are on every wall, her piano is to be left open and there will never be a moment when I don't remember her and want her.'

'I know.'

'You too, darling, that's how you feel isn't it?'

'Will you ever go back to Italy?'

'I don't know. I can't think of it at the moment, if I go back it will never be the same, and all the time I'll be reminded of the accident when she died. Perhaps it would be better if I got rid of the villa and bought something else a long way away from it.'

'Where?'

'Well, there are lots of places. Not necessarily in Italy.'

'I'll never look like her, will I?'

'Perhaps not, but you'll have your own sort of beauty, at the moment I don't really want to see your mother in you.'

Such sentiments didn't surprise her and he was saying, 'So what do you propose to do with your time this Easter?'

'Spend it with my horse. Daddy, why don't we have a dog? Sally says they have two and they take them everywhere.'

'Your mother didn't particularly like dogs, she preferred cats, I suppose that's why we never had one.'

'But you like dogs.'

'Yes, but I'm a very busy man and they can be very tying. Do you want me to come with you to the stables?'

'No. I might not ride him today, but I do want to see him.'

From the window he watched her hurrying through the gate and then running down the hill to the stables. There seemed so little for them to talk about. He didn't want to discuss Olivia or the accident, and Vanessa had asked no questions. Perhaps Mina had been right, it might have been better for her to have gone to London with all it had to offer, rather than mooning around the countryside, afraid to discuss the person dearest to them in case such conversation caused too much pain.

The office felt empty, he was accustomed to seeing Margaret's dark head bent over her desk, calm, uncluttered Margaret wrapped up in her work, and yet in that moment of ridiculous fervour, just a few weeks ago, he had seen a different woman, one not averse to a more intimate association. He'd regretted it, and now that there was no Olivia and they worked alone together, would she expect more of the same?

Tomorrow he'd go to the bank and test the water. See if the old life could continue or if there might be something else, something to take him away from what he now regarded as an end to normal existence.

Margaret Gates's mother was happier than she'd been for years. She enjoyed watching her daughter drive away every morning to what she called a normal life. She enjoyed listening to office gossip between the girls. The films she saw on the odd occasions she stayed on in town, and the odd office party to celebrate birthdays, or some retirement.

This was what she'd always wanted for Margaret, not some cloistered existence in a house with a man she was besotted with, a man with a wife.

She was taking more interest in clothes, and she had her hair done during her lunch break. Altogether a new Margaret was emerging, she only hoped that it was not so that she could show a new and more glamorous image when Richard Lorival returned to the land of the living.

It was the president's secretary who informed Margaret that Richard Lorival was in the building and she wished she'd been able to hear the news calmly without the anxiety of wondering when he would call in to see her.

It was late in the afternoon when Kevin Simpkin put his head round the door to enquire if she'd sorted out her work arrangements.

Staring at him blankly she said, 'Work arrangements? I'm not sure what you mean?'

'Don't tell me he didn't call in to see you,' he said.

'I haven't seen him, perhaps he was in a hurry.'

'And perhaps he's undecided what to do. I expect he's still in a bit of a trauma.'

'Was he with the president?'

'Most of the time. I only saw him for a few minutes but they had quite a long conversation. Don't worry, Margaret, I'm sure he'll be in touch very soon.'

She'd promised to stay on for a meal with two of the girls but somehow the prospect no longer interested her. Instead she made her apologies and arrived home, much to her mother's surprise.

'I thought you were eating out this evening?' she said, thinking that Margaret seemed less than at ease.

'I had a bit of a headache, Mother, so I decided to come home. You needn't worry about a meal, I'll get something later.'

Something was worrying her. She had little conversation and yet when the telephone rang halfway through the evening she jumped up quickly to answer it, as if she'd been expecting the call. Her mother was sure it was him, but Margaret had closed the door after her and all she could hear was her daughter's voice.

It seemed to have been so long since she'd

heard his voice but it was brisker than usual. Every day since Olivia's death she had agonized over what she would say to him, now somehow his talk was all of business and she got the distinct impression that he wanted her to say nothing.

'I'm sorry not to have seen you at the bank, Margaret, but I was in rather a hurry and not looking forward to the traffic build-up. Now, how do you feel about the job?'

'I'm sorry, I'm not quite sure what you mean.'

'Well, are you happier at the bank or do we go on as before? I take it you've been quite happy working for Evesham.'

'Yes I am, Richard, but it was only a stopgap until his secretary got back. It was just something for me to do, after all there was nothing here and I was getting my salary.'

'Of course. So where do we go from here?'

'Do you want me back or are you looking for a change?'

'I'm handling this very badly, Margaret. Things will get back to normal and of course I would prefer you to work for me, we're used to one another. I've got Vanessa at home for Easter so obviously she'll expect me to spend time with her, so I suggest you stay with Evesham until Easter and then come back to me for the time being.'

'Very well, Richard, I'll do that.'

'Goodbye then, Margaret, enjoy Easter.'

She couldn't say, 'You too, Richard', not to a man who had just buried his wife, so all she said

103

was goodbye and returned to her chair in the sitting room with a decidedly doubtful expression on her face.

Her mother missed none of it. 'I suppose that was him?' she said shortly.

'Yes, Mother. I'm to go back to working for him after Easter.'

'It's a mistake, Margaret. These last couple of weeks you've seemed more like yourself, enjoying the company of other women and men, not drooling over a man who can never be yours.'

'I never expected him to be mine, he had a wife.'

'He hasn't got one now, but don't think he'll suddenly turn to you. In a few months' time he'll realize he's a free agent, can go where he likes and meet who he likes, I don't want to see you getting hurt.'

'Mother, I'm a grown woman, I know the score and I really don't want to hear you going on and on about it all the time. I'm having my job back, it's a job I like and if you're going to go on and on interfering like this then I'll get a flat somewhere.'

'Where will you find a flat around here?'

'You'd be surprised. They're converting the old vicarage into flats and they may be very nice, at least that's what I've heard.'

'The vicarage isn't all that big, they're sure to be pokey.'

'Oh Mother, if I moved into one you'd find everything wrong with it just like you do with my life and my job. I'm tired of it.'

'I won't say another word then.'

'You will, you can't help it.'

She thought about her telephone conversation with Richard. What had he meant 'for the time being'? Did that mean that changes were afoot? It was no use worrying until she'd seen him, it would all work out. After all, Olivia had gone from his life and she wasn't coming back.

Over the weekend she met Mrs Peterson shopping in the village, and she was quick to realize that Mrs Peterson knew no more than she did.

'He's restless,' Mrs Peterson said. 'Of course it's only to be expected. He's been out riding with Vanessa most mornings but it's the nights when he seems at his worst. He should go down to the pub, but he doesn't want to face the men there, and he's mooning round the house looking at her pictures, leafing through photo albums, wandering round that studio of hers.'

'How has Vanessa taken it?'

'It's hard to say. I don't think there's much conversation between them, but then Vanessa seemed so unsure about her mother.'

'Unsure?'

'Well, I don't know if that's the right word or not, but wantin' to be like her, then angry with herself.'

'Oh well, Vanessa's at that gawky age of growing up, she'll never be like her mother, but she could be just as beautiful in her own way.'

'That's what I say. Time'll tell.'

105

Ten

Vanessa stared at her reflection in the mirror and didn't like what she saw. A tall, gangling girl with dark red hair wearing a short grey flannel skirt and pale blue blouse, the school uniform she'd grown up with and which she'd come to hate.

For two and a half weeks she'd been surrounded by photographs and pictures of her mother wearing silks and chiffons, her pale, porcelain face framed with silver fair hair, her eyes startlingly blue, her smile gentle but always assured, and when there were no pictures of Olivia there had been others that she'd painted, which her father gazed at long and often, which made her want to scream, 'Look at me, Daddy, I'm here!'

She shrugged her arms into her long trench coat and decided to go downstairs. Miss Gates was back in her office and her father was probably with her so she would have to ask when he intended to leave.

Miss Gates looked up from her typewriter and indicated that her father was speaking on the telephone so she went over to the window and stared out across the garden. The early morning rain had stopped and a pale, watery sun was struggling to break through the clouds. When Miss Gates joined her at the window she turned to say, 'Are you coming with us, Margaret?'

'No, Vanessa, I have work to do here. Your father won't be long, would you like coffee before you leave?'

'No thank you.'

'When will schooldays be over for you?'

'A year and a half.'

'Have you thought what you'll do then?'

She longed to say that she'd marry a rich man and live the life of Riley, but instead she said, 'I don't know yet, it's something I have to think about.'

Margaret smiled politely. There had been a time when she'd thought she was making friends with Vanessa, but nothing had materialized. Instead she found the girl tetchy and distant, and with a brief smile she returned to her desk.

Richard put down the telephone and said, 'Well, my dear, are we ready to leave? I brought your case down and put it in the car, you haven't forgotten anything?'

'I don't think so.'

'Well, say goodbye to Margaret then, she'll see you in the summer no doubt.'

Margaret watched them leave from the window, reflecting that her day would be like so many others of late, either alone or with a man whose mind was miles away. She'd offered her sincere condolences on his loss, which had been received with a brief smile and a change of subject, since then he'd confined all their conversation to work, when nothing of a more personal nature had been allowed to intrude.

Her mother had been keeping a discreet silence about her job and her boss, but she knew she was far from happy with the situation. If Margaret was honest with herself, she too was not happy with it either. She missed the vitality of the bank, the girls and their titbits of gossip, the men and their sly jibes at her position with Richard now that there was no Olivia, and when she thought about the future she felt she couldn't see the wood for the trees. Was there a future?

She left the office early and decided to look at the flats going up in the village. She hadn't been serious about them, she had mentioned them simply to shut her mother up about Richard, but she passed them every day on her way to work and she thought they were looking rather nice. One of the builders working outside said there was a flat on the first floor that was finished and she could look at that, and although she admitted it was pokey, it did have possibilities. She pictured it with her own furniture and carpets, the ornaments she had treated herself to over the years, and she began to think it was time she flew the nest.

Her mother would be appalled, but she would surely know that she would be there for her if she was needed. Anyway, girls left home now as soon as they'd finished school almost, so surely a woman in her twenties should be allowed to without too much prejudice.

From the window she could look across the fields to Richard's house, she could see the lights in his windows, she'd know when he was at home, and if he was out she'd wonder where he was and with whom. It was stupid to think about a flat, and why should she care whether he was out at night or not? But the awful truth was that she did care.

For heaven's sake, it was early days yet, Olivia hadn't been dead long and time healed many things. He saw her every day, knew her perhaps better than he knew anybody else, why couldn't she hope that one day he'd realize life was for the living and he had to move on?

She smiled at the builder on the way out and he said, 'Take yer fancy then, miss?'

'I think they could be very nice.'

'That they will when all the units and the like 'ave gone in. Thinkin' ye might be 'avin' one?'

'I'm thinking about it.'

As much as Margaret loved her mother, it would be wonderful not to have to explain or excuse everything she did. Her mother too would be able to sort out her life; she wouldn't be deserting her mother, simply giving both of them some space.

She made up her mind to call in at the estate agent's the next day to make enquiries about the flats.

She did it in her lunch hour and a pushy young man tried to sell her one on the spot, advising her to make up her mind quickly since they were in great demand.

She was late getting back from lunch but Richard didn't seem to notice. He noticed precious little these days, she thought, but apologizing for her lateness she decided to ask his advice.

'The young man at the estate agent's is responsible for my lateness,' she said, 'I hadn't realized the time.'

He looked up to stare at her. 'I hadn't realized you were late, Margaret, it doesn't matter anyway.'

'I was so busy thinking about the flat I lost all count of time.'

'Flat, what flat?'

'Oh I'm sorry, didn't I say? I'm thinking of buying one of those flats at the junction of Acinroy Street.'

'Aren't you happy living with your mother?'

'Oh, my mother's a darling, but we do need our own space, I think, and it would be very handy for my work here.'

'Well, you're not too far away as it is.'

It was all going wrong. He didn't want her any nearer, he didn't care a toss where she lived, but she had to go on. 'Perhaps my time at the bank gave me a new sense of freedom I seemed to have lost recently. My own flat would be nice.'

'Were you happier at the bank, Margaret?'

'No. I'm happier here.'

'Well, nothing's for ever, is it, I've realized that very potently recently.' He smiled bleakly and returned to the letters before him.

She sensed his restlessness. Halfway through

110

the afternoon he pushed the papers away and rising to his feet said, 'I'll take a walk to the stables, I promised Vanessa I'd keep an eye on her horse.'

Of course it was early days, she recognized that, but as the weeks wore on and he showed no interest in whether she intended to purchase the flat she began to have doubts about whether she was doing the right thing or not.

Her mother was sulking. She asked no questions about the flat either and even their neighbours seemed distant whenever they met her in the street.

The flats were largely completed now and the estate agent, who had made sure he kept in touch with her, was already warning that the choice was rapidly dwindling.

One morning as she drove to work she saw Richard standing on the road looking up at the flats. She brought her car to a stop and he came over to the window to say 'They look quite pleasant, have you made up your mind about them?'

'Not really.'

'Which one are you interested in?'

'The one in the middle on the first floor.'

'Well, why don't we just take a look?'

So together they climbed the stairs and found the door unlocked and a young couple looking around.

Margaret stared at them doubtfully, and the young man said, 'We're just looking at this one and the one at the end of the corridor.'

'And have you made up your mind?' Richard asked.

'No. We're looking at several others.'

When they had gone Richard smiled down at her, saying, 'It would seem that you do have to make your mind up quickly.'

'What do you think about it?'

'Well, it's very nice. Small, but then what would you want with a mansion? It's handy for work and for seeing your mother. What does she think about it?'

'She hasn't seen it.'

'Do you have the furniture for it?'

'Some, but then I really wouldn't like to rob my mother's house for this place, I'll buy some new stuff, I can afford it.'

'And I could well have one or two things at the house I could let you have.'

She stared at him in some surprise. 'Why would you want to part with anything, Richard?'

'Oh, there are one or two things tucked away on the top floor, things that were my mother's and which Olivia didn't want. She had her own taste in furniture, my mother's things she con- sidered too conservative.'

'I'd be quite happy to buy something you don't particularly want, Richard.'

'My dear girl, I'd give them away. I don't want to sell them, we'll talk about it when you've made your mind up.' She made her mind up at that moment. She would have the flat and the furniture Richard didn't want, and Richard would advise her. It would give him something more to think about than Olivia, and perhaps when she moved in he'd visit her and they could dine together.

It was a dream world she was living in and she said nothing of her plans to her mother outside the fact that she had decided on the flat, even when her mother said it was pokey, no lift, no garage for her car and she didn't like the kitchen.

In late summer Margaret moved in and admitted to herself that the flat looked tasteful and homely. The furniture Richard gave her added a great deal of charm to the living room and the tiny hall. His mother's walnut bureau was classy and charming, the hall table equally impressive, and when her mother saw them she said acidly, 'How much did you pay him for those?'

'Nothing, Mother, he gave them to me, his wife never liked them.'

'I've seen things like that in one or two of the good antique shops, they cost a lot of money. Why did he buy them if she didn't like them?'

'They belonged to his mother.'

'Oh, I see, she preferred something more modern and trashy.'

'No, Mother, there was nothing trashy about Olivia, they were simply not her style, that's all.'

'You've not said a word about our summer holidays.'

'No, I'm sorry, Mother, I was so wrapped up with the flat. Have you anything in mind?'

'I'm going to Weymouth with some ladies from the church, you hadn't shown any interest so I don't suppose you mind.'

'No, Mother, of course I don't.'

'So what will you do then?'

'Absolutely nothing. Enjoy my flat, take walks into the country, drive around. Perhaps buy one or two extra things to enhance the flat.'

'What sort of things?'

'Vases perhaps, or a picture or two.'

'Well, I'm sure there'll be plenty of those at his place.'

'He won't part with any of her pictures, Mother, I wouldn't expect him to.'

It was one evening when she was leaving her office that Richard asked, 'Happy in your flat, Margaret? I'll have to take a look at it one day.'

'Yes thank you, Richard, it's really very nice. You're very welcome to eat dinner with me one evening if you would like to.'

He smiled. 'Thanks Margaret, I'm pretty busy at the moment but we'll see.'

She felt rebuffed by his answer, it hadn't been what she'd expected. She felt a fool for reading more into his interest in the flat than he'd intended, but like Kevin Simpkin mentioned on the telephone, she must give him time, it was early days yet.

There were days when she knew he was out of the house that she wandered around the empty rooms picturing Olivia still up in her studio painting. She could still smell her perfume whenever she went in and on one occasion when Mrs Peterson found her on the landing survey-ing one of the pictures the housekeeper said,

'She's still around here, isn't she? I can feel her, smell her perfume, hear her footsteps across the hall. I went in the studio the other day and the linseed oil was overpowering. If I can sense her how do you think he feels?'

'It's your imagination, Mrs Peterson.'

'I suppose so, but don't say you don't feel it too.' Mrs Peterson was regarding her with a slightly mocking smile. 'He'll never get over her in this house, you know, he should get back to workin' in the City, move house if he feels he must.'

'Move house!'

'Why not, it's only bricks and mortar, too many memories and Vanessa doesn't like it.'

'Why do you say that, has she said so?'

'Not in so many words but I can sense it.'

'Oh Mrs Peterson, I'm sure you're wrong, Vanessa loves the house, she's got her horse down at the stables and her mother's things around her, she adores the house.'

'If you say so, Margaret, but I'm sorry not to agree with you.'

Mrs Peterson didn't often use her Christian name, preferring to call her Miss Gates, but the use of it today somehow seemed to make her views more potent.

Richard had left no message as to when he would be back so she decided she would leave early, at the same time she didn't want to go home. It was a warm, golden spring day when she should be somewhere enjoying the sunshine and the fresh air, and yet she had deliberately

115

made no plans.

It seemed to Margaret Gates that she was marking time.

It was much later when she saw his car returning to the house and she knew instinctively what he would do. Go into the office, then prowl around the house looking at Olivia's pictures, then slink into a chair to think bitter thoughts about the blow that fate had dealt him.

One day surely he must come back into the land of the living, and would she be around waiting for that day? Her mother thought she was a fool, there was speculation among the people at the bank, and even Mrs Peterson regarded her with grim awareness. Where would it all end?

Eleven

It was Saturday, a Saturday when the sun shone in glowing splendour on a town bursting with life, with crowds round the market stalls, the brass band in the park and people emerging from the chill gloom of winter days into a spring promising long summer days and all they might offer.

Margaret spent the afternoon planting pansies in the window boxes on her tiny balcony and

116

contemplating what to do with the rest of her Saturday.

Her mother had gone on a coach ride to the Melrose House thrown open to the public on every Saturday until the end of September. It was something she did with the Mothers' Union every year, and on the two occasions Margaret had gone with her it had always followed the same pattern: afternoon cream teas in the conservatory followed by a walking tour of the gardens.

The married girls at the bank would be out with their husbands and families, the single girls enjoying other activities she too had once partaken in.

Mrs Peterson emerged from the front gate and passing the flats she looked up with a smile, saying, 'Not going out then?'

'Perhaps later.'

'Oh well, it's too nice to stay indoors. I'm visitin' my sister over at Oakwell.'

'For the weekend?'

'Yes. He said he didn't mind. I never knows what he wants to do with himself these days.'

'No, of course not.'

She was glad when the sun went in and the town quietened down, glad to put the lamps on and draw the curtains, exasperated that there seemed nothing to watch on the television until later and although she wasn't given to self-pity, somehow she felt close to tears as she contemplated the emptiness of her life. She wasn't bad looking, indeed many people thought her

117

attractive. She was reasonably intelligent, could hold a good conversation, and she was generously kind, so why on a Saturday night was she terribly alone when so many other people had so much?

She made herself eat a modest meal and after she'd cleared away she sat in front of the television to watch a silly film she realized she'd seen before and hated then.

She dozed fitfully in her chair and was suddenly wakened by the shrill ringing of her doorbell. Consulting her watch she saw that it was almost eleven o'clock and wondered who had come so late unless it was her next door neighbour who was something of a borrower, from cups of sugar to change for her meter.

She opened the door and stared in amazement at the sight of Richard standing in the doorway smiling at her defensively and holding a bottle of wine. Holding the door wider she invited him in and he said swiftly, 'I saw your light on, Margaret, I hope you don't mind. I was feeling rather lonely and thought we could perhaps share a drink together.'

'Oh yes, that would be lovely.'

'I'm surprised to find you in on a Saturday evening.'

'I haven't been in long,' she lied.

'Well, I'm all alone, Mrs Peterson's gone off to her sister's, and I don't look to Molly for company.'

She took the wine and he followed her into the kitchen and while she found the glasses he opened the bottle which they then took with them into the living room. They drank and watched the television, they chatted and as she had expected their talk went on to Olivia. He talked about the letters of sympathy he had received from far and wide and offered to let her read them if she would like to.

When his conversation turned to Vanessa she said quickly, 'Poor Vanessa, she must be simply devastated by all this.'

For several minutes he stared at her; then he said, 'I don't know what to think about Vanessa, she's said little, she's shed few tears, as far as I know, and she must still be smarting from the villa episode.'

'Have you decided what to do about the villa?'

'Of course. I never want to go back there. I'll hang on to it for a while, perhaps let it in the summer, perhaps allow Vanessa to go with her friends, but I never want to set foot in it again.'

'But it was so beautiful there.'

'I know, but it was never mine. It was Olivia's father's villa, he never left it and neither will she. I don't want to forget Olivia, I simply want to remember us together without any third party, even if it is a ghost.'

'Is that how it's going to be all your life, Richard? You in that house living with a ghost?'

He stared at her, suddenly contrite. 'Oh, I don't mean I'll never get over her, Margaret, of course I will. I'll never forget her, but I'll pull myself together and get on with my life. I'll have to, won't I?'

119

It was well after two when Richard consulted his watch and rising to his feet said, 'I say, I'm sorry to have kept you up so late, Margaret. Good job it's not Monday or you'd never have been ready for the office.'

She smiled as she held the door open for him and stood listening to the sound of his footsteps going down the stairs. She was very sure at that moment that he would come again. Richard regulated his life or she did it for him. Certain days for certain things, certain people on certain days, as inevitable as Christmas Day and Boxing Day. Would it now be Margaret's flat on Saturday evening around eleven for drinks and talk of Olivia?

She was hating herself for feeling bitter, why couldn't she simply accept him for what he was: a sad, grieving man, selfish of course? But she knew if she didn't love him she wouldn't really care one way or the other.

It was in her power to stop all this. She could resign, move back to the bank or to some other bank, tell him enough was enough, but she wouldn't. Not while there was a shred of hope that one day he just might see her as a warm, living human being. Recognize that Olivia had gone and she was not coming back.

She debated with herself as to whether she should invite herself over for coffee on Sunday morning, but when she saw him driving off in his car soon after ten all she could think was, Where is he going and who is he going to?

Half an hour later she hated herself when she

120

saw Molly walking down the street and asked, 'I saw Mr Lorival going off in his car, Molly, is he going to see Vanessa?'

'Eh, Miss Gates, I never asks and he doesn't tell me. Mrs Peterson's at her sister's so like as not he's gone off somewhere for his lunch.'

'Yes, of course.'

'I'm glad, I can go out now if I wants to, there's nobody in the house to tell me what to do.'

At first he only came on Saturday when he was left alone in the house. He always brought a bottle of wine and they chatted and watched television, then the one night became two nights and more before the inevitable happened and they spent the night together.

Margaret knew it wasn't love on his part, it was merely grief and loneliness that propelled him into her arms, but she didn't care. One day he would realize that she loved him, that she would always be there for him, and on the nights he didn't come she lay in torment wondering why, and who he might be with.

She was receiving odd looks from Mrs Peterson and on her weekly visit to her mother she could tell from her mother's accusing expression that she knew something about the affair.

To break the silence, Margaret said, 'You haven't been to see the flat now that I've furnished it to my satisfaction, Mother, you only saw it when it was halfway there.'

'I was coming last Sunday after church with Mrs Crawley but we were just getting out of the

121

car when we saw your boss at the door carrying a bottle of wine. I surmised he was coming to you.'

Disconcerted, Margaret said quickly, 'You've met him, Mother, you could have joined us. It was merely a courtesy call to see my flat.'

'And how many courtesy calls have there been? More than that one I'm sure.'

'Can't you understand that he's feeling very lonely?'

'I know that men who are lonely are often looking for something and somebody to make them less lonely.'

'I can be lonely too, Mother.'

'I know. Is it likely there might be something more or are you the stopgap he's looking for?'

'You can be pretty unkind, Mother. You don't know him and yet you're forming all sorts of judgements about him.'

'I know you, Margaret, I know how you feel about him and I don't know how it's going to end.'

'Don't you think it could end like I want it to end?'

'I don't know. For your sake I'd like to think so but I can't help being pessimistic. I can't think it's going to be that easy.'

Margaret believed their love-making was perfect so what her mother said depressed her. Surely Richard must care for her or it would show? Her love for him showed in every kiss, every moment of their time together. Now she began to wonder how much Mrs Peterson suspected. Every weekend he gave her time off to go to her sister's and Molly was off with some boyfriend or other and hardly a problem.

One morning Mrs Peterson said, 'I don't know where he spends his weekends but he tells me he doesn't need me for meals or anything else. If he's got another woman it's not taken him long.'

She didn't know that his other woman was a sitting tenant who had been waiting in the wings for years.

When Margaret didn't respond to her doubts she said, 'I know it's none of my business but if there is somebody you have to admit he hasn't wasted much time.'

'I shouldn't think there is anybody, Mrs Peterson.'

'Doesn't he talk to you?'

'Only about business.'

'I'd have thought he'd want to see something of his sister, I wonder what she'd have to say about him and his goings-on?'

'Mrs Peterson, aren't you surmising quite a bit? I'm sure there aren't any goings-on.' She knew that Mrs Peterson was not convinced but probably thought she'd said enough as she turned away.

The long summer evenings meant that it was light much longer so inevitably they would have to be careful, Molly was up and down the road, and any titbit of gossip she would delight in passing on to Mrs Peterson.

Sunday was the best time, when they drove out into the country and ate in charming country inns, luckily without ever meeting a soul they knew.

It was on one of those Sundays that Richard remembered his daughter, and Margaret asked, 'Have you decided what you will do during her summer holidays?'

'Not really, but I suppose I'll have to start thinking about it.'

'Will she have thoughts on the villa in Italy?'

'I don't think so, I told Vanessa that I intended to dispose of it.'

'Didn't she mind?'

'I really don't know. It's very hard these days to know what Vanessa thinks about. She was disappointed not to be visiting the villa but made no mention of it when last I saw her.'

'You are still selling it?'

'Heavens yes. I never want to go there again, it's part of the most agonizing time of my life.'

He was no nearer forgetting Olivia than he had ever been, so much Margaret realized, but she had to ask, 'Don't you think the initial pain is beginning to ease a little?'

'Perhaps, I don't know.'

She wanted him to say that indeed the pain was going thanks to her but Richard was unable to do that. He was well aware that he was using Margaret. He wanted her company, her devotion and their love-making, but he knew in his heart that he didn't love her, could never love her. He liked her, which made him feel very guilty, and one day it would have to end, how he would end it he didn't as yet know, only that he would.

Vanessa wrote to him every week, which was something the school encouraged, but her letters were bland, she wrote about tennis and sport, about the netball team, which was doing very well, and she asked if he would be agreeable to her spending a couple of weeks with Sally and her parents in Bournemouth during the school holidays. She never mentioned her mother.

Margaret's mother was asking about her holiday plans, keen for her to accompany the Mothers' Union to Weymouth, but she was hoping Richard would suggest something and her mother's frustration was very evident.

'You want him to ask you somewhere, don't you?' she accused her.

'No, Mother, he does have a daughter you know.'

'I know that, that's why I can't understand why you keep putting off making any plans.'

'It's because I'm not sure when I can take my holidays, Mother.'

'You've never had trouble before.'

'Things are different now.'

'I know that, do you think I don't?'

'Well, it really doesn't affect you, since you're going away with friends,' said Margaret in an attempt to end the conversation.

'People are beginning to talk, you know. They know you're in a flat near his house, they know I hardly ever see you at the weekends and they think you've got a funny arrangement as regards your job. They ask questions and I don't know

125

what to tell them.'

'Why should you tell them anything, Mother? It's none of their business.'

Every time they met it was the same old argument and Margaret knew that one way or another she would have to think about her summer vacation.

She broached it with Richard in the hope that he would suggest that they spend it together, instead he merely said, 'Make whatever arrangements you want, Margaret, I can make no plans until Vanessa comes home, and even then I'm not in a holiday mood.'

She agreed to accompany her mother to Weymouth in August and Richard thought it was a very good idea, a complacency that angered her considerably but she realized she expected nothing more in spite of her hopes.

She stood in the window of her office watching him unload Vanessa's luggage from the boot of his car, and she stared with some surprise at the girl getting out of the front seat, a tall, slender girl who seemed suddenly to have developed a new grace. Her dark auburn hair fell in shining waves on to her shoulder and as she looked up and smiled Margaret saw in Vanessa a beauty that would never be Olivia's but which was just as potent.

During the first week of Vanessa's holiday Margaret never saw Richard after they had dealt with the morning's mail, and she left everything on his desk for him to sign when he decided to attend to it. He left notes for her and in the

126

evenings she visited her mother to discuss their travel arrangements and how they would spend their time in Weymouth.

It was the Friday afternoon before she left for the start of her holidays that Vanessa came into the office, and perching on the edge of her father's desk she said, 'My father says you're going on holiday with your mother?'

'Yes, to Weymouth.'

'I've never been there, actually I haven't been to many places, but I'm going to Bournemouth for two weeks this year.'

'How lovely, Vanessa, with your father?'

'No, with my school friend's family.'

'When is that then?'

'The week after next. Didn't you know?'

'No. So your father'll be here alone?'

'I don't know what he'll be doing, he hasn't said.' Margaret stared down at the papers on her desk and Vanessa looked at her long and hard before saying, 'Are you having an affair with my father, Margaret?'

The suddenness of her question made Margaret look up with amazement to find Vanessa looking at her with a strange amusement, and before she could utter a word the girl said, 'I shouldn't have said that, so please forget it, it isn't important.' Then with a swift smile she left her alone.

Confused, Margaret sat back in her chair. What wasn't important, that Vanessa didn't mind, or that she wasn't important in Richard's life, she would like to have asked her.

It was later that afternoon when Richard entered the office and with a bright smile said, 'Ready for Weymouth, Margaret?'

'I suppose so.'

'You'll enjoy it. When do you go?'

'In the morning. What will you do while Vanessa's away?'

'Spend some time at the bank. Necessary I think.'

'You're not going away?'

'No. Like I said, I'm spending time at the bank.' He leaned forward and pressed a roll of notes into her hand, and even when she thanked him for it she didn't want it. Always the day before her holidays he'd given her a gift of money to spend on some frippery or other but this year it made her feel like a woman who was being recompensed for her favours.

He sensed her reluctance and said lightly, 'It's your holiday bonus, Margaret, something the bank likes to do for its loyal employees.'

Twelve

The hotel in Weymouth had an old Edwardian charm about it. Most of the guests were her mother's age, and it seemed that Margaret was the youngest person in the dining room on that first evening.

The ladies had dressed for dinner, the men wore correct lounge suits or dinner jackets and they all smiled polite greetings and she felt she may have imagined the scent of lavender.

There were no children in the dining room and her mother said, 'They can be so disruptive and Weymouth is such a lovely place, but hardly suitable for children, at least not at this hotel.'

The last person to take his seat in the dining room was a man in his mid-forties, obviously well-dressed and immaculate, smiling his good evenings at the people sitting round him, and Mrs Gates said meaningfully, 'He seems nice, obviously on his own.'

'You don't know that, Mother.'

'Well, he is on his own, probably a widower. You should set your stall out, Margaret, no telling who you might meet.'

'I didn't come here to meet anybody, Mother.'

'Well of course not, but it could happen.'

'Please stop this, Mother, let the poor man be and keep me out of it.'

After dinner some of the guests played bridge while others listened to a man playing the piano in the lounge. It was all very genteel and while her mother chatted to two other ladies from the Mothers' Union Margaret thought about Richard and wondered what he would be doing.

Her mother found new friends to chat to, mostly around her own age, and Margaret had no doubt that they would be learning that she worked in banking, very high up position working for a senior executive, and if she mentioned that she worked for him in his own home she would no doubt glorify the position without displaying her antipathy to it.

She preferred to sit in the sun lounge and gossip so Margaret walked along the promenade or looked in the shop windows in the little town.

On their second day Mrs Gates informed her that she had been speaking to the gentleman, he was a bachelor, just lost his mother and was a solicitor.

'He's very nice, a little lonely I think, probably looking for some young lady to accompany him to places of interest, he has a nice car.'

'Did he say that, Mother?'

'Well no, I surmised it.'

The next morning Margaret encountered him in the town and they walked back to the hotel together.

'Your mother tells me you are in banking?' he said by way of conversation.

'Yes. My boss works privately at home.'

'My brother's in banking, he's out in Hong Kong, seems to like it there.'

'My mother tells me you've recently lost your mother?'

'Yes, three months ago. She'd been a semi invalid for some time.'

'I'm sorry.'

'I miss her very much, but life goes on, doesn't it? My brother says I should visit him in Hong Kong, see a little of the world, perhaps I'll take him up on that.'

'Oh yes, I'm sure that would be wonderful.'

Her mother was right, he was nice, a gentleman, but her mother was wrong if she thought he was looking for romance, that had been stamped out of him a long time ago.

Her mother was curious. 'Did you spend the morning together?' she asked.

'No, we simply met on the way back.'

'He's very nice, isn't he?'

'Yes, Mother. Lonely after losing his mother. He's going to Hong Kong to see his brother.'

'He didn't tell me that.'

'He told me. He's not looking for love, Mother, he's restructuring his life. By the way, I see there's a concert in town this evening and we're to be taken by coach.'

'Oh yes, some singers from the local operatic society. I'm not sure if I want to go.'

'Why not? You like things like that.'

'Are they all going?'

'I don't know, but I expect so.'

131

'Is he going?'

'We didn't discuss it.'

Her mother was so transparent Margaret felt she could read her like a book. Her mother would make some excuse not to go to the concert and hope Margaret and the man would go together, it was all so silly.

Their drive home after the holiday was over was taken largely in silence. It was when they stopped for lunch that her mother said, 'I feel I'm going home to an empty house. Just me in it, nobody to talk to, nobody to cook for, and what are you going home to?'

'Mother, you know I'm always there for you when you want me.'

'It's not the same.'

While her mother unpacked Margaret made tea and sandwiches and gathered some flowers from the garden which she put in a vase in the hall, so that her mother said, 'You see what I mean, don't you? I can't be bothered with flowers, the house never looks lived in, everybody tells me they can't understand why you needed to move.'

'Mother, I simply felt like some space, the need to do things for myself, my own home, my own furniture.'

'You had furniture here. You could have taken it with you.'

'And leave this place half empty so that you would need to replace it?'

'I can see it's no use talking to you. You'd best get off to that empty flat of yours, no doubt he'll have left work for you to do, or does he bring it round?'

'I'm on holiday, Mother, he'll probably be on holiday too.'

'With his daughter?'

'Possibly.'

It was dusk when she let herself into the flat, picking up the post from behind the door and there seemed so much of it. Probably a load of rubbish, circulars and catalogues, but when she looked through the window Richard's house seemed unlived in. No lights shone in the window, but then Mrs Peterson's domain was at the back of the house, and Richard would be away, or out.

She unpacked and put away her clothes, and she decided she hated the flat. It was impersonal, cold new stuff, even the curtains and the few ornaments. She decided to watch the news on the television, then she'd go to bed, but she'd only just settled down in front of it when there was a ring on her doorbell. Richard, she thought joyfully, and she leapt quickly to her feet to answer the door, staring in amazement at the stranger smiling at her on the threshold.

'I'm sorry to intrude,' she said softly, 'I'm Mary Barrow, your next door neighbour. I hope you don't mind allowing me to use your telephone, but mine hasn't been installed yet and it is rather urgent.'

'No, of course not, please come in.'

She showed her where the telephone was and went into the kitchen so she wouldn't be able to hear the conversation. After a few minutes there was a knock on the kitchen door and her neighbour was there offering to pay for the call.

'No, it really isn't necessary,' Margaret said. 'Have you moved in while I've been on holiday?'

'Yes. I don't know any of the other occupants but I've spoken to one or two people in the village. The lady from the big house knows you, she said you worked there.'

'Mrs Peterson. She's the housekeeper there, I work for Mr Lorival.'

'Yes, she told me. He's a banker I believe?'

'That's right.'

'I believe he's away in Italy at the moment.'

Margaret felt a quick surge of anger that she should be hearing of his absence from a complete stranger. Why couldn't he have left her a note, and when would be expect her to pick up the pieces of her job?

'The flats are rather nice, aren't they?' her visitor said. 'I believe you lived in the town before you came here?'

'Yes, with my mother. Would you like coffee? I've unpacked and was about to make some when I heard the doorbell.'

Mary made herself comfortable in the living room while Margaret served her with coffee and biscuits, and it quickly became obvious that Mary Barrow was intrigued by a woman who worked privately for the man at the big house across the way.

'His housekeeper said he was a widower, quite

recent isn't it?' she asked.

'Yes. She was killed in a car accident in Italy.'

'Oh dear, that's awful. Artist, wasn't she?'

'Yes.'

'I've seen him once or twice during last week, he's good-looking and quite young, he'll probably marry again.'

'Would you like more coffee?' Margaret asked.

'Yes please. This is nice, isn't it? I was hoping there'd be somebody in the flats I could relate to. Will you be on holiday until he returns?'

'I'm sure he's left plenty for me to do. I intend to go to the office on Monday morning.'

'Is that necessary?'

'I think so.'

'Doesn't he have a daughter?'

'Yes. Vanessa.' Margaret was getting tired of her questions. It was obvious her companion was curious about a great many things regarding her work and her boss, so to change the subject she said, 'I take it you're not from around these parts?'

'No. I'm a teacher, I've got a job at the junior school in the village, eight-year-olds, I start in September.'

'I'm sure you'll be very happy there.'

'Well, I hope so. As yet I've only met the headmistress, Miss Ives. Do you know her?'

'No, but I do know one or two of the teachers, I'm sure you'll fit in very well.'

She stole a quick look at the clock, and seeing it Mary said, 'Well, I expect you've got things to do after being away on holiday. Thanks for the coffee, I do hope you'll call in to see me very soon.'

Margaret smiled as she walked with her to the door. She wasn't happy that she had a neighbour who she felt sure was capable of gossiping, keeping an eye on her comings and goings and had already chatted to Mrs Peterson.

Richard was in Italy, why had he gone there and why couldn't he have invited her to go with him? Then as soon as she had thought it she realized the stupidity of such fantasies. It was too soon. What would they think at the bank, what would her mother say, would he ever have considered such a move?

As she let herself into his house on Monday morning its emptiness struck her forcibly. He had left notes for her with correspondence that needed to be answered. One note hoped briefly that she had enjoyed her holiday and stated that he would be away for several weeks in Italy. Vanessa would stay with her aunt after her holiday in Bournemouth.

It was all so businesslike and impersonal. None of it had anything to do with their snatched nights of passion, nights that had meant so much to her and probably hardly anything to him.

Mechanically she attended to her work, surprised several days later when she received a visit from John Eastman.

'I've come to pick up a file or two, Miss Gates. Lorival said you'd be here and would know where to find anything I needed.'

She served him with coffee but even after he laid aside the files he had been working on he seemed disposed to chat.

'So Richard's gone off to Italy then,' he said dryly. 'He did say he'd never go back there, I wonder what changed his mind.'

'He's put the villa up for sale, it could be that he's found a buyer for it.'

'Maybe. Ever get the feeling that changes are afoot, Miss Gates?'

'I'm not sure what you mean, Mr Eastman.'

'This job, this house, the bank. He's restless, he needs to move on, it's my bet he's thinking this way.'

She stared at him doubtfully. 'He's said nothing to me about moving on,' she said.

'Oh, perhaps not immediately, after all it's early days, but mark my words, Lorival's a high-flyer. It was Olivia who kept him close to her, even to banking from home, now she's gone and he'll need to fill the void in his life with something to take her place.'

She stared at him with her mind in turmoil. Had she been a fool to think that she was filling Olivia's place? She could imagine the talk at the bank, the speculation, but none of them knew about her involvement in his life, to them she was simply good old Margaret, loyal secretary, even friend, never destined to replace the perfection that had been Olivia.

He was watching the expressions flit across her face, and thinking that he had perhaps said too much, he said evenly, 'Don't worry about it, I could be wrong, but in any case if he does go off into the blue your job is safe. The bank think a lot of you, whatever he decides won't affect your future with us.'

'He does have a daughter to consider, Mr Eastman.'

'Well, of course, but you know what young people are these days, she probably already has her future mapped out and although I've only met the girl once or twice she seemed like a girl very much on her own.'

'She's not the easiest girl to get close too, I really don't know how much she's missed her mother.'

'My wife always said there wasn't room for anybody else in Olivia and Richard's life, and that I think included their daughter. Of course, you'll know better than I do if she's right about that. Living so close to the family you obviously know things about them that I don't.'

He was looking at her expectantly and Margaret knew that whatever she said would be passed on to Mrs Eastman, and she decided to change the subject.

'Are you going straight back to the bank today, Mr Eastman?'

'No, I'm going home. My wife's got a bridge party on this evening and I've had strict instructions not to be late. Do you play bridge, Miss Gates?'

'Very ineptly, I'm afraid.'

'My wife's mad keen on it. It's the first thing

138

we do on a cruise liner, look for the bridge tables, same in hotels we've stayed in. She's happier at the bridge table than anywhere else.'

'Perhaps I should have tried harder.'

He got up from his chair and handed the files over, saying, 'I'll get off now, Miss Gates, I've enjoyed our little chat, but what we've talked about is between the two of us. I wouldn't like Richard to think we've been sorting his life out for him.'

She smiled. 'Perhaps you're wrong about him.'

'Time will tell. I suppose I could be, but I have an instinct for these things and my wife has an even better one.'

Margaret accompanied him to the door when he said, 'Funny situation, Miss Gates, you in this big house all alone. Isn't the housekeeper here?'

'No she's visiting relatives, I really don't mind, I'm used to it.'

He smiled again and walked off to where he had parked his car, then with another wave of his hand he was driving away down the long drive towards the gates.

Thirteen

Richard Lorival sat on his terrace waiting for his visitors to arrive, dreading the interview before him, and at the same time praying they had not changed their minds.

Somebody called Spencer Hetherington had shown an interest in buying the villa and wished to view it during the afternoon. Richard had given his permission although no specific time had been mentioned. Consequently every car that passed along the winding road that followed the coast enlivened him.

Maria had served him with a light lunch and now he felt his impatience growing with the rising heat of the afternoon sun. His interest quickened at the sight of a large black Bentley ascending the hill up to the villa and he stood up and moved nearer to the steps. A large man got out of the front seat and he turned to speak to a small, stout woman who had emerged from the passenger seat. Richard's first reaction was that they seemed an unmatched pair, but he went down the steps to greet them, holding out his hand to each of them in turn.

Spencer Hetherington was affable, saying, 'We didn't state a time so I hope this one is suitable. We've spent the morning in Naples, Julie here wanted to shop.'

Julie was probably half his age, pretty in a blowsy way, but it did not take Richard long to surmise that she was totally enchanted by her companion.

As they wandered from room to room all Julie could say was that it was wonderful, she'd never seen anything more beautiful, that it would be heaven to live there and he said very little until they paused in front of Olivia's painting of the Bay of Salerno from the terrace.

'That's it,' he exclaimed, 'that's what I saw her painting, it's still here.'

Faced by Richard's surprise, he said quickly, 'I've been coming here for years, it's my favourite part of Europe and I always looked at this villa and wished it was mine. I came here about five years ago and saw a lady painting pictures in the garden and I walked up the hill to talk to her. My, but she was beautiful, and talented, I asked if I could buy that picture when it was finished but she said it wasn't for sale.'

'The lady was my wife, Olivia.'

'Really? Then you ask her, she'll remember it I'm sure, she was very amused I remember.'

'I regret I shall not be able to ask her anything about it, she died in a car accident on that road there last year.'

'Oh my goodness, I am sorry. I think I read something about it, but I didn't connect it with the lady I spoke to. Is that why you're selling the villa, too many memories?'

'Something like that.'

'Do you have a family?'

'One daughter.'

'Well, Lorival, I want to buy this villa if we can agree about the price, I also want to buy that picture. What do you say?'

'I'd have to think about it.'

He waved them off from the terrace before he returned to the villa to look at the picture. Had he really thought he might take it back to England where it would surely have no place on the walls of his house there? Every time he looked at it he would be reminded of what had happened to them on that winding coastal road.

The picture captured perfectly the sun setting over the exquisitely shaped bay, gleaming on the white-walled villas clinging to impossible cliffs, red roofs catching the crimson glow of the sun with tall, stately cypresses etched against the glowing sky.

Spencer Hetherington could have the picture along with the villa, which he wanted very badly. He didn't think he would quibble at the price Richard was asking, he could afford to be magnanimous about the picture. He wanted the whole thing over and done with so that he could return home, but he had come to the realization that it was home where his troubles might be beginning.

Vanessa didn't know what she wanted. She had no views about a career that her education should have prepared her for. She didn't want to go to university, and she was growing up too fast. One minute she'd been a child, now she seemed too soon a woman, headstrong and complicated.

Then, too, there was Margaret Gates. He liked her but he didn't love her, she was simply the good secretary he'd always had, even when he knew she wished to be more. Their affair should never have started, but how to end it without tears and recrimination was a problem he needed to face.

In the morning Spencer Hetherington would think himself a lucky man to have purchased the villa he'd always wanted, and on Richard's own part there would be few regrets. He'd visit Olivia's grave in the afternoon, cover it with flowers, beg her forgiveness for the many things he'd done in an endeavour to obliterate her memory, then what?

His life had to change, but he needed time to think about it. Margaret would be there expecting him to pick up the pieces as if they'd never been away from each other, and it seemed like a thousand worries were pressing down on him: his daughter, the house, even Mrs Peterson, who he suspected had an idea about himself and his secretary.

He was glad the villa would soon be gone, it was one worry off his mind, but there were others to replace it, problems that had to be resolved before he could move on.

Move on! That's what they all kept saying to him, his sister and her husband, his colleagues at the bank, his friends at the village pub, only

Margaret thought that he had moved on to her.

As soon as he got home he'd go into the bank and talk to the Big Man; his career needed sorting out. He couldn't possibly confine the rest of his life to working at the office in his home, he might as well write the rest of his life off. It had been all right when there was Olivia there, now he felt like a caged tiger.

It had been a perfect summer's day, and even now at nine o'clock in the evening the warm sunlight spread itself across the country road and hedgerows, on old leafy trees and stone houses, and on Richard's house singularly empty and lonely.

Margaret had sat on the small balcony of her flat to eat her evening meal, that way she could hear his car coming up the road, see him unloading his luggage, but she didn't know when he was coming home, and he had not thought fit to tell her.

The sun was setting in a blaze of glory as she piled everything on to her tray and prepared to take it into the kitchen when she heard the sound of a car being driven fast along the road. She knew the sound of his engine, and she watched as the long black tourer swung through the gates and up to the house, then she continued to watch while he unloaded the car and went into the house.

Lights were being lit now so that they shone across the terrace and the garden, but Margaret hurried into the kitchen to put the crockery away and wait. Oh surely he must come, when he'd had time to put things away, when he'd had a word with Mrs Peterson, when he'd looked through the window and seen the lights on in her flat, reminding him that she still lived close by and was waiting anxiously for him to call.

It was at least half an hour later when she heard the sound of the doorbell, but her face dropped when she viewed her visitor, the woman from next door. She didn't want her here when Richard came, she wanted her gone, and the expression on her face made Mary Barrow say quickly, 'I'm so sorry to intrude but I've just made coffee. I was hoping you might join me.'

'I'm so sorry,' Margaret said quickly, 'but I'm expecting a telephone call so I need to stay in right now.'

She felt ashamed of her excuse, but she had to be in if Richard came and yet from her neighbour's expression she felt she wasn't believing her.

'Oh well, it was just a thought,' Mary said. 'I think I saw your boss returning a little earlier, you'll be very busy from now on.'

'I expect so.'

'Oh well, I'll let you get on. Some other evening, perhaps.'

'Yes, of course. I'll look forward to it.'

How slowly the time passed, and what was there to do? Surely he'd either telephone her or come to see her, if only to discuss matters relating to the bank. Shortly after eleven she went on to her balcony so that she could look up to the house for any sign of life. In one of the upstairs rooms there was a light, but the night was hot and sultry and it had started to rain. She went back to her chair in the living room and incredibly she fell asleep. It was the crashes of thunder that woke her and flashes of lightning illuminated the room. Looking at the clock she saw that it was after four. He would not come now, but could she go to bed and even try to sleep again when there was so much on her mind? She thought about her conversation on the telephone with Vanessa several days before and the girl's obvious anger.

She'd been telephoning from Bournemouth and had asked to speak to her father; when Margaret had told her he was in Italy there had been silence, then Vanessa had said angrily, 'Why is he in Italy? He didn't tell me he was going there!'

'He didn't tell me either, Vanessa, I was away on holiday with my mother when he left, I didn't know until Mrs Peterson told me when I got home.'

'Apparently he didn't want to take you any more than he wanted to take me,' Vanessa had snapped.

'But aren't you on holiday with your friend?'

'Yes. I've been invited to spend more time with them at their home, I was ringing Daddy up to ask him for some money.'

'Well, I can send you some, it isn't a problem, Vanessa.'

'You needn't bother,' she said quickly. 'I'll telephone Aunt Mina. My father doesn't care about me, or you.'

The telephone suddenly went dead and she knew Vanessa had slammed the receiver down in a fit of pique. Now in the early hours of a storm-tossed day she knew Vanessa was right. Vanessa was his daughter, of course he cared for her, but did he care for anybody else, or was he likely to?

She sat in her dressing gown drinking coffee. It was still raining, beating savagely on the windowpanes, and it was too early to go to her office. She was dreading her meeting with Richard, wanting desperately to quarrel with him but knowing if he was kind and considerate she would forgive him everything.

The sound of distant traffic made her decide to get ready for work and she decided to leave early, after all he would surely expect her to be at her desk on their first morning together for several weeks.

She found herself leaving the flat at the same time as Mary Barrow and as she left Mary at the bus stop the other woman said, 'I'm sure it was your boss's car going down the road around seven. The thunder woke me up and I went to the window to make sure I'd closed it. I'm sure the car came down from the big house, driving very fast he was, I haven't seen it come back.'

Margaret merely smiled politely and Mary said, 'I may be wrong, of course, but we don't get much traffic up here and it was coming from the house.'

'Oh well, I'll soon know won't I? I didn't think your school started up again until September.'

'It doesn't, I'm simply going in to see if I can prepare anything. I'm a new girl, I want to make a good impression.'

'I'm sure you'll do fine.'

She walked quickly up the drive towards the house, noticing that there was no sign of Richard's car, which he invariably left on the drive in the summer months.

She was picking up a mountain of post at the door when Mrs Peterson came into the hall and in some exasperation she said, 'I don't know where he's gone this time. He tells me nothing, you neither for that matter. He came home last night, left some washing for me, packed another suitcase and was off again this mornin'.'

'You say he's taken another suitcase?'

'Yes. I heard him on the telephone last night to his sister I think, he didn't sound too pleased, and then off he goes without a word.'

'You're sure it was his sister he was talking to?'

'Well, I took him in some tea and sandwiches and he seemed pretty angry, and he called her Mina, that's his sister right enough.'

Margaret felt sure that this time it was Vanessa, insecure and difficult, obviously causing problems, that would warrant him leaving for London so early in the morning.

Mrs Peterson was disposed to chat. 'Don't you

148

have the feeling that changes are afoot?' she said darkly. 'I don't know what they are but I'm never very far wrong about these things.'

'What sort of changes, Mrs Peterson?'

'I'm not sure but I know I'm right. I thought at first he was beginning to get over her but now I know I was wrong. A little while ago he didn't seem as restless, it was as though he'd come to terms with her being gone. Now I have the feelin' he's back where he started.'

'Perhaps his visit to Italy has brought it all back to him,' Margaret offered.

'Perhaps, and then if Vanessa's playing up, I don't rightly know, I only know something's afoot, no doubt these next few weeks'll sort it all out.'

Margaret walked over to his desk and picked up one or two of the unopened letters lying there and Mrs Peterson said, 'He couldn't even be bothered to look through them, simply tossed 'em back on his desk and left 'em there.'

Margaret looked at them with dismay. There was little she could do without him. She was his secretary, hardly capable of taking on the work he normally attended to. Oh, she could tidy up his desk and the office, but then what? Stand around hoping he'd telephone to say when he'd be back? Then where would they go from there?

It was two o'clock in the afternoon and still no word.

Mrs Peterson served her with coffee and sandwiches, and her expression as she laid the tray on her desk spoke volumes.

149

At three o'clock, angry and frustrated, Margaret decided she was leaving. Sitting around marking time was useless – as useless as waiting for him the night before in her flat had been.

She drove aimlessly, it was too soon to go back to her flat, and in any case what would she do there except look for jobs that didn't need doing, sit around desolate, hoping he would phone?

She couldn't even think what drew her to Marcello's window. She hadn't even been there since purchasing the dress for the Lorival Christmas party.

As usual the window was adorned with two dresses suitable for a bride's mother, one large cream hat awash with pink roses and then the assistant was smiling at her as she laid a cream, soft leather handbag on a chair next to the dress.

Her smile was an invitation to go inside and then Margaret was accepting a cup of tea and talking to the chief assistant as though she was an old friend.

'It is Miss Gates,' she gushed charmingly. 'We get so many customers but I remember you bought that most beautiful gown for that party you were going to over Christmas. We haven't seen you lately, Miss Gates.'

'No, but then I live some little way away.'

'Of course, but that gown you bought must have been the envy of everybody present.'

'There were a great many beautiful gowns there, a few of the others bought from here.'

'Well yes, of course.'

Margaret made a pretence of looking through the stacks of clothes hanging in the cupboards, and the assistant asked, 'What exactly are you looking for, Miss Gates, perhaps I can help you decide?'

What would the woman have said if she'd said, 'I'm not looking for anything, I'm killing time until my boss remembers my existence. I don't want any of your gowns, he's never even noticed the ones I've already bought from here'?

'Is it something businesslike?' she persisted 'We have something very chic here, very businesslike and very up-market. For somebody in your profession it would be perfect, over here, Miss Gates.'

Margaret allowed herself to be ushered in the direction of a cupboard holding a selection of darker clothes and from it the assistant produced a black suit and white silk blouse, both beautifully cut, and evidently designed for some top executive which Margaret certainly was not.

How to keep her dignity without appearing naive and stupid? How to make this fawning woman realize that the clothes she was showing her were too expensive and hardly suitable for a woman whose boss was the high-flyer and who would undoubtedly leave her behind without a qualm?

She was relieved when the shop door opened, but less relieved when she saw that the newcomer was Mrs Eastman. 'Why, Miss Gates,' she said with some surprise. 'Having a day off then?'

'No, simply a little time at the end of the day to see if they had anything for me here.'

'And have you found something?'

'A very nice suit and blouse. I'm thinking about it.'

'Is that it then?'

'Yes. What do you think?'

'Oh smart, very smart. I'd buy it if I were you, it might even encourage Richard to take you with him when he moves on to better things.'

'Better things?'

'Why yes. He's decidedly restless. He was destined for much more than he ever found here, but it was Olivia who kept him here, chained to her, you might think.'

Margaret didn't speak, she felt anything she might say would be passed on to whoever cared to listen and in any case, what did she know? Undeterred by her silence however, Mrs Eastman said, 'My husband said when Richard was younger he always had a yen for the Far East, Hong Kong, Singapore, China even. Has he never said anything to you?'

'No. I'm his secretary, not his confidante.'

'I thought being his confidante was part of your job, my dear. Anyway, there's nothing and nobody to stop him now so I'm thinking things might be changing. I'd buy that suit and live in hope.'

She liked the suit but there was no way she was going to buy it on Mrs Eastman's instigation, instead she looked quickly at her watch, saying, 'I really must get away, I have a call to make on the way home.'

The only call she might have made was to see her mother but instead she drove the long way home and felt decidedly guilty when she passed her neighbour waiting at the bus stop, pretending not to have seen her. What was the matter with her? She was becoming mean and devious. She'd be particularly nice to her neighbour when next they met and she'd take her mother some flowers, but Mrs Eastman had upset her.

How could Richard be thinking about leaving the bank? He was in London, not necessarily at his sister's or with Vanessa. At this very moment somewhere in London he could be accepting a contract to work in the Far East without having given her a thought.

She was not to know that Richard sat facing his sister, both of them upset and agitated, even when the cause of their agitation had stormed out of the house an hour ago.

'She's my daughter and I don't understand her at all, why is she going on and on about Italy? She's had a holiday with Sally's family, and Italy was not mentioned when they decided on that holiday.'

'Didn't you promise she and Sally could go to Italy and then you went off on your own?'

'I went to sell the bloody villa, I never wanted to set foot in it again.'

'Then why did you promise she would go there?'

153

'That was when Olivia was alive, after she died everything changed, surely you can understand that?'

'I can, but can Vanessa?'

'Surely she is old enough and grown-up enough to understand?'

'Did you ever talk to her about selling the villa? Did you ever talk to her about anything beyond Olivia?'

'Heavens above, woman, Olivia was her mother!'

'Richard, you've immersed yourself so much in your own grief have you ever really thought how much it has affected Vanessa?'

'Well of course I have, but she's been at the school, with caring teachers and an army of friends. I've seen to it that she's had money for her holiday and she's short of nothing, that horse of hers has cost me a small fortune.'

'Material things, Richard.'

'I don't know what more she wants. It was bad enough losing my wife, now I feel I've lost my daughter too.'

'And which is the most painful?'

'I don't think I need to really explain that, Mina. Olivia was my wife, and I adored her. We were destined to grow old together, belong together, while one day our daughter would leave us and make a life of her own. Surely the world can understand that?'

'But Olivia's death has changed all that, Richard. You're still comparatively young, you could meet another woman, fall in love again,

154

Vanessa is the here and now.'

'I don't know what you want me to do.'

'How much does Vanessa figure in the rest of your life? What are you going to do with your life, Richard, stay in the house and work from there? I don't think so.'

Looking at her sharply he said, 'So you've been presuming, Mina. What did you come up with?'

'Nothing concrete, except to believe that what you have now isn't going to be enough, it never was enough, Richard, you told yourself it was because you had Olivia.' He stared at her without speaking until she said, 'How does Margaret Gates fit into your future plans?'

'Margaret! Why do you mention Margaret?'

'Because she's worked for you a long time, loyally, devotedly perhaps, will she be moving on with you?'

He didn't answer, instead he went to stare through the window at the build-up of early evening traffic, immersed in the turmoil of his own thoughts.

'I'm thinking of taking up a job in Hong Kong that's been offered me. You know it's what I had in mind when I first went into banking, now it's become a possibility.'

'Which it never would have been when Olivia was alive.'

'No. It didn't matter then.'

'So now you're getting away from familiar things, from the friends you have here, from me, but what of Vanessa?'

'When she leaves school she will have the chance to join me there, the possibilities for her are endless.'

'Would Margaret Gates be going with you?'

Why Margaret again? he thought angrily, then meeting her questioning gaze, he said firmly, 'No. I doubt if she would take to the idea. Anyway her life is here and she has a mother she would be reluctant to leave. There will always be a job at the bank for her, she's very well thought of.'

'And the house and Mrs Peterson?'

'I shall keep the house and the housekeeper. I shall return for holidays and Hong Kong is closer now, the world is shrinking thanks to air travel.'

'You seem to have got it all worked out, Richard. When do you propose to make your plans common knowledge?'

'Well, I need to speak to them at the bank, they'll be expecting it I'm sure. There are many things to do before I can shake the dust of England off my feet.'

He was aware of the sorrow in her eyes, sorrow tinged with memories of the children they had been, the games they had shared, the quarrels they had endured, memories that made parting bleak and painful.

How would Vanessa take this latest drama?

'When will you tell Vanessa?' Mina asked gently.

'I'll speak to her this evening, she'll have had a chance to calm down by then. Mina, she's my

156

daughter and I'll always do the best I can for her, but I have to think a little bit about me too.'

Mina didn't answer him but she couldn't help thinking, Would my brother be thinking about himself if Olivia was still here? She knew that he would not.

Fourteen

Philosophically, Mina's husband said, 'Don't interfere, let Richard tell her on his own, don't even think of saying anything.'

'But the Far East, Nigel, the child will feel abandoned.'

'She's not a child, Mina, try to get that into your head.'

'Well, she's little more. She's lost her mother and now she'll think she's losing her father.'

'I've told you, Mina, stay out of it. Let Richard handle it.'

Richard faced his daughter in Nigel's study overlooking the park. He had told her his plans, now he waited for her response, and looking at her pretty, sulky face he was not optimistic.

At last she said, 'Does that mean that during school holidays I'll be in that big house on my own except for Mrs Peterson? I don't suppose Miss Gates will even be there.'

'In less than twelve months, Vanessa, you will

be leaving school and you will be able to join me in Hong Kong. Think about it, darling, the Far East, Singapore, Bangkok, China, all the places most young girls would die for. I'd see to it that you had a marvellous time.'

'What about my horse?'

'Well, you know Miss Hetherington at the stables looks after him very well, I'll continue to pay for his welfare and you could always come to stay with Aunt Mina, she'd like that, you know she would.'

'Daddy, I don't know, it's all going to be so strange, a different world, nobody in it that I'll know except you. Why are you doing it now, I never heard you talk about Hong Kong before?'

'Because it wouldn't have been possible, but when I first went into banking that is what I wanted, the Royal Bank of China, I had an interview for that one and it was offered to me.'

'But you didn't take it. Why was that?'

'Well, I got married, and it wouldn't have worked out. Your mother was already becoming well known as an artist, then war came and for the next few years familiar things changed for everybody.'

'But when the war was over, Daddy, didn't you think about it then?'

'Yes, but it wasn't possible. There was your mother and there was you.'

'There's still me, Daddy.'

'Darling I know, but one day you'll have your own life to think about and I shan't expect you to consider me. Vanessa, you know I'll always be here for you and Hong Kong isn't a world away. Tell your friends at school about it, they'll all be very envious I'm sure.'

He wondered why her expression should be so cynical, but Vanessa was thinking of her friends who had close-knit families in an England her father was leaving behind. Surprising him, she said, 'What about Miss Gates?'

'Well, she'll go to the bank, they think very highly of her there. I'll be very sorry to lose her, but these things happen in everybody's business life.'

'She'll be unhappy.'

'Why do you say that?'

'I know she will. I think she was in love with you.'

He made himself smile, saying airily, 'Well of course she wasn't in love with me, dear, she was my secretary, nothing more.'

There would be many times in Vanessa's life when she thought about her father's indifference to Margaret Gates. It was her first introduction to a man's often cynical disregard for the feelings of a woman who had loved him.

Richard wanted to move on from the subject of Margaret Gates. He knew that she loved him, the truth was he didn't love her but then he'd never professed to love her; all he'd done was use her and of that he was ashamed.

Vanessa sensed his embarrassment and, still angry with him, she took a degree of pleasure in it. 'When will you tell her?' she insisted.

'When I have something concrete to tell her.

In any case the bank will handle everything very well.'

'You mean you'd rather they told her than you?'

'Really, Vanessa, I can assure you that my going will cause Miss Gates very little pain. She'll probably get promotion at the bank and possibly a better boss than I've ever been.'

'When are we going home?'

'I have to spend a few days in London. You'd like that, wouldn't you?'

'Doing what?'

'Well, there are the theatres, think of a show you'd like to see. Your aunt tells me you like dining out and she'll love having you shopping with her.'

For the time being Vanessa appeared to be appeased. At least the immediate future would be less stressful, and in the days to come his future in banking was the most important issue.

When he telephoned his secretary the following morning he was aware of the expectancy in her voice, and the silence when he informed her he was spending the next few days in London, largely on business.

Why, if he needed to be in London surely the bank would have deemed it necessary to inform her? They would surely not like paying her salary for work a junior clerk could quite easily have done, and Mrs Peterson merely echoed her thoughts.

'There's somethin' going on we don't know about,' she said darkly. 'Do you think he might

160

be thinkin' of selling up here?'

'Of course not. Vanessa's still at school, they both love this house.'

'Well somethin's going on. I'd like him to be straight with me, isn't that what you want too?'

'And I'm sure he will be, whatever it is.'

But the thing was she *wasn't* sure. She should never have entered into an affair with him, now she wanted the old days back when she came to the house to do the job she was paid for. She had thought Olivia's death would bring them closer but now it seemed it had only alienated them, and made her increasingly worried about her job with the bank.

She had too much time on her hands. She drove into the country and took long walks into the surrounding villages, and on one reckless afternoon she bought the suit she had admired in Marcello's, and on the way back she called to see her mother, taking care to leave her parcel in the car.

'What are you doing out and about at this time of day?' her mother accused her. 'A few people have told me they've seen you around, I could not make head nor tail of it.'

'Have they nothing to do but gossip, Mother?'

'They weren't gossiping, they simply saw you around and mentioned it because you're my daughter.'

'Richard's in London, Mother, he has business there, and he's been to see his sister. There's also his daughter to think about.'

'I saw that woman who has the flat next to

161

yours the other morning, she said he was away and you were out and about.'

'It would seem I'm living in a goldfish bowl.'

'She's very nice, she wasn't being unkind about anything. Good neighbours are hard to find.'

'Did she say anything else?'

'Only that she's invited you in for coffee several times but you've been too busy to accept.'

'That's true.'

'Except that you seem to have plenty of time on your hands. Is it him that keeps you company in the evenings?'

'Mother, I've told you he's in London. I intend to invite her in one evening when I feel like it, and isn't she at the school on evenings when there's something going on there?'

'I'll make us a cup of tea, or are you in a hurry to get back?'

'A cup of tea will be nice, Mother.'

'You did say I could bring Mrs Jarvis round to your flat for tea one Sunday but you didn't mention it again. I did tell her but nothing more.'

'We'll arrange something, Mother. I'll know better where I am when Richard gets back from London.'

The shock came several days later when she saw Mrs Eastman leaving Marcello's and her first words were, 'I've been thinking of the suit you were looking at but I was too late, apparently you decided to buy it.'

162

'Yes, I did like it, perhaps I was feeling extravagant.'

'Or you were thinking it was the thing for impressing high-flyers in exotic places.'

'And where would I find those?'

'You might well, my dear, it will largely depend on how well you play your cards.' Faced with Margaret's blank expression, Mrs Eastman said hurriedly, 'I must go, we have a dinner engagement this evening and there's so much to do. Think about what I've said when you decide to wear that suit.'

Margaret thought of little else. The woman was a gossip, known for it, and she was remembering that Richard had once said, If you want something to get out, tell Mrs Eastman; if you want to keep something private, give her a wide berth.

Three days later Richard's sister came to the house, bringing Vanessa, and Margaret heard their laughter and their footsteps in the hall outside her office. It was several hours later when Vanessa came into Margaret's office, her pretty face wearing a decidedly veiled expression.

Margaret smiled and Vanessa said, 'I wasn't sure you'd be here with my father being in London.'

'Work goes on, Vanessa.'

'Yes of course, but not as much, surely.'

'You'll soon be back to school. Will your aunt be taking you?'

'Oh no, my father will take me. I wanted to see my horse and pack my case for school. Nothing

163

much changes around here, does it?'

'Not really. I suppose you'll soon be thinking about what you want to do when you leave school?'

'I think my father's already having thoughts about that.'

'Really, and what is it to be?'

'Oh, some high-flying job in some far distant land, I'll have my own ideas about it when the time comes.'

'Yes, I'm sure you will.'

In some strange way she felt that Vanessa was baiting her, talk of distant lands, and that half-smile on her pretty face, dispelled in the next instant when Vanessa said, 'Isn't it awfully boring for you here all on your own?'

'Not really, I find I have work to do.'

'I suppose so.'

'Is your father coming home this evening?'

'Yes, he said it would be quite late and we're off back to the school in the morning so you probably won't see him.' The last piece of infor-mation was given with a degree of malevolence she had often been treated to by Vanessa over the years. At one time she'd thought of it as a kind of jealousy but it had been there even before suspicions about Margaret's feelings for Richard had entered her mind.

It was after eleven when the lights from Rich-ard's car swept along the road and then suddenly there were more lights from the windows of the house, and although in her heart she was willing him to come to her she knew he wouldn't.

164

He could have invited her to join them on their journey back to the school – she'd done it when his wife was alive why not now when she was dead? – but she knew he wouldn't. Perhaps it was Vanessa who prevented it, but in her heart she knew it was something else. Anyway, after tomorrow there had to be explanations, his job and hers couldn't go on in this ridiculous fashion indefinitely.

As she closed the door of her veranda she was aware of her neighbour walking out on to hers where she started to water her plants, and closing her own door hurriedly Margaret drew the curtains. She didn't dislike Mary, indeed if the circumstances were different she felt they could have been friends, but the woman would pose questions she couldn't answer, and now that she had met her mother she had to be careful.

Richard and Vanessa left soon after lunch so there had been plenty of time for him to invite her to join them. She watched them go from her living room window, saw Vanessa sitting beside him in the long black car. Neither of them looked up at her flat and then looking down she saw her neighbour setting out to do her weekend shopping, heading for the bus stop. They could have gone together, after all, anything was better than mooning around her empty flat thinking about him. No doubt Mary would go to the cinema or have tea in one of the small cafés, perhaps visit some friend she'd made in the village. She certainly wouldn't be wasting her time thinking about a man who'd chosen to forget her existence.

She was feeling sorry for herself. She had a key to the house, she could walk up there and see if he'd brought any work home but she didn't want Mrs Peterson putting two and two together and making five. There wouldn't be anything different in the office. After all, he'd only been home one evening, hardly time to attend to any of the matters waiting on his desk. On Monday it would all be back to normal.

Richard was a nice man, he'd explain a great many things and apologize for some of them, then they'd get back to how it was. There'd be intimate dinners in favourite places and drives out into the country. She'd wear her new suit and she'd see the admiration in his eyes and know that it was all going to be all right.

Perhaps even on Sunday he'd call in to see her. After all, what else would he do in that great big house with only servants around? He'd see her flat, know where he might find her and life would begin again. She wished she'd invited her mother and Mrs Jarvis to tea. After all, when Richard came back and settled down to work it might not be possible.

The long, lonely day stretched out in front of her and she found herself remembering the restaurant she had dined in when she had accompanied Richard to Vanessa's school. He'd probably dined in the same place, and then he'd be travelling home alone. Would he have any memories of that day, or were all his memories concerned with Olivia?

As she gazed soulfully through her window she saw that a car had stopped near the pavement below and almost immediately her next door neighbour was running from the front door, waving and smiling before she took her place in the front seat. She didn't know if it was a man or a woman driving the car but it was evident Mary had found a friend, and her own feelings of desolation intensified.

Her thoughts went back to the days when she had worked at the bank and when Saturdays had been something to look forward to, days to be spent with friends and very often the odd young man – never meaningful, but often fun.

She had been proud of the fact that the girls had envied her move to work with the high-flying Richard Lorival, who most of them fancied. Now she was the one who needed to envy them, girls who had married like-minded young men and career-minded girls who believed she was one of them.

She saw Mrs Peterson leaving the house to spend her usual Saturday with friends or her sister, followed soon after by Molly trotting down the road in her ridiculous heels to be picked up further down the road by a young man driving a battered old car.

She went into her bedroom and opened the wardrobe to take out the expensive suit she should never have bought. She'd wear it on Monday morning, far too pristine for a day working at her desk, but it would be another day, hopefully the start of something more profound in their relationship. If wearing the suit would help, then why not?

She did not see Richard's car all Sunday so she simply assumed he was staying somewhere near Vanessa's school, and the desolation returned. If he'd thought anything about her at all why couldn't he have come home to spend it with her? One thing was sure, she'd keep well away from her mother until life got back to normal.

Fifteen

It was still only seven o'clock when Margaret stood in front of her cheval mirror looking at her reflection in her new suit, well pleased with what she saw.

Her hairdresser had cut her hair shorter and added some paler highlights to it. She had a good figure, she was tall, at least eight inches taller than Olivia had been, and she had a good bust and trim waist. It was true she didn't have Olivia's chocolate-box kitten looks, but she was attractive rather than beautiful. What was wrong with hazel eyes and a cool, straight gaze some men had found attractive?

She would go into the office early, show Richard that she was keen to get started on an overload of work. Consequently, eight o'clock found her walking up the road towards the large house and Richard's car standing outside the front door.

So he was home, Margaret thought, but why wasn't it in the garage? Surely he wasn't contemplating going out again today.

She opened the door to meet Mrs Peterson picking up the mail from behind the door and her surprise was very evident.

'My, but you're early,' she said, 'it's nowhere near nine o'clock.'

'I know, Mrs Peterson, but I thought it will probably be a very busy day, better to make an early start.'

'Yes, well, since you're 'ere you might as well take the mail in.'

'I don't suppose he's had breakfast yet.'

'He asked for it early. He's already in there.'

'Oh, well, you see, we probably both had the same idea.'

Mrs Peterson favoured her with a long, hard look before hurrying off across the hall.

Margaret stared at Richard, who was standing at her desk cramming piles of correspondence into his briefcase before he turned round, his expression at once surprised and embarrassed.

'Good morning, Richard,' she said formally, and after a few moments he said, 'You're early, Margaret, is that the morning mail?'

She handed it to him, at the same time staring at the bulging briefcase. Quick to explain, he said, 'I can't be bothered with all this so I'm taking it into the office this morning. I've siphoned out all the important stuff, let somebody else

169

take a look at the rest of it.'

'That's why I came in early. I thought you'd want to look at it with me.'

'There's too much of it, Margaret.'

'Well, of course. You've been away and I couldn't handle it.'

'No, of course not.' His embarrassment was very obvious, the embarrassment of a man who had secrets he wasn't ready to divulge, and yet behind the embarrassment there was a strange remorse. He was aware of her standing beside him, aware that she was looking more attractive than he remembered her, and he could smell her perfume, reminding him of more intimate moments that he was trying very hard to forget.

'Did you say you were going to the bank today?' she asked him.

'Yes, I have an appointment with the Big Man and the committee, he's flown in specially to meet me today.'

'I see.'

She didn't see and he was not going to explain. Instead he said, 'Get Mrs Peterson to make you some coffee, I don't suppose you've had much breakfast.'

She stared at him blankly. Breakfast! Why should he concerning himself with her breakfast? She watched him go through the door, heard the sound of his footsteps crossing the hall, then his voice before the closing of another door and then she sat down weakly on his chair, stunned and close to tears.

A few minutes later Mrs Peterson arrived with

her coffee, saying, 'Mr Lorival thought you'd like some breakfast, said you'd probably not had any.'

'I don't want any, Mrs Peterson, just the coffee.'

'So 'e's off to London?'

'Apparently.'

'What's goin' on, I'd like to know, and I'm sure you would.'

'We'll know in due course, I'm sure.'

'Not good enough. Is he movin' away, is he changin' his job, and where do we fit into it?'

Margaret didn't speak and Mrs Peterson said mournfully, 'I'd 'ave thought he'd tell you even if he didn't tell me, although he should be tellin' us both. You're his secretary and I'm his housekeeper. He's unsettled, I can say that much for him, he's lost his wife and he can't come to terms with it.'

At that moment the door opened and Richard said calmly, 'I'm getting off now, Margaret, the morning traffic will have eased off and we'll have words when I get back.'

'When will that be, Mr Lorival?' Mrs Peterson asked.

'I'm not sure, Mrs Peterson, it will depend how long the meeting lasts, possibly a few days. Look around for something to do, Margaret. I'm sure you'll find something and there really won't be any need for you to come in at eight in the morning or stay late in the evenings. Get off early.'

For the first time he smiled the smile that she

171

remembered, then he was gone.

'Well, that's that then,' Mrs Peterson said sharply. 'Don't ask any questions, just wait until you're told. Then what do we do if our life's changed?'

'I can't think that will happen, Mrs Peterson.'

'Can't you? I can.' With that dour remark Mrs Peterson left her to her own thoughts.

Was it fate that sent her to eat lunch next to Marcello's the next day? She'd found nothing to do in her office apart from separate the morning mail, and it was an advert in the morning paper of an autumn early sale at the dress shop that made up her mind to see what they had. She had looked in the window but seen nothing there to her liking when she decided the much patron-ized restaurant next door was a good idea. Her mother had always considered it too expensive for them so they'd never eaten there, but she knew that Olivia had dined there with friends on several occasions and Richard had informed her that she'd spoken well of it.

It was quiet because most diners had already eaten, but a waiter showed her to a table in a corner near the window and she was poring over the menu when a voice said, 'I'm so pleased to see you here, Margaret, I wasn't looking for-ward to dining alone.'

Margaret looked up to see Sophie Simpkin smiling down at her and in the next moment she was occupying the chair opposite, unloading her shopping on the floor and saying, 'Why don't we have a drink before we dine? My treat.'

Margaret didn't dislike Sophie Simpkin, she was the only wife at Olivia's Christmas parties who had always been friendly, never patronizing, but at the same time Margaret would have preferred to dine alone. She didn't want any questions about her job or her boss. It was a forlorn hope, however.

'I don't blame you for taking time off Margaret, I suppose it's a good idea when Richard's in London.'

'Well, I did have his permission.'

'I'm sure you did, and he's been spending so much time there recently.'

'Yes.'

'My husband would talk about the bank all the time if I would listen to him, but he knows I'm bored by it. There is something going on, however. Kevin's quite excited at the moment, says Gresham's pushing himself for promotion and they're bringing in a new man. I suppose Richard's told you all about that?'

'Well, bits and bobs, that's all.'

'Well, I only half listen, but changes are afoot. Do you think Richard's quite got over Olivia now?'

'Perhaps not, it's pretty recent, isn't it?'

'I suppose so. The Eastmans have the most to say, particularly her. She even voiced one or two opinions about you, Margaret.'

'That doesn't really surprise me, Sophie, but I'm sure nobody listens to her.'

'Well, we all know what she's like and we all know how much Richard idolized Olivia,

173

though of course she's gone now.'

'And he hasn't forgotten her.'

'Well, no.'

Throughout their lunch Sophie talked about their holidays, the clothes she'd bought and Margaret realized she'd learn nothing from her about changes at the bank; Sophie wasn't interested, as long as the bank contributed to their somewhat lavish lifestyle.

As soon as they'd eaten Margaret made an excuse to leave, saying that in spite of her boss's absence in London there was still plenty to do.

'I'll probably see you round and about,' Sophie said. 'I rather think those dinner parties at Christmas will have ended.'

Margaret smiled but offered no comment of her own.

The meeting in London was over and Richard sat in the manager's office only too aware that there was more to come.

'You're sure about all this Richard?' John Gregson began.

'Yes. It was something I wanted when I went into banking, then the war came and so many things were altered.'

'And not least of all your marriage. It wasn't something Olivia would have wanted.'

'No, and I realized that she had her own career. She knew nothing about the Far East, her entire world was here in Europe where she became well known.'

'You haven't surprised me.'

Richard smiled. 'Davidson seems keen to take my place, are you happy with him?'

'I think so. He's a lot like you, ambitious and fancy-free.'

'He isn't married?'

'No. He's a couple of years younger than you, ambitious, all high-flyer, no permanent woman. I've heard he's quite a ladies' man, and I'm wondering how he'll take to Margaret Gates.'

Richard stared at him in surprise, and John Gregson said, 'She knows all about your plans I hope, otherwise she's going to have something of a shock.'

'I haven't told her. I've seen little of her, I had to think about my daughter and so many other things. I will tell her now. Have you spoken to Davidson about her?'

'Yes. He said if she'd been good enough for you she'll be good enough for him. It rather surprised me, I would have thought his thoughts would fly to someone a little more glamorous than Miss Gates. Perhaps glamorous isn't quite the word, Miss Gates is an attractive woman, but somebody younger I'd have thought.'

'He's hardly a teenager, and she's only in her twenties.'

'No. He's two years younger than you. When do you propose to take Miss Gates into your confidence?'

'When I get back home in a few days.'

'I'll telephone her in the morning, suggest that she comes here to see me and meet Davidson. When you meet her again I shall have put her in the picture.'

'Hardly gallant on my part, John.'

'No, but I'll let her down lightly, Richard.'

'I should tell her first, I feel pretty dreadful about all this.'

'Well, it can't be helped. Davidson's only here tomorrow afternoon and the next morning. Richard, you've burned your bridges as far as the bank and your secretary are concerned, it's a whole new start. My old headmaster used to say, "Don't linger too long in the moments that have fled."'

John Gregson was a materialistic man, not given to sentimentality. He would break the news to Margaret in a purely matter-of-fact manner, unaware that she might be shocked to the core. He hated himself for being a coward, he hated his dishonesty to a woman who had loved him and he was dreading the meeting that was inevitable. Would there be scorn in her eyes, anger, hatred even? Was it something he would remember in his new, challenging world?

John Gregson had commanded her presence in London, but Margaret was very sure that Richard too would be present. He had made up his mind to return to the City, he was asking her to join him there, saying that apart from the change in venue nothing else would have changed, and of course she would agree with him.

Mr Gregson's secretary had greeted her with a smile and Margaret reflected that she had once moulded herself on Miss Jenkins, her calm

176

efficient manner, her quiet good taste in clothes and her serenity. Now the older woman was saying, 'Did you drive up to London, Miss Gates?'

'No. I left my car at the station and came by train.'

'Very sensible. We're just waiting for Mr Davidson, he won't be long.'

'Mr Davidson?'

'Yes. Our latest acquisition. He's very nice, I'm sure you'll enjoy working for him.'

Margaret looked at her in dismay, suddenly aware that her heart was beating furiously and a tall man was smiling down at her, holding out his hand saying, 'Miss Gates isn't it? I'm Eric Davidson, Mr Gregson's expecting us.'

Was she really getting to her feet and following this stranger across the room and through the door? Then John Gregson was smiling, holding out his hand and inviting her to sit down.

'Well, I can see you've already introduced yourself, Eric. Mr Davidson is our new high-flyer, Miss Gates, destined to do great things and you will be working for him here in London. Makes a considerable change from your position over the last few years but I'm sure you'll soon settle down.'

She stared at him in dismay and he was well aware that he had dropped a considerable bomb-shell on a woman who was not interested in whether Eric Davidson was a high-flyer or no, or on whether she would settle down into something she had not asked for or wanted.

'I'd like you to join us here as soon as possible,

Mr Davidson expects to join us next Monday. Will that be possible for you, do you think?'

'Mr Gregson, I don't know. I don't know anything about this.'

'No. Mr Lorival will, I'm sure, explain things to you but he's had a great many problems – the death of his wife, his daughter, and the entire complexities of moving abroad, leaving England, his house, his job to work in Hong Kong.'

'Hong Kong?'

'Yes. An opportunity most men would die for, ask Eric here. He's spent time in the Far East, I'm surprised he's decided to come back.'

Eric merely smiled.

Both men were aware of Margaret's pallor, of her hand trembling on the arm of her chair and Davidson's thoughts were considerably more cynical than the thoughts of the older man. John Gregson thought she'd been shocked to learn she was leaving the comfort of a job she loved to travel and work in the City; Eric Davidson's were considerably more earthy. Lorival and this coolly elegant woman had had an affair and it was over.

Gregson rang the bell on his desk and when his secretary appeared he said, 'Can you order some tea for us, Miss Jenkins? I've given this young lady here a considerable shock and I'm sure she'd enjoy a cup.'

The tea arrived, the two men chatted, Margaret responded to their questions automatically and again Gregson said, 'I'd like you to think about next Monday, Miss Gates. Lorival is staying in

178

London for one or two days, then I'm sure he'll return home to put you in the picture. Don't be too hard on him my dear, he's had a difficult few months, this is his way of coping with it, to get right away, away from memories and hopes of a fresh start.'

She finished drinking her tea, agreed to let them know if Monday would be convenient and then she shook hands with both of them and was ushered out of the room.

She was aware that Miss Jenkins looked at her doubtfully, but she was out in the vast corridor, running down the shallow, curving stone stairs into the hall below, oblivious of people she passed on the way, people who stared at her curiously, concerned by her pallor, her faltering footsteps, her tear-filled eyes and a despair alien to her surroundings.

She remembered little of the journey home, the crowded train, the late afternoon sunshine or the child who ran his toy train up and down the table in front of her.

The first thing she was aware of was a loud hooting of horns as she drove her car out on to the road without ensuring that it was clear, and the angry driver who shook his fist at her through his window.

All Margaret was aware of was her anger, her disbelief that in the short space of one afternoon the love that she had nourished for so long, and which she had believed stood a chance of being returned, had turned to hatred.

Two emotions so far apart and now so real.

Sixteen

There was no sleep for Margaret that night. It seemed that in one brief afternoon everything she cared about had been swept away. The job she'd been so proud of, the man she'd thought she was in love with, and in its place there would be new people and the older people who would either feel sorry for her or gloat at her comedown, which is how they would see it.

John Gregson had told her she would be just as important in her new role as she had been in the past, but she didn't believe it. She'd be one of a dozen girls doing the same sort of job under different men, whereas before she'd been so much more, or so she had thought.

Half past six found her in the kitchen making coffee and she had already made up her mind that she would go across to her office early to tidy out her desk. She didn't want to see him, she wanted to be out of the office and out of his life before he returned from London.

Her key wouldn't open the door at eight o'clock so she had to ring the bell and Mrs Peterson greeted her with amazement.

'My, you're early. I take it he'll be coming

back today?'

'I don't know.'

'Would you like coffee?'

'No thank you, Mrs Peterson, I've only just had some at home.' She knew that the woman was hoping to ask more questions but she went quickly to her office, closing the door sharply behind her.

She had never been an untidy person and even over twelve years the drawers were hardly crammed with memories. Pencils and pens, stationery bearing his private address and which she'd used for more personal correspondence, and the usual bric-a-brac which she could probably consign to the waste paper basket.

In the second drawer she came across an envelope containing some photographs which she instantly recognized as those taken at the last Christmas party. She hadn't taken them home because she hadn't wanted her mother to see them, now she looked at them again. The men with their wives, holding glasses of champagne, all smiles and jollification. Sophie Simpkin and Kevin, highly gratified to have been included at last, and the Eastmans, he pompous standing next to his hostess, and his wife looking up at Richard with evident admiration.

There was one of Olivia on her own, holding the enormous bunch of roses they had presented to her, beautifully assured, silver fair hair exquisitely coiffeured and smiling as only Olivia could smile, gentle, gracious.

Without a second's hesitation she tore each

photograph in half, then putting them back in the envelope threw them into the waste bin. Let him find them, he'd get the message.

It was half past nine and the drawers were empty so she set about putting the top of her desk in order so that only her typewriter remained with its cover intact. She hoped the bank would find her one as good because for so long it had given good service and it was one thing she would like to have taken with her. In any case it probably belonged to the bank so she could have a word with Mr Davidson.

She stared through the window at the sound of a car's engine and to her consternation she recognized Richard's car coming to a halt on the drive and realized that she would have to face him.

She heard his footsteps crossing the hall. If he went into the kitchen to see Mrs Peterson she might just be able to slip out of the front door, but the footsteps were coming back then the office door was opened and he stood staring at her and she sat down weakly at her desk and started to open the drawers again as if she was looking for something.

She heard the closing of the door; then he was standing looking at her and she was unprepared for the sadness in his voice. 'Margaret, I'm sorry,' he said. 'I should have talked to you, told you my plans, you deserved that of me but it all happened so quickly. You must be very angry with me, I'm not sure I can make you understand.'

She looked up at him but there was no softening of her expression, the hatred and the anger she had felt the night before were still there and he knew at that moment that anything he might say would be inadequate.

After a few seconds he said, 'I can see you are very angry, Margaret, you're not the only one. My sister and my daughter are angry but you could at least let me explain a little.'

'You mean there is an explanation? I've got a job I didn't ask for, working for a man I don't know. Oh, I know I don't have to take it but if I'd known what was going on at least I'd have had a choice.'

'Such as what, Margaret? The bank employs you, it is doing the best it can for you, I've made sure of that.'

'Then I must thank you, mustn't I? You did care enough for that.'

'Well, of course I care. I think very highly of you, but it isn't enough, is it? Not for you and not for me. I've lost the person I cared for most in the world and this house suffocates me, it's too soon, Margaret. I need to get away for a while, find something new, snatching at straws could never have worked.'

'So I was one of the straws you snatched at?'

'Margaret, I'm very fond of you, we worked well together, we were friends. More than any woman I know I respect you but it isn't enough for me and it isn't enough for you.'

'So you think you might find it in Hong Kong?'

'I'll find new interests, a different environment, it's a start. I wanted to work in the Far East years ago, but the war came and Olivia. Her life was here, she was known here, and there was Vanessa.'

'And what of Vanessa now?'

'She'll finish her education, then hopefully come out to join me. The world could be her oyster.'

'And will she, do you think?'

'I don't know. She's at a very difficult age, resentful, rebellious, she's not in the least like her mother.'

'That bothers you most, doesn't it, Richard?'

'It worries me quite a bit. I'd like her to join me, whether she will or not is in the lap of the gods. My sister isn't hopeful, and to be honest neither am I.'

They looked at each other long and hard; then Richard held out his hand, saying, 'Perhaps you'll forgive me in time, Margaret. I wish you well, I shan't forget you and everything you have done for me.'

She took his hand, then picking up her bag she walked to the door. She didn't look back.

At that moment all Richard could think about was that very soon he would be leaving the last few months behind him for a new life. It couldn't come soon enough.

Back in her flat Margaret contemplated the long, empty day ahead of her. She needn't have waited until Monday, she surely hadn't expected Richard Lorival to quarrel with the bank's decision.

She was hating Richard for everything, the flat that was too near to his house and no longer an advantage; the fact that she'd once more be one of a million girls travelling by train every morning into a City where she would just be like everybody else, then travelling home in the evening. Before she'd felt different, now she'd be faceless.

She blamed him that soon the days would be shortening, the autumn leaves would be falling and winter would be laying its icy hand over the landscape surrounding her. It was then that she decided she would visit her mother. Her mother could be relied upon to put into words her feelings about the man she thought she had loved.

She let herself into her mother's house with her own key and her mother was staring at her with amazement before she said, 'Why aren't you at work? A few people have been telling me they've seen you around the village and elsewhere.'

'I'm not working until Monday, Mother.'

'Why is that, I suppose he's away again?'

'Not at the moment, Mother, but I'm going back to work at the bank. I know you'll be pleased about it.'

'You mean you're both going back to the bank? Well, I didn't think he'd get much joy from working at home after she'd gone.'

'I'm going to the bank, Mother; Mr Lorival is going to work in Hong Kong.'

Her mother's expression was comical, so comical that in the next second Margaret burst into tears and sank miserably on to the nearest chair.

She didn't hear her mother get up from her chair, but in the next moment a glass of sherry was placed in her hand and her mother's voice commanded her to drink it.

'Now what's all this? You've got a good job, he's not leaving you without work. Surely you didn't expect him to take you to Hong Kong with him?'

'I didn't know, Mother, he never told me anything about it, he left it to the bank to tell me and I'll be working for a man I don't know. Why couldn't he have told me what he had in mind when I bought that flat so convenient to his house, why did it have to be like this?'

'Well, I for one am delighted that you're going back to working at the bank. You're more annoyed than you should be because you were in love with him, don't think I haven't seen it all these years. You had expectations when he lost his wife, now they've come to nothing, but you'll get over it, Margaret. One day you'll be glad it happened. Who is this new man you're going to work for?'

'Eric Davidson, he's new.'

'Is he married?'

'Oh, Mother, I don't know. I don't know anything about him.'

'You've met him though?'

'Very briefly.'

186

'Well, was he nice to you? Is he good-looking? How old is he?'

'Mother, I don't know. I was too dazed, too angry to think about anything. I don't care how old he is, I don't care if he's had half a dozen wives, and I wish I was going to work anywhere but the bank where they'll all be feeling very sorry for me.'

'Why would they be sorry for you?'

'Because before they envied me, I was the one who was different, I was the one who got invited to dinner parties, special things, they thought I was more of a friend, now it's all over.'

'Surely they can't all be sniggering about it, you had some friends among the girls.'

'No, not all of them, Mother, I do have friends, but there are the others who will find some amusement in it all.'

'So when do you start your new job?'

'Next Monday. I'm dreading it.'

'What's he going to do about his daughter, surely she'll be as miserable about all this as you are?'

Not for a moment had she thought about Vanessa. After all, she had surely been Richard's first concern. His moving to Hong Kong might even be the sort of adventure she would delight in at her age.

Richard faced Vanessa's headmistress in the warmth of her study on a blustery Sunday morning, already aware of the consternation his news had given her.

'I'm assuming you've already discussed all this with Vanessa, Mr Lorival?' she asked cautiously.

'Well, yes of course!'

'And how did she respond to it?'

'I have to tell you, Miss Gordon, that I have been finding Vanessa difficult these last few months. She's been secretive and rebellious, my sister seems closer to her at the moment than I am.'

'She's recently lost her mother, Mr Lorival, it is bound to have had some repercussions in her life.'

'I know that, but there's something else, I can't put my finger on it, only to say I don't understand my daughter these days. You see more of Vanessa than I do, haven't you noticed some change in her? She seems to be sulking about one thing or another, how long is it going to go on?'

'You've tried, Mr Lorival. I'll keep my eye on her, and perhaps have a talk to her when the occasion arises. I don't want to do it too soon or she'll only think you and I are pressurizing her.'

'I'd be very grateful, Miss Gordon. She's missing a woman to talk to, a woman like her mother. Olivia would have understood her, known how to get through to her.'

They parted in the school hall with Miss Gordon wishing him well, then she watched him running lightly down the steps towards his car. In some strange way she felt sorry for him, for his inadequacy in dealing with a troubled girl on the threshold of womanhood, and for the catastrophe that had deprived him of the wife he had adored, but then she too had been inadequate. A beautiful, talented woman obsessed with herself and unable to reach out to the daughter who was growing up without either of them.

Vanessa's words to her friend Sally would not have surprised Miss Gordon unduly if she could have heard them later that afternoon. They were sitting in the art room after some slides of Italy had finished and Vanessa said wryly, 'That wasn't the Italy I saw when I was there, I never went to Rome.'

'But we were going to go to Rome, Vanessa. You remember how we said that one day we'd go to Rome? Venice too, then you said how we'd start with Naples.'

'Yes, now all Daddy can talk about is Hong Kong and I'm not going there.'

Part Two

Seventeen

Richard Lorival stood on the terrace outside the Peninsular Hotel looking across Victoria Harbour at the skyscrapers on Hong Kong Island and the mountains that soared even higher behind them.

It suited him to live in Kowloon where the pace was calmer, the throb of tourism not so urgent and from where he could escape into the New Territories emerging from the old China.

He had been four years in Hong Kong, in which time he had caught up with the ambitions of his youth but had been unable to extricate himself from the past. He missed England: he missed its bustling cities and the quietude of its timeless villages; he missed Mrs Peterson's incessant grumbling about unimportant things; and he missed Margaret Gates and her quiet efficiency. Most of all he missed Vanessa, and this was palpably evident by his sense of guilt.

He had begged her to join him in Hong Kong, promised her a life far exceeding any she could hope to have in England, had flown back home to encourage her to believe in the truth of it but it had all been to no avail.

In the end it had been his sister who had said,

'Leave it, Richard, she doesn't want Hong Kong or anything else you are offering. She wants to stay here in England.'

Vanessa had seen that she had won, promised to visit him, but that had been two years ago and her promise had come to nothing. She wrote sporadically, she wrote about times she spent in London at his sister's house, her horse, even once telling him she had spoken to Miss Gates, who she'd met in London and who was enjoying her work at the bank, which Richard read as an innuendo that he felt sure had been prompted by some cynical notion of her own.

Tonight would be the scene of another banquet, and there were so many of them in a place where there was so much money, so much commercialism and so much extravagance. Hong Kong had lived up to his expectations; at the same time there were moments when he longed for the quietude of his house in England and his life with Olivia which refused to go away.

As he entered the lift to go to the banqueting hall he paused to allow a woman to step inside before him. He had seen her several times at some function or other but he did not know her name, only that she reminded him forcibly of Olivia, not so much her face but her figure and the way she walked. She favoured exotic clothes that Olivia would not have worn, she invariably wore some sort of adornment on her head, either chiffon or feathers so he had no idea what colour her hair was. Her eyes were an unusual amber

and he felt intrigued by her without real substance to his feelings.

She was quickly surrounded by a bevy of men
in the banqueting hall and she chatted to them
vivaciously but as her eyes met his across the
room she smiled and the smile on her kitten-soft
face was too familiar.

Later in the evening he asked one of his
colleagues who she was and the man smiled
cynically, 'Leanne Valois, her father was a
financier, her husband a banker.'

'Isn't her husband with her?'

'She's a widow, he died four years ago in
America.'

'She seems to have plenty of admirers.'

'She's played the field pretty well since her
husband died, he was a dull sort of chap and
nobody can ever call Leanne dull.'

When Richard didn't immediately speak his
companion said, 'Why don't I introduce you
since you seem interested in the lady?'

'Not really. I just don't recollect seeing her
before.'

'You must have, Richard. She's never away
from the fleshpots or the places they frequent.'

Richard smiled and moved away but it was
later in the evening when he found himself
standing next to her and with a smile of amusement on his face his previous companion per-
formed the introduction. It soon became obvious
to Richard that Leanne Valois knew more about
himself than he'd known about her.

Fixing him with a singularly charming smile

195

she said, 'And have the last four years endeared Hong Kong to you, Mr Lorival?'

'It's confirmed all the expectations I had about it.'

'And you intend to soldier on?'

'For the time being, yes. And you?'

'Oh, I'm a bird of passage, I go where the spirit moves me.'

'And where will the spirit move you on to, Mrs Valois?'

'Please call me Leanne. I was never very happy being Mrs Valois. Indeed, I would much prefer to revert to my maiden name.'

'So, where is your next port of call, Leanne?'

'I'm not sure. It depends how bored I get with what is on offer at the moment.'

Her smile was provocative, but determined not to respond to its invitation, he said lightly, 'I've no doubt we shall meet again at some function or other, always providing Hong Kong maintains its attractions.' He smiled and moved away, only too aware that Leanne Valois was not accustomed to any form of indifference.

She watched him walk across the hall, occasionally stopping to chat to groups of people, and if she was conscious of pique she was also conscious that she needed to talk to him again.

The occasion presented itself at a racecourse meeting several days later where she was unmissable in her floating gown and large, flower-encrusted hat.

They spoke briefly, but then several days later there was another banquet and he found himself sitting next to her. Against a halo of white gardenias he was surprised to see that her hair was a dark auburn and he felt somehow cheated, just as Vanessa's auburn locks had always cheated him.

Conversation came easily between them, he found her witty and amusing but it was much later when they stood together on the terrace looking out across the harbour that she surprised him by saying, 'I intrigue you don't I? You don't really know what I'm about or if you should get to know me better.'

'Is that what you think?'

'Yes. I sense that one minute you want to know me better, then there is disappointment, I don't quite measure up. Do you know what I mean?'

'For me to find something lacking in you would hardly be cordial, Leanne.'

'Oh, I agree, but now you are beginning to intrigue me, Richard. What exactly did you hope to find in me?'

'I find you beautiful, charming and amusing, what more could I possibly be looking for?'

'I've been finding a little out about you, Richard.'

'Really?'

'I'm unused to men shrugging me off like some bothersome fly. Was it meant to trouble me or excite me?'

He was staring at her now, aware of the amusement in her amber eyes, the taunting smile on her red lips, and with a regretful smile he said, 'I'm sorry if my manner offended you, Leanne. Perhaps I'm out of practice when it comes to handling beautiful women.'

'Shall I tell you what I have learned about you?'

'Is it appropriate, do you think?'

'I think so if we are to be friends.'

'Then perhaps you should tell me the names of the people who have given you such information. How well do they know me, how long have they known me?'

'I learned only superficial things, Richard, but enough to make me want more.'

'So tell me what you learned.'

'That you are a widower, your real home is in England and that you are successful and ambitious, highly respected in your chosen career. You can see it isn't very much to be going on with. I don't want to know about your ambitions, I want to know more about you, the things nobody could tell me.'

For several minutes he stood silently staring out across the harbour and she waited patiently, aware that she was dealing with a private man who felt a great reluctance to involve her in a past that was still too painful.

At last he looked down at her, saying wryly, 'What they told you more or less sums me up, Leanne. I am ambitious, but only because there didn't seem to be anything else. My wife was killed in a motor accident about five years ago. I've moved on, but not enough perhaps.'

'Was it the loss of your wife that made you

198

want to come out here?'

'Not really. I always hankered after coming out here, but before Olivia's death it was never possible. I have a daughter who doesn't want to join me here and I still have my home in England for whenever I get tired of it here. I don't know what else I can tell you.'

'Only that you have it in you to forget the past, or at the least find something to replace it with. Tell me now why I intrigued you, I know that I did.'

'I saw you several months ago here at one of the banquets, you walked out of the lift in front of me and you reminded me of Olivia. Oh, not so much your colouring, or your face, it was your stature and the way you walked. Really you're not very much like her as regards your dress or your attitude to life.'

'What do you know about my attitude to life? Very little, I suspect.'

'Well, perhaps not very much, but it will be very different from Olivia's.'

'Tell me about her then.'

'She was very talented, an artist who painted wonderful pictures people wanted to buy, and she was beautiful.'

'There have been men who have considered me to be beautiful.'

'Of course, and I would never say anything to the contrary, and in many ways you do resemble her, but the resemblance is illusive.'

'She had auburn hair?'

'No, she was blonde, a Scandinavian pale

fairness and her eyes were blue, perhaps the difference is in the colouring.'

'What is your daughter like?'

'Tall, independent and auburn-haired. She likes horses and wouldn't know a paintbrush if she saw one.'

'Nothing like her mother at all then?'

'No.'

'A disappointment to you?'

'Of course not. Vanessa is her own girl, I was hoping she'd come to live with me here.'

That was the moment when they were joined on the terrace by a group of people who immediately put an end to more probing, much to Richard's relief and Leanne's exasperation.

It was much later in the evening when they met up with each other again, she with her escort for the evening, he alone. He knew that she lived on Hong Kong Island and as they parted at the doorway to the hotel she said, 'No doubt we'll meet again, Richard, another banquet perhaps.'

He smiled and said, 'Yes, I'm sure we will.'

The next day he lunched with a colleague and asked with all the innocence he could muster, 'What do you know about Leanne Valois? I sat next to her at dinner last evening.'

His companion smiled. 'I thought you seemed to be getting on rather well with the lady,' he said dryly. 'Well, I can't tell you much that you don't already know. French husband, American father, witty, popular, I don't know anything to the lady's detriment.'

'No lovers?'

'Not that I know of that are meaningful, but then Leanne Valois is a sophisticated woman who knows well how to be discreet.'

'You mean there have been lovers?'

'I mean I've never heard of any. Are you interested in getting to know the lady better, Richard?'

'Not particularly.'

'You've been on your own for five long years, here is a widow on her own, rich, attractive, popular, nobody would find it at all incongruous. I don't know if the lady intends her solitary state to be permanent or not; do you?'

'I haven't met anybody I wanted to give it up for.'

'Well, it's worth thinking about. Set a few tongues wagging, here and in England.'

'In England?'

'Well, of course. The banking fraternity and no doubt your friends and neighbours.'

In the weeks that followed both fate and friends made it easy for Richard and Leanne to spend time together. She was always available and it was one evening on Victoria Peak when he decided to invite her to have dinner with him without the presence of others.

She looked at him in some surprise before saying, 'I got the impression that you were content to keep women at arm's length, why this change of heart?'

'Shall we just say that your impression was wrong,' he answered with a smile.

201

'Then I shall look forward to our evening together and I will try very hard to live up to any expectations you might have.'

She had told him that her favourite restaurant was a huge junk ship renowned for its ambience and its food and as they crossed the harbour in the small boat that took them there he was aware of her mounting the gangway in front of him wearing a long, floating silk coat and with her hair covered by a pale chiffon scarf.

After that evening they were constantly together and inevitably he began to see her as a woman he couldn't live without. A woman who was intelligent and passionate, a woman who fashioned herself into being everything he needed until in the end he began to ask himself if he had ever really known Olivia.

Comparisons were useless. Olivia belonged to the past and Leanne was erasing every single incident of their life together, now all he could think about was their next meeting, how necessary she was to him, how vital in a world that he believed had grown suddenly cold.

There was gossip. Leanne Valois was not a woman to be overlooked, she had been around too long, and inevitably there were men who envied him, men who questioned his involvement and among the women in particular there were feelings of doubt and suspicion. They talked among themselves about her obvious desire to capture him and just where his affair would lead him. They brought up memories of Jules Valois that were hardly commendable, and asked each other if a woman who could ever have married such a man would be the right sort of wife for pristine Richard Lorival. They discussed his daughter who they had never met, asking each other if she would accept Leanne in her mother's place, particularly when at one stage he had told them so much about the attributes of his first wife.

Both Richard and Leanne knew they were the topic of much censure from one half of the community and a certain good will from the other. Neither of them cared, they had gone beyond that. Richard thought it was time to inform his sister that he had met a woman he wanted to be a permanence in his life but he hesitated, unsure how it would affect Vanessa.

Vanessa was living most of her time with Mina and she wrote to say she was having a wonderful time with her cousin's friends, going here there and everywhere and she was hoping to find a job in London.

He felt guilty about Vanessa, but at the same time he had a life to live, a job he needed and yet all he was doing for his daughter was keeping her well supplied with money. One day it would all be different. They would return to England, Vanessa would love Leanne, who would take the place of her mother, and their lives would begin again.

He talked to Leanne about Vanessa and found her sympathetic. She wanted to meet her, suggested that they return to England for a holiday so that she could become acquainted with his friends and family, but Richard didn't think it was the time. Richard had memories of Vanessa's rebellion, which he had never understood, but he believed it was a rebellion that might come between himself and Leanne and he was not prepared to risk it.

The intense loneliness had gone, Leanne saw to that. She filled their time together with endless excursions to places he had only read about, and there was laughter and excitement to be found in the warm, sultry nights when they wandered through the thronged streets of Hong Kong, down streets where songbirds in golden cages filled the stalls and fortune-tellers delighted in telling their future in grains of sand.

'I don't believe a word of it,' Richard said, laughing.

'But of course you have to believe it, darling,' she'd answered him. 'How can you be so dubious?'

'That we are to live a hundred years and have twenty children, that our paths to heaven are lined with gold and paradise itself will not be more wonderful? The man is a fake.'

Leanne was quick to reassure him that it would all come true.

Eighteen

Mrs Peterson was displeased. Half an hour ago Vanessa had arrived in the company of three other young people, two men and a girl, and now they were making their way to the stables where Vanessa's horse was stabled, leaving the hall cluttered with their luggage.

She had no idea how long they intended to stay but she should have let her know when they were coming and when they intended to leave. This was becoming a regular occurrence and she thought that it was time to have a word with the girl's aunt to see what solution she had to offer. Of course it was Vanessa's home and she had every right to be there, but it was the haphazard coming and going that was annoying her.

It was later in the afternoon when she heard them laughing and joking in the drawing room and she decided to confront Vanessa with her problems. They were spread out over the sofa and chairs and she was met with four pairs of faintly hostile eyes when she opened the door.

She decided to take the bull by the horns by saying, 'I wish you'd let me know when you decided to come and bring people with you, Miss Vanessa, I need to get extra groceries in.

You know there's only me and Molly here.'

'Really, Mrs Peterson, there's nothing for you to bother about, we're eating out this evening, all we need is breakfast and we'll see to that.'

The fact that they were larking about in her kitchen the next morning did nothing to appease her, particularly when she viewed the state they left it in. No crockery had been washed, the pans too were stained with oil and as she and Molly viewed the remnants of a hastily consumed breakfast she said, 'Somethin's got to be done about this, either I'll write to her father or to his sister.'

She had enjoyed living in the house with just Molly, her time was her own, she had the run of the place and her pay was hardly much less than it had been when she'd had Richard to look after. Mr Lorival had always been generous, she didn't want to leave his service, but there were limits to her endurance.

Mrs Peterson would not have been surprised to hear the views expressed round the breakfast table at the home of Vanessa's aunt Mina.

'It was nice to be able to get into the bathroom without banging on the door this morning,' Mina's son, Alex, said with a wry smile.

'Perhaps we should install another bathroom,' his mother said. 'It doesn't bother your father and me because we've got our own, but you and Vanessa are always arguing about something.'

'How long do we have to put up with her, Mother?'

'Oh, don't say it like that, dear. She's a sweet

girl really, you used to like her.'

'She's out of control, Mother, she should be with her father.'

'What do you mean, out of control?'

'Well, she's off with that Hardcastle chap, we all know what he's like.'

'I thought he was a friend of yours? What do you mean, Alex? Is there something wrong with him?'

'No morals, too much money and two much swank.'

'Vanessa likes him.'

'Of course. She likes his money and she likes his lifestyle, which he's prepared to flaunt in front of anybody who's prepared to listen to him.'

'He seems very fond of Vanessa.'

'No, Mother, he's fond of himself, she's just a good-looking girl with a rich father who's never around. If she's aiming on marrying him she's in for a big disappointment. Don't say I didn't warn you.'

He got up from the breakfast table and after kissing her cheek he said, 'I'm off now, folks, I shan't be in for dinner, some meeting with the high-ups.'

When he had gone his mother said feelingly, 'He's got me worried about Vanessa. Surely she's intelligent enough to know what that boy's like?'

Her husband gave his full attention to the *Financial Times*, and realizing he didn't wish to be involved, she said plaintively, 'I can see I

207

shall get no help from you,' but at that moment Alex came back into the room and tossing the morning mail on the table said, 'There's a letter from Hong Kong, Mother. Perhaps he's coming home, that would solve all your problems.'

While his father gave his full attention to the mail he found of greater interest Mina opened the letter from her brother. She read it quickly in disbelief, then after reading it again she laid it down in front of her and stared down at it without speaking.

Her husband was accustomed to hearing all the news Richard's letters usually contained, now he looked up with some surprise at her silence. 'Is something wrong?' he asked. 'You look dumbfounded.'

She stared at him. 'He's married, some woman he's met in Hong Kong. Here, read it for yourself.'

She watched while he read it, then he chuckled. 'Well, this lets you off the hook, old girl, she wants to come to live in England. Hong Kong is losing its enchantment, in less than six months they'll be here. Vanessa'll have a stepmother and you can wash your hands of everything that's bothering you.'

'But who is she, Nigel? He's never mentioned her in a single letter, now to have married her, I can't believe it.'

'Her name's Leanne, he says she's beautiful and when we meet her we'll understand why he fell in love with her.'

'Oh, I wonder how I can tell Vanessa.'

'Well, she's got to be told, this might be the making of her.'

'Olivia wasn't the making of her Nigel, they were so besotted with each other their daughter had little chance.'

'Oh, he won't be so besotted the second time, this time it'll be different.'

'I'm not so sure. Oh, Nigel, there's been so much anger and bitterness in that girl, and the last time I spoke with Margaret Gates I sensed it in her also.'

'You mean there was something going on there?'

'I'm not sure. There may have been, after all she was always at the house, closer to him than anybody else at the time he was very lonely and vulnerable.'

'And then he ups and leaves for the other side of the world. If something was going on I can understand her anger, can't you?'

'Yes, of course I can.'

'And now to bring a new wife home, doesn't Margaret Gates live in the vicinity?'

'Yes, she works at the bank in London, I suppose they'll know about it and if they do she will.'

'Well, it's nothing to do with us. He's entitled to marry anybody he wants to marry. Evidently he wasn't over the moon about his secretary, she probably realized that a long time ago.'

Mina nodded, Nigel would be philosophical. Mina felt her worries were just starting. How would Vanessa take it? How was she going to tell her? But Vanessa made it very easy for her.

She came into the house when Mina and Nigel were sitting down to afternoon tea, full of the events of the weekend, talking about the restaurant they'd dined in, the fun they'd had on the horses, the way they'd managed to placate Mrs Peterson, and faced with their silence and Mina's obvious anxiety she said, 'Is something wrong? You both look so dismal about something.'

'Do sit down, darling,' Mina said. 'Help yourself to something from the trolley, we've got some news for you.'

While Vanessa poured the tea Mina brought out her father's letter and seeing it, Vanessa said, 'From Daddy. Don't tell me he's pestering me to go out there again?'

Silently Mina passed the letter over and watched nervously while Vanessa read it, then laying it down in front of her she said, 'So she's beautiful and we're all going to love her. Not me, but it does mean that I can please myself what I do with my life, he'll be so preoccupied with her he won't care what I'm doing.'

'Really, Vanessa, of course he'll care, he's always cared.'

She was aware of Vanessa's cynical expression before she said, 'Oh well, perhaps it's just as well. I was never going out there and he might be home in time to give me away. I'll be off his hands for good.'

'Give you away, Vanessa? What do you mean?'

'I'm going to marry Tim Hardcastle. I shan't need my father's money or his blessing. The new wife has really fallen on her feet, no step-daughter to contend with, no second claim to anything she believed was hers and a son-in-law who'll keep me in the manner to which I've become accustomed.'

'You mean Tim Hardcastle has asked you to marry him, Vanessa?'

'Not in so many words, but he will.'

'I never heard anything more ridiculous,' said Alex that evening. 'He's not the marrying kind, he boasts about his conquests, Vanessa's simply one of them.'

'Perhaps this time he's in love, Alex.'

'No, Mother, he's not. He's happy to be with her, a pretty girl hanging on his every word, idolizing him, he wants that, but he's not look-ing for commitment.'

'How can I convince her he's unsuitable?'

'You won't.'

'You don't like her very much do you, Alex?'

'I did once, Mother, but she's changed. She's not a bit like the little girl who used to come here for holidays.'

'I just don't want her to get hurt, Alex.'

'Well, perhaps her father'll talk some sense into her when he comes home.'

'Alex, he's got married again, some woman he's met in Hong Kong, that was the news in his letter.'

'Well well, how did she take it?'

'I'm not really sure except that she said she would be marrying this boy and her father's marriage was nothing to do with it.'

'Will they be coming home?'

'Yes, I'm not sure when, but soon I would think.'

He put his arm around her shoulders, squeezing her affectionately before saying, 'Mother, there's nothing you can do about Vanessa. You've already done more than your share. Let her sort her own life out.'

It seemed to Mina that she was living in limbo waiting for news from her brother, worrying about Vanessa and feeling a certain anger – when would it all be resolved?

A visit to see Mrs Peterson provided little comfort.

They sat in the morning room drinking tea while Mrs Peterson poured out her frustrations regarding Vanessa and her friends, their sudden appearances and the upsetting of her routine, their thoughtlessness and the music which went on through the night.

'What are they like, these young people?' she asked.

'Well, I've never really spoken to them, they're young, careless, keen on having a good time.'

'But the young man who she says is special, what about him?'

'Oh, that one. He's good-looking, full of himself, too much money.'

'Why do you say that?'

'His attitude. Swanks about his cars, where he's been, what he's done. I can't help but over-hear him, either in the garden or the conserva-tory, whenever he's got an audience.'

'You don't like him?'

'I shouldn't be saying that, I don't really know him, but I can't help forming some opinion, can I?'

'No, Mrs Peterson, you can't. I hope my brother comes home very soon, but things might be very different for you, Mrs Peterson.'

'Oh well, if I don't get on with the second Mrs Lorival I can leave, I've had several offers since I've been here. I don't think I'll have any problems in finding something else.'

'I'm sure it won't come to that, Mrs Peterson. My brother always spoke very well of you, I'm sure your job here is safe.'

'I wonder what she's like, this new wife of his.'

'I'm as much in the dark as you. He says she's beautiful, all he could wish for. I just wish I knew what he wished for. Tell me, Mrs Peterson, do you ever see Miss Gates, she lives quite near, I believe?'

'Oh yes, in those flats along the road there. I only see her now and again because of course she's working in London now. Her mother seems quite happy about it, says she likes her job and she's made new friends there.'

'I'm so glad.'

She had the impression that Mrs Peterson would like to have said more on the subject, but

213

after a few seconds she changed the subject. 'I just wish Miss Vanessa would tell me when she's coming down, I could prepare for them, make meals. As it is they help themselves and leave everything upside down.'

'I'll have a word with her, Mrs Peterson, but I can't promise it will do much good.'

Nineteen

On Monday morning Margaret Gates returned to her office at the bank after spending a week recovering from a very bad cold, and immediately she was aware of an elusive atmosphere. She was well accustomed to office gossip, but somehow on this morning she had the strangest feeling that it concerned her.

There were whispering groups who separated when they caught her looking at them, and apart from their asking if she felt better, no desire to communicate further. It was later in the morning when her boss requested her presence and facing him she was instantly aware of his knowing smile before he said, 'I'm not sure if I've got to you before the office gossips have had their say, notice anything different in there?'

'Yes, but I don't know what it is.'

'Then do take a seat and I'll tell you. It concerns your friend Richard Lorival. I know he

214

was your boss, but I'm assuming after all the years you worked together that he was also your friend. Am I right?'

'In a way.'

'Well, whatever way it was I should tell you that our friend Richard has outgrown his enchantment with the Far East and intends to return to England. Does that surprise you?'

'Not really. The things we want don't always live up to our expectations.'

'That's true, but it would seem he's also decided he's had enough of the single life. He's elected to get married again.'

She was aware that he was watching her intently with a gleam of speculation she had come to associate with him, but he on the other hand was unaware of her racing heart and that her hands were clenched tightly under his desk.

For five long years she had told herself she was well and truly over Richard Lorival. She was fancy-free, with a good job and no romantic intrusions into her life. Now he was coming home to a house close to her own little flat and not alone.

Eric Davidson waited for her response. An astute man, he could see that his news had shaken her in spite of her attempts to hide it, and deciding to avoid mention of the new Mrs Lorival he said, 'I feel that Lorival bequeathed you to me, Margaret. Now that he's coming back here I've been wondering if he'll be asking you to work for him privately again. Would you be interested?'

'No, Mr Davidson. I'm happy at the bank, I would never go back to the job I had before.'

'That's what I wanted to hear.'

'Will he be coming back here?'

'Oh no, I'm sure he won't, he'll stay with the Bank of China, but he'll still be needing a secretary.'

'But not me, Mr Davidson.'

'Good. Now you can go in there and face all the busybodies with the information that you know all about it and you're not in the least bothered.'

She had never been more relieved to see the end of her working day. It was the beginning of October and already the days were shortening, making her glad to light the gas fire and draw the curtains. It was only when she did that she looked up towards the big house beyond the wrought iron gates, a house that stood in darkness apart from a discreet light above the door.

Soon now there would be lights everywhere, cars driving up to the front of the house and what would she be like, this new Mrs Lorival? Why hadn't she had the courage to ask her boss if he knew anything about her? She tried using her imagination. Tall and slender, dark hair and brown eyes, and obviously sophisticated. A woman with ready laughter and the capacity to make friends and impress people.

When there was a ring on her doorbell around nine o'clock she thought immediately that it would be her next door neighbour, who invariably chose this time to descend on her. She quite liked Mary Barrow, but on this occasion she'd been wrong when she opened the door to find Mrs Peterson standing on the door mat.

'I hope you don't mind my comin' round, Miss Gates, but I just felt I wanted to talk to somebody. I don't suppose you've heard the news?'

'About Mr Lorival? Yes, I heard today, simply that he was coming back to England and that he was married.'

'Well, that's as much as we know, even his sister doesn't know much more.'

'Well, do sit down, Mrs Peterson, and I'll make coffee – or tea, if you'd prefer it?'

'Coffee will do very well, Miss Gates. This is a nice little flat, somethin' like this might be what I'll be needin' now.'

'Oh, surely not. None of this will make any difference to you. He's going to be very glad to have you and so will she.'

'Well, I'm not too sure. He's met her out there you know, how she'll settle in here is anybody's guess.'

'Do you know anything at all about her?'

'Well, his sister did tell me she's American, widow, her husband was French. She's lived in Hong Kong some time, she doesn't know what she looks like, only that she's wonderful. He would say that, wouldn't he?'

'I suppose so.'

'I never thought he'd marry again, he was so besotted with her, but if he did I'd hoped it might be somebody like you, nice but ordinary, if you know what I mean.'

'I'm sure you never thought he'd marry me, Mrs Peterson, however nice and ordinary.'

'Don't get me wrong, they're nice things to be, I can get along with that. I really did think that at one time he was gettin' to look at you twice.'

'No, Mrs Peterson, you're wrong.'

'But you did like him?'

'As my boss, yes. Now I have a new boss who I like equally as well and that's all.'

'So you won't be coming back here to work for Mr Lorival?'

'No. He won't be working for the same bank any more, he'll have a new secretary, he probably won't be working from home.'

'Oh dear. I was hoping you'd be coming back, at least it would be halfway to being like old times.'

'I don't think we can ever go back, we move on. I wonder how Vanessa will take it?'

'Badly, I shouldn't wonder. I'm worried about that girl, it's none of my business but that young fellow she's goin' around with isn't exactly my cup of tea, he's too full of himself by half.'

'Well, perhaps it isn't serious.'

'Well, it's my bet they're sleeping together, I can't even begin to think what her father's going to say when he finds out.'

Margaret decided not to comment, and Mrs Peterson said dourly, 'It's a different world from the one I was brought up in, even her aunt is worried about her.'

'Then perhaps it's as well her father is coming home.'

'Perhaps, but with a new wife, I'm not so sure.'

One Saturday morning halfway through November Margaret encountered Vanessa riding her horse along the road outside her flat where she was backing her car out of its parking space.

She never quite knew where she was with Vanessa. Sometimes she would smile, at others turn away, but this particular morning she halted her horse and smiling down at her said, 'My father's expected home tomorrow, did you know?'

'No, only that he was expected home soon.'

'I've been ordered here to meet them, I'm not looking forward to it.'

'Who issued the order, Vanessa?'

'My aunt. She said it would be expected of me. What will be expected of you, I wonder?'

'Absolutely nothing, Vanessa. We now work for different banks. My job with your father finished when he left for Hong Kong.'

Vanessa smiled. 'Aren't you a little curious as to what she'll be like?'

'I'm sure she'll be very nice, I hope you and she will get along together.'

'I don't expect to be here, not for any length of time at any rate.'

'You're staying in London, then?'

'After I marry, yes. That's something I have yet to talk to my father about.'

'I didn't realize you were engaged, Vanessa, I do hope you will be very happy.'

Vanessa smiled and rode on, but as she drove into the village Margaret felt troubled. Vanessa should have been happy, filled with joy at the future that awaited her; instead she had sensed in her a defiance, a piquancy both resentful and mischievous.

What would the new Mrs Lorival make of Vanessa? She despised herself for feeling qualms of pity for Richard. Irritably she argued with herself that he deserved to be troubled. She hated him for months of depression, for his casual handling of their affair and yet she was honest enough to know that hatred and love were close bedfellows, emotions that were too strong to be cast aside as unimportant.

She had purposely not told her mother that Richard was coming back but she didn't want her to discover it casually. She decided that now that his return was imminent she should tell her so she called on her way to the shops. Since they lived apart they were more comfortable together, and of course now with Richard out of her life her mother had been prepared to let sleeping dogs lie.

As always her mother set about making tea, inviting Margaret to sit near the fire, enjoy the freshly-baked scones, and then she proceeded to tell her the church gossip and all that was happening to her neighbours. After all that was exhausted Margaret dropped her bombshell, which from her mother's expression she deemed it to have been.

'You're not going back to work for him I

hope?' her mother said sharply.

'No, Mother, I'm not, there's no question of that.'

'Why's he coming back then?'

'Most people come back in the end, Mother. Besides, he's remarried.'

For several minutes her mother didn't speak, then she said adamantly, 'There now, what did I tell you? He never had any thoughts about you even when you had plenty about him. I'm glad you've got him out of your system. What's she like, this new wife of his?'

'I don't know, I've never met her. Nobody knows.'

'What about the bank, don't they know?'

'None of them have met her. Mr Davidson says she's American, a widow, her husband apparently was French.'

'Oh, well that figures, she would have to be something different.'

It didn't trouble Margaret now that her mother used sarcasm in her tirades about Richard – she felt the same way about him – but this morning she was deriving little comfort from it. Thoughts of him made her angry, yet inwardly she despised the fact that her anger only meant she still cared. Indifference would have been a greater comfort.

It was later in the afternoon when she met Sophie Simpkin at one of the market stalls. She would dearly like to have avoided her but it was too late, and there was a determined look in Sophie's eyes as she descended on her.

'Margaret,' she cried. 'I've been so longing to see you, but now that you're working in London our paths never cross. Kevin tells me about you, you've settled down very well, I hear.'

'Yes, very well.'

'I rather like Mr Davidson, he's really quite dishy.'

'Is he? I hadn't noticed.'

Sophie laughed. 'Oh, come now, perhaps not as dishy as Richard but he's no longer available. What do you think about the new wife, Margaret?'

'Nothing at all. I haven't met the lady.'

'He's coming back. Do you suppose we might expect an invitation to the usual Christmas dinner party?'

'Oh, I really wouldn't think so. After all, he'll no longer be working for the same bank, they'll have new friends, new acquaintances.'

'No reason to forget the old ones, though. Oh, I expect Richard will pick it all up as if he'd never been away. She's American, I believe. Well, they're great socializers, aren't they, so I expect she'll soon make her presence felt.'

Margaret wished she could make her excuse and move away. She didn't want to hear anything about Richard's wife, an American beauty once married to a Frenchman, sophisticated and elegant as she was beginning to imagine her.

'Oh, I'm dying to meet her,' Sophie was gushing. 'You live so close to them, when you see her do tell Kevin what she's like so that he can tell me. Better still, why not call to see me one day so that we can gossip together?'

Margaret made no promises and was relieved to be driving home in the misty misery of a November afternoon.

Richard's sister and her husband watched Richard leave the house in the company of his new wife with mixed feelings. Nigel had found her witty, charming and altogether acceptable; Mina had her reservations.

'I couldn't believe it when I first saw her,' she said thoughtfully. 'She looked so much like Olivia, small, and dainty, but it was only later when I realized she wasn't really like Olivia at all. Perhaps I should phone Vanessa, tell her we've met, give her some indication of what she looks like.'

'She'll see her for herself tomorrow, love. If I were you I'd let tomorrow take care of itself. Why don't we eat out this evening, take your mind off all this, forget your brother and his new life?'

As she got ready to go out later, Mina thought about Leanne, her enthusiasm for the few days they had spent in London, their hotel, the shops, the theatres, but how would she like living in the village north of London in the large house Olivia had loved and where every nook and cranny spoke of her?

She was determined not to spoil their evening by her concerns about her brother and his future.

Twenty

Vanessa had heard the car approaching while she sat in the morning room reading a magazine, but immediately she jumped to her feet and ran out into the hall and up the stairs.

From her bedroom window she was now able to look down at the arrival of the big black Bentley and her father climbing out of the front seat. He didn't look any different from the last time she'd seen him. He was handsome, she'd always listened proudly to her school friends enthusing over his good looks. Nearly six years hadn't altered them. He was still tall and slender, still dark-haired and elegant, and now he was walking round the car to open the door for a woman to step out. It was then Vanessa stared with anguished eyes at the small, slender figure standing beside him.

There was a sudden knock on her door and then her father was in the room, holding her against him, then holding her away from him to say, 'Gracious, Vanessa, I thought I was coming back to a little girl, not a beautiful woman. Leanne is waiting for us downstairs, darling, then we have all the time in the world to get to know each other. You'll like her, darling, she's warm and sweet and funny, we'll be a family again.'

'I have to get back to London tomorrow, Daddy, I've only been given tomorrow morning off so that I can travel back. There's only to-night.'

Richard stared at her in disbelief. 'But Vanessa,' he said gently, 'this is your home, not with Mina. Why are you going back?'

'I'm taking a course on art at a gallery in London, they took me because of my mother, they knew of her, but if they expected me to follow her example I'm going to disappoint them.'

'They expected you to paint?'

'Not really. But I'm learning about art, how to appreciate it, what it's all about.'

'But you're not happy?'

'No.' Now was not the right time to tell him about Tim Hardcastle. She'd given him quite enough to be going on with.

'Oh well, there'll be other times,' he said philosophically. 'Come and meet Leanne.'

Vanessa swallowed her anger that her father should be so dismissive of her life. And so it began again...

Leanne, in the meantime, had been surveying the drawing room, which was largely as she'd imagined it would be. It was not to her taste.

She'd had enough of Chinese carpets and oriental rugs. They didn't go with pictures of Scottish lochs and Highland cattle, nor was she enamoured with velvet drapes at the windows

225

and huge stone fireplaces. While she waited for Richard to return she visualized how she intended to change things.

She turned as the door opened and a beautiful but rather sulky young woman followed Richard into the room.

'Ah, you must be Vanessa! I'm delighted to meet you at last. Your father's told me so much about you.'

Leanne moved toward Vanessa with her arms open, but the young woman extended her right hand formally and said rather stiffly, 'Really? I'm surprised he found the time. He seems to have been very busy.' She shot an accusing look at her father, who laughed it off and moved to his wife's side, putting his arm around her.

Leanne swallowed her irritation at Vanessa's apparent determination to dislike her new stepmother and turned to Richard, saying, 'Darling, I'm awfully tired after the journey, and you and Vanessa must have such a lot to catch up on. I'm going to have a lie down and then perhaps—'

'You needn't go on my account,' Vanessa interrupted. 'I have to go and see to my horse.' And with that, she left the room.

On her way to the front door Mrs Peterson caught Vanessa, eager for some information about the new Mrs Lorival.

'Miss Vanessa, Miss Vanessa!' she called, hurrying after her. 'Did your father mention if they'd be dining here tonight? And do you know how long you'll be staying for yet?'

Vanessa halted in her tracks and heaved a sigh.

226

'They didn't mention supper, and I'll be going back to London in the morning.'

'Oh, so soon? Don't you want to get to know your new stepmother?'

'No. Does it matter?'

'Not to me it doesn't, but I think it might matter to your father.'

'Oh, I don't know, he's got her now, hasn't he?'

Nothing of the house surprised Leanne, the Englishness of it, the richness of walnut and the sheen of silver, the gleam of crystal and the allure of velvet and brocade. When they entered the studio at last Leanne looked around at the stacks of canvases, the easels and the unfinished drawings and Richard said, 'This is the first time I've been in here since Olivia died, there's nothing we can do with it except lock the door and forget about it.'

Oh no, thought Leanne, that's not what we'll do with it. We'll get rid of all this, turn it into another bedroom and forget it was ever here.

Everything had to change, but she had to be careful. She had no means of knowing how his daughter would react to change, and there had been something about Vanessa that had unsettled her.

What she would do for now was get to know his friends, people in the village. Richard had said that Olivia had never been one for visiting neighbours or the local inns, not because she was a snob but because it simply hadn't been her scene. Well, he had a new wife now and she would be all the things Olivia hadn't been.

She made a great effort to entertain Vanessa over their evening meal until Vanessa wished she would shut up. She didn't want to know about the delights of the Far East or the dozens of young men she might have met and who she would have found quite enchanting. 'But then,' Leanne added, 'I'm sure there must be some young man here equally as captivating. Are we going to hear about him?'

Her father was looking at her with a half smile and Leanne said, 'Don't keep us in suspense, Vanessa. I'm sure your father's itching to know what you've been up to these last few years.'

Vanessa had debated with herself how soon she should tell him about Tim but now wasn't the time, not with Leanne smiling provocatively across the table. Instead she said, 'I have to get off early in the morning, Daddy, so I'll pack my case and go to bed early. I'm sure you want to spend the evening alone.'

'When will we see you again, Vanessa?' her father asked.

'Oh, whenever I get time off. You will keep an eye on my horse, won't you?'

'Of course, darling! But it seems so wrong for you to be living with Mina and Nigel. I feel you should be here with us.'

'I don't think so. I'm a grown woman now, and perhaps one of these days I'll have my own place and my own job. You have a wife to consider now.'

Richard found Leanne sprawled out on the settee in front of the fire, her red velvet robe startlingly bright against the more sober cushions. Bestowing him with a bright smile, she said, 'Nice girl, darling, not what I expected.'

'What did you expect?'

'The little girl you'd left behind. I don't intend to take the place of her mother, I doubt if she'd want it.'

'I'd like you to be good friends.'

'Was she very close to her mother?'

'Well, I was away during the war and there were just the two of them, they were close then, then somehow later it all seemed so different. Maybe they never quite cared the same way again.'

In some strange way Richard had believed life with his new wife would take up the pattern of the old. He quickly began to realize that this would not be so.

In the few weeks leading up to Christmas Leanne talked about dinner parties and guests, asking, 'Surely you had dinner parties at this time of the year, why don't we continue with them?'

'We had the usual one for staff at the bank, but I no longer work with them and I haven't yet got to know the new people in London. Perhaps we should simply invite Vanessa and my sister and her husband.'

'Oh no, darling,' Leanne cried. 'Vanessa will want to be with her boyfriend and your sister has her own ideas about Christmas. Don't you have a list somewhere of people you invited? Did Olivia do the preparing or did you have caterers in?'

Somehow or other Richard was swept up in a tide of partying he had never experienced and he began to have doubts as to how well invitations to old colleagues would be received. He need not have worried. Apart from his erstwhile secretary they accepted his invitations with great pleasure.

Margaret Gates stared at her own invitation with disbelief. She regarded it as insensitive. How dare he feel he could simply invite her along like an old workmate and expect her to comply?

Strangely enough it was her mother who surprised her by saying, 'You know what they'll be thinking if you don't go, that you're jealous of the new wife, that there was something going on between you. And what's more, it's something she's going to think.'

'I thought you'd be the first to say I should stay away,' Margaret said.

'Yes, well, perhaps I do think that, but at the same time I can imagine what they'll all be thinking.'

'I'll think about it, Mother.'

'Well, you don't need to buy anything new, you bought a new dress every year, that last one was very expensive.'

'Mother, it's six years old, and in the last six years I haven't felt the need to buy another because I haven't attended anything that demanded one.'

'Oh well, you'll please yourself I suppose, and you'll want to keep your end up.'

Margaret's acceptance of the invitation was the last to arrive on Richard's doorstep and Leanne looked at it with a smile. The secretary, without an escort. What was she like? How well had they known one another? She decided not to question Richard, but innocently she asked Mrs Peterson, 'You would know Miss Gates, Mrs Peterson. She's accepted the dinner invitation, how well will she know all the other guests?'

'Quite well, and now she's working with most of them.'

'I suppose you knew her very well?'

'She came here to work every morning, I served her with coffee in the morning and tea in the afternoon, she was always very nice.'

'She wasn't married?'

'No, she lived with her mother.'

Mrs Peterson decided to say nothing of Margaret's removal into her flat, let Mrs Lorival find out for herself, but she felt a sly amusement that Leanne felt it necessary to ask questions.

'What age of a woman is she?' Leanne asked.

'Oh, she's in her early thirties.'

'Attractive?'

'Quite nice-looking, intelligent, Mr Lorival thought highly of her, she was good at her job.'

Of all the guests they had invited, Margaret Gates was obviously giving her the most cause for thought.

231

In all innocence Leanne said to Richard over their evening meal, 'I do think we ought to have suggested Miss Gates bring an escort, darling, she's the odd girl out. Do you know if there is anyone?'

'Leanne, I've been out of the country for the last six years, she could have a hundred escorts.'

'Is she likely to have, do you think?'

'I never knew of anybody, but time alters many things.'

'You thought well of her, Richard?'

'She was an admirable secretary.'

'I'm looking forward to meeting her.'

'I thought you were looking forward to meeting them all, why Miss Gates particularly?'

'Oh, darling, you know about secretaries and their bosses, I want to reassure myself that your secretary was not a femme fatale.' Richard smiled uncomfortably.

Eric Davidson had a malicious sense of humour, which was evident when he said to Margaret, 'So you're invited to meet the new wife? Why don't I pick you up?'

'I didn't know you'd been invited, Mr Davidson.'

'Apparently he thinks I qualify, and since we're both unattached it seems like a good idea.'

So Margaret described where he would find her flat and felt indescribably relieved that she would not have to arrive at the dinner party alone.

She liked Eric Davidson, She had been warned that he liked women but had no intention of getting involved with a single one of them. He enjoyed his single life, his golf club, his skiing holidays in Europe and the luxury of cruise liners. Margaret had no doubts that if he ever got tired of the single life he would not be looking for some thirty-plus-year-old, but rather a nubile young woman other men might envy him for.

She decided that she would not tell her mother anything about the new arrangements. Her mother would speculate and this time it would have her approval. A rich man, single, with a good job, then would come the questions about his family, his background and where it was all going.

Margaret knew where it was going: nowhere. Picking her up had been a kind gesture. She had been dreading meeting Richard and his new wife, standing in the hall to receive their guests, singularly alone. Now at least Eric Davidson would be the right sort of escort, and perhaps even give Richard Lorival room for contemplation.

Twenty-One

Eric Davidson was a stickler for punctuality so she knew he would not be late. That he looked remarkably handsome and elegant made her warm to him, entirely without the attraction she had felt for Richard Lorival.

'You look lovely, Margaret,' he greeted her, ignoring for the first time the Miss Gates he would normally have used.

'Thank you,' she said with a smile. 'I need to do justice to such a handsome escort.'

He laughed. 'It's a good idea to give them all something to talk about, what do you think, Margaret?'

'Well, the office watchdogs will be on the prowl on Monday morning but tonight at least I think we might be spared.'

'I'm not too sure about that. One or two of the wives have reputations we should distance ourselves from.'

'You know about them?'

'Of course, as a single man without strings attached I'm quite sure I've been the object of their speculation for some considerable time, and you didn't escape either.'

'I didn't?'

234

He laughed. 'Come along, we mustn't be late, I'm anxious to meet the new Mrs Lorival, and I expect you are too.'

What would he have said, she wondered, if she'd said that she didn't want to meet her, not tonight, not ever? She was dreading the evening ahead, dreading seeing the inside of the house again, Richard's grave, charming smile and the replacement for Olivia. She wanted the evening to be over and never repeated, but by this time he was holding the car door open for her and she was directing him to the gates of the house.

'Quite a place,' he said softly.

'Yes,' she replied, 'quite a place.'

Memories were piling up as she viewed the large Christmas tree in the hall and the array of flowers everywhere. In those first few moments it seemed to Margaret that nothing had changed, with Richard playing the perfect charming host and the dainty figure of his wife beside him.

It could have been Olivia from where she stood at the door watching them at the foot of the stairs. It was only when she took their out-stretched hands that she realized Leanne Lorival was not like Olivia at all. Her gown was too flamboyant, her smile was speculative, lips that smiled while her eyes did not, and as Richard took her hand she hated the feelings that engulfed her.

How was it possible to hate him and love him at the same time? Then the old anger was back and she was grateful for it.

Eric Davidson received the full measure of

Leanne's charm and Margaret watched cynically as he responded to it with amused aplomb.

After she had deposited her wrap she joined the other ladies in the drawing room and at that moment Mrs Eastman was the first person to ask in a whisper, 'Well, what do you think of her, Miss Gates?'

'I've only just met her, Mrs Eastman.'

'Of course, dear, haven't we all, but there's been so much speculation, people saying she has been round too many corners.'

'Whatever do you mean by that?' another woman asked.

'French husband, the high life in Hong Kong, rich American stock. We'll just have to wait and see, won't we?'

The waiters were serving them with drinks and Richard and his wife were now circulating amongst them. Margaret stood near the window. She didn't feel like one of them now, just as she'd never felt one of them before. They were the wives of the senior executives; she had merely been Richard's secretary and she'd risen no higher in the hierarchy. She was glad when Eric Davidson paused to say, 'You all right, Margaret?'

'Yes, thank you.'

'You'll know everybody, of course?'

'Yes.'

'Perhaps we'll be sitting together over dinner, in any case I'm sure everybody will mingle.'

'Yes, I'm sure they will.'

Richard smiled at her across the room occasionally, but otherwise he was keeping his distance, and as she viewed the men talking business, the women making polite conversation, she was asking herself savagely, 'Why have I come? Why did I buy this stupid dress? Why am I still hurting?'

The meal was excellent, as in the old days, the waiters were efficient, the wine flowed freely, and she noted with some cynicism that Eric Davidson sat next to his hostess and she was relieved when Sophie Simpkin was placed next to her.

'Just like the old days,' Sophie said with a smile.

Margaret agreed.

'Is this the first time you've met her?' Sophie asked.

'Yes. It was an excellent meal.'

'Oh, yes it was. She seems to be quite taken with your boss, how do you get on with him?'

'Very well.'

'I thought when you arrived together something might be going on for you.'

'No, Sophie, it isn't.'

At that moment another wife, who Margaret knew only slightly, attracted Sophie's attention across the table, so she turned away after returning her brief smile.

Dinner over, Margaret walked into the large conservatory, which was mercifully empty of guests. But she was not alone for long before Leanne joined her, saying with a smile, 'You're all alone in here, tired of bank gossip?'

'Well, there's a lot of it I don't understand and the wives all know each other very well.'

'Of course. You worked for Richard, didn't you? It must have come as quite a shock when he decided to go out to the Far East.'

'In some ways, yes.'

'You worked here at the house I understand? I've seen the office, Richard's decided to keep it on as a study but we'll change the furnishings and make it cosier. I'm still very new here but I do intend to knock a few walls down and change a few things around.'

'I can understand that.'

'Well, yes. The colour scheme's not mine and all these pictures, some of those will have to go.'

Faced with Margaret's doubtful stare she smiled brightly, 'Oh, I know Olivia was famous as an artist and her pictures are probably quite valuable, all the same they're not to my taste. I had an artist in Hong Kong who painted the sort of things I liked. She was Chinese. She painted orchids and humming birds, lotus flowers on a pool and bamboo. I've brought some of them here with me so no doubt they'll find a place on the walls when Richard decides what to do with the others.'

'Thank you for inviting me Mrs Lorival,' Margaret said, trying to hide her shock. 'It was most kind of you.'

'Yes, well, Richard gave me a list of people who always came just before Christmas so I decided not to alter a thing. Are you quite happy working for Mr Davidson?'

'Yes, thank you. We have no problems.'

'Did you ever have problems with Richard?'

'No. I did my job and he never complained.'

Margaret had the distinct impression that her words were not what Leanne had wanted to hear, her expression was bland, at the same time her eyes were mocking, and somewhat hurriedly Margaret said, 'It looks as though some of your guests are ready to face the elements.'

'Gracious, yes, it's well after midnight and some of them do have some way to travel. I'll join Richard in the hall.'

Meeting Eric Davidson at the door Leanne said, 'If you're looking for Miss Gates she's waiting for you. I'm so glad to have met you, Eric. You don't mind if I call you Eric, do you? It's so much less formal.'

Eric smiled, and across the room Margaret read the cynicism in his eyes.

She collected her wrap and together with some of the others they moved out into the cold December night. They were climbing into the car when a low-slung sports car came through the gates and drove up to the house at breakneck speed, coming to a halt with a screeching of brakes outside the door.

The guests had stopped to stare at the two people climbing out on to the drive, a young man and a girl, laughing and obviously not a little drunk. Laughing, they waved to the departing guests; then Richard was there to order them into the house.

'Rather late visitors,' Eric said with a smile.

'That was Vanessa, Richard's daughter.'

'In for a few strictures, I shouldn't wonder. What sort of a girl is she?'

'Not easy, perhaps rebellious.'

'How will she take to the new stepmother, do you think?'

'I don't know.'

'Did you like her?'

'She was very pleasant.'

He threw back his head and laughed, and when Margaret looked at him sharply he said, 'You found her pleasant, friendly, perfectly circumspect, while I found her worldly, flirtatious and decidedly ambitious. Strange how differently women and men assess each other.'

'I wasn't out to assess her, I was simply a guest for the evening.'

'You'd rather not have gone all the same.'

'Why do you say that?'

'Because I feel sure you and Richard Lorival were particularly close, nothing came of it, but you're only human, Margaret, you had to know what she was like and now you're pretty sure he's made the biggest mistake of his life.'

'I don't think any such thing!' She was not a little taken aback at his powers of penetration, and she fought the blush that threatened to reveal just how accurate he had been.

'Well, if you do think that I heartily agree with you. When I said she was flirtatious I meant it. If I'd been that way inclined I feel sure the lady would have been flattered where a new wife could have been expected to feel reserve.'

'So you laid on all your charm and you believe she responded?'

He laughed. 'Something like that.'

'I was warned you were quite a charmer, Mr Davidson.'

'Well, just between us, Margaret. I doubt if you'll ever call me Eric and when we next meet in the office you'll go back to being Miss Gates. A very good idea, don't you think?'

'Yes, I do.'

'Well, here is your flat. Give me your key, I'll escort you to the door and bid you a warm good-night. I've enjoyed this evening, the men's talk and the tittle-tattle of women, the charm of our host and the duplicity of his wife, and of course the meal and the wine were excellent.'

'Why do you say his wife was duplicitous?'

'Because I have the strongest feelings that the months to come will prove me right.'

He opened the door to her flat, handed her the key, and smilingly kissed her hand. Then he was striding back to his car and after a brief wave was driving down the road.

She made herself a cup of chocolate and sat down in front of the electric fire in the kitchen to drink it. The evening she had dreaded was over. For the last six years she had told herself that she was over Richard Lorival, he didn't exist any more, and yet once or twice during the evening she had found him looking at her – oh, not with any look of love, but with a degree of uncertainty that had been more confusing.

He had a new wife, and all they had had was a

brief affair when he was lonely and vulnerable. She had loved him, he had never loved her. His need to get away from her, the bank and England only confirmed her feelings and yet she couldn't help thinking about the words she had exchanged earlier with his wife.

All evening Leanne Lorival had been the gracious hostess, perhaps more at home with the men than the women, but she had played her part and it couldn't have been easy for her when all around her were memories of Olivia.

From her bedroom window Margaret could look up the hill to where Richard's house stood blazing with lights. The sports car was still standing outside the front entrance and all the other cars had long gone. She could only hazard a guess at what was going on behind the closed door of the house, with Vanessa and the young man facing an irate Richard, and a wife who could easily feel resentful.

Why should she concern herself with how Richard felt, how he might view his daughter's behaviour or her choice of boyfriends? She'd thought she was well and truly over him, now simply because he'd come back into the area it didn't mean that old anxieties had to be rekindled, old flames to be relit.

In the weeks and months to come Richard would find his life, his home and his future would change considerably, the old Richard would not take kindly to it, but the new Richard, the newly married Richard, would have to accept it.

There had been so much certainty in Leanne's expression when she had talked about the changes she intended to make, so much assurance towards the woman she was least sure of. The other women were the wives of the men there, but Margaret was unmarried, had been part of a life she could only speculate about, and at a time when Richard was most vulnerable. Margaret had been the unknown quantity and grimly she thought to herself that Leanne Lorival, having met her, would feel reassured that she had nothing to fear. A secretary who was no raving beauty, into her thirties and unmarried, she would be more than reassured, she would be ecstatic.

She made herself go to bed although she was not tired, and after a night of tossing and turning she was ready to face the next day at seven o'clock in the morning, though she had no plans and no work to distract her.

As she was collecting her newspaper Mary Barrow came out of her flat burdened with packages and Margaret said, 'Is there something special at the school, Mary? I'm looking at all your parcels.'

'It's the nativity play, I've got costumes and all sorts of things here, it's going to be a hectic day.'

'Do you want any help?'

Mary looked at her in surprise. 'Well, yes please, if you're available, we're always looking for an extra pair of hands.'

'I'll get my car out, you'll never manage that

lot on the bus. I've nothing else on today.'

It was Saturday, market day, and as they drove down to the school Mary said, 'I saw you setting out for your party last night, he looked very nice.'

'He's my boss.'

'Really? He still looked very nice.'

'Yes, I suppose he is. It was nice of him to give me a lift.'

'Was the party a good one?'

'Very good. They've all been good.'

'But this one was different, wasn't it? New wife, is she nice?'

'Quite nice.'

'And you don't want to discuss her, I can understand that. His housekeeper looks none too happy.'

'Really? I can't see why.'

'Well, things are bound to change. It's early days yet but a new wife is bound to make changes.'

'I just hope she gets along with Vanessa.'

'I've seen her round and about with a young man, have you met him?'

'No. I've seen him briefly, that's all.'

'He's young, good-looking and very full of himself. He drives a fast car and seems to have plenty of money, he's also very confident and she seems besotted with him.'

'Where have you seen all this?'

'Oh, they've been round and about in the village, on their horses, in the car, walking along the lanes. I wonder how you've missed them.'

'Well, I'm usually in my car, and I tend not to stay around at the weekend.'

'I've been teaching children for years, perhaps I've developed a second sense with people. I'd be surprised if he was marriage material, too much of a playboy. But like I said, she was the besotted one.'

Twenty-Two

Vanessa slept badly that cold December night. Furious with her father and her boyfriend, she tossed and turned in her bed, going over and over the scene of the night before.

Tim had stood just inside the door, angry, petulant, unused to being reprimanded, while her father had accused them both of irresponsibility, that Tim had been unfit to drive, that they should both have had more sense and Tim's face had grown more and more sullen and she had become tearful.

Her new stepmother had kept well out of it, but in the end her father had suggested they retire to their rooms to sleep it off. It was then Tim had said he didn't intend to stay, he would drive home and Vanessa could please herself. No amount of remonstrating that he was unfit to drive had the slightest effect and he had left, storming out angrily, and all she could hear was the screech of his car hurtling towards the gates.

Of course Tim was angry. His parents allowed him free rein, their spoilt only son was the epitome of perfection. Whatever he wanted he got: money, cars, foreign travel. All his parents saw was his handsome face and his charm when he cared to use it, and he was always surrounded by like-meaning friends who saw no further than his charisma and his affluence.

Vanessa was afraid that he would still be angry, be capable of ending their relationship. She wanted to marry him, she had told her aunt and her friends that they intended to marry, but would Tim countenance a marriage to a girl whose father had spoken to him in such a fashion, treating him like a fool, when his own father would merely have been amused by his behaviour?

Today they were supposed to be going back to London to a bevy of parties and now here she was in her father's house while he might not even wish to come back for her.

There were sounds of movement in the house and she decided to go downstairs. She had to see her father sooner or later but hopefully without the presence of his wife.

The curtains were still drawn in some of the downstairs rooms but there were sounds from the kitchen and then suddenly the kitchen door opened and Mrs Peterson was staring at her across the room.

'Good morning, Mrs Peterson,' Vanessa said. 'I don't suppose my father's about yet?'

'I think you'll find he's in his study, I've just come to draw back the curtains. When did you arrive?'

'It was very late.'

'Not for the dinner party then?'

'No. I didn't even know there was one.'

She waited until the curtains were drawn to let in a stream of pale sunlight and Mrs Peterson said, 'Will you be staying on for Christmas then?'

'Oh no, I'm going back to London today.' She wasn't at all sure she was going back to London, so many things had to be resolved.

She went to the study and after knocking on the door she opened it to find her father gazing morosely out of the window. He turned and for several moments they stared at each other until he said, 'Have you had breakfast, Vanessa?'

'No.'

'Did you sleep well?'

'No. I was upset.'

'I was upset too, Vanessa. I was upset that I had had to chastise you like I did, but that boy should not have been driving in his condition – supposing you'd had an accident?'

'But we didn't and the roads were quiet.'

'And how many times had you driven with him in that state?'

'We'd been to a party, you had a party here and your guests were drinking.'

'And they all know when to stop. How well do you know that boy?'

'He's not a boy, Father, he's twenty-three and

247

he's a friend of my cousin's.'

'I asked how well you knew him, Vanessa.'

'Very well. I like him.' She wanted to scream at him that she intended to marry him, that they were in love, but now wasn't the time. She wasn't sure how he would take it, she wasn't sure of Tim.

'I don't want us to quarrel, Vanessa,' her father said calmly. 'I only want the best for you. I suggest we have breakfast and then talk about the rest of the day.'

'I'm going back to London, there's a big party this evening.'

'And how are you getting there?'

'Tim will come back for me.'

'I see.'

'Daddy, I don't want you to go on again about last night when Tim arrives, it isn't fair. Besides, it was the first night you'd met him.'

'Not a very auspicious start to our meeting. I'll make up my mind later about that young man.'

'I want you to like him, you're expecting me to like her.'

'"Her"?'

'All right then, Leanne.'

'I hope you will like her. Suppose we join her for breakfast?'

They were halfway through breakfast when Leanne joined them and Richard said with a smile, 'We started without you, darling, I expect you were tired, you put so much effort into dinner last night.'

'I think it went very well, don't you?'

248

'Oh yes, very well. Vanessa arrived just as they were all leaving.'

'I know. I heard a little of the furore. Where is the young man?'

'Oh, he left, Vanessa tells me he's returning today to drive her back to London.'

'Do we have you for Christmas, Vanessa?' Leanne asked.

'I don't think so, there's so much more going on in London,' Vanessa answered her, and as their eyes met Leanne thought savagely, She's so right. Those had been her thoughts in distant Hong Kong: so much to do in London, the banquets, the shows, the London she'd visualized, not this quiet town miles away and this enormous house surrounded by countryside and with too many memories.

Vanessa was watching her, knowing and understanding her and yet in the younger girl's eyes Leanne read only cynicism and resentment.

'I would have thought you'd be spending Christmas with us, darling,' Richard was saying. 'You can still go to your parties but come back for Christmas day and the rest of the holiday.'

'I don't think so, Daddy. I told Aunt Mina I'd be with them.'

'I'll speak to your aunt, Vanessa, I'm sure she'll understand why I'll want you to stay with us. Besides, I'd have thought you'd want to see your horse.'

Vanessa didn't speak, but Leanne with a bright smile said, 'I can understand the parties are important, darling. Perhaps later Vanessa and I can have a talk about the things I want to do with the house.'

'You're doing things at the house?' Vanessa asked in some surprise.

'Well, of course, dear, I want to feel at home here, I want to make it my house, and your father's too of course, but ours together.'

'So what are you going to do?'

'Change the colour scheme, get rid of the old office and keep it as your father's study, do something about the studio.'

'That was my mother's studio.'

'Well, of course, but we don't want a studio now, do we? I'm no artist and we could turn it into something else, another bedroom, a music room, a change. I've got things of my own I want to bring here, ornaments, pictures, all sorts of things.'

'My mother painted those pictures.'

'I know, dear, and they really are very good. I have pictures though that I would like to bring and after living so long in the Far East I do have a collection of valuable ivories and some jade.'

Instead of answering her Vanessa looked around the room, at her mother's watercolours adorning the walls, the lustre of velvet and the carpets her mother had loved. Dryly she said, 'My mother loved Chinese and Indian carpets, I would have thought you'd like them too.'

'Oh, I do, but the colours are not to my taste. Your father and I will talk about it in the New Year. So when can we expect to see you again?'

'I'm not sure.'

It was late morning when Tim arrived at the house and Vanessa went out nervously to meet him. He had hoped she would be waiting for him dressed for travelling but she said quickly, 'You're invited for lunch, Tim, I couldn't say no.'

Climbing out of the car he said stiffly, 'I'm surprised your old man wants to set eyes on me again.'

'Please be nice, Tim, forget about last night.'

'I will, but will he, do you think?'

Richard greeted him graciously and Leanne was introduced. Lunch was a civilized if awkward meal. Richard inwardly disliked his daughter's boyfriend as equivocally as he had the evening before, and it was left to Leanne to entertain them with her amusing anecdotes of the times she had spent in the Far East.

Farewells were said and Vanessa heaved a sigh of relief when they were driving away and Tim was saying, 'Oh well, I suppose that went off reasonably well. But he doesn't like me, Vanessa.'

'But of course he does, Tim, you have to get to know him, that's all.'

'She's quite a woman, isn't she?'

'You liked her?'

'Well, you have to admit she's been around a bit and it shows.'

Doubtfully Vanessa said, 'Are you saying there's something wrong with her?'

'No, she's the sort of woman I like: sassy, worldly, the sort of woman I hope you'll grow

251

into. I'd keep close to your stepmother, Vanessa.'

Vanessa bit her lip doubtfully, his words were not what she'd wanted to hear.

As Richard and Leanne moved back into the house after seeing them off she said quietly, 'He's not at all the sort of young man you want for Vanessa, is he, Richard?'

'No. Was it very evident?'

'To me, yes, and probably to him.'

'Did you like him?'

'I had a surfeit of young men like Timothy when I was growing up in America, too much money, fast cars, overrated egos and raging hormones. I shouldn't worry, Richard, nothing will come of it.'

'Why are you so sure?'

'I think she's crazy about him, but it isn't reciprocated.'

'Why do you say that?'

'Because, my dear, she may not be aware of it, and she probably doesn't want it, but there must be a lot of Olivia in Vanessa. She's pretty, looks more like you than her mother, but inside her there have to be somewhere the characteristics of her mother.'

'Are you saying that would be a bad thing?'

'For some men – you, for instance – it would be admirable; for Timothy it would be disastrous.'

'Then she's going to get hurt.'

'But of course, we all get hurt sooner or later.'

'I'm her father, Leanne, I don't want her to get

252

hurt by him. I feel she's been hurt enough, she lost her mother when she was very young, I went off to Hong Kong leaving her here and even now I don't seem to be able to get close to her.'

Leanne smiled. 'Richard, you say she lost her mother, but had she ever found her mother? And when you went away did she really mind?'

'She was very close to her mother, and she must have minded terribly when I left the country. Leanne, you don't know the half of it.'

Leanne looked into his eyes and smiled cynically. She knew the sort of man Richard was, she'd been aware of his characteristics almost from the first moment she'd met him. His English reserve that had been so at variance with her American forthrightness. His reticence and her frankness, and even now that they were married she sensed in him sometimes his disapproval of her need to be in the limelight.

Deciding to change the conversation she said, 'I've had some ideas about your office, Richard, I've been thinking about it this morning. Shall we take a look and I'll tell you what I think we should do.'

He followed her into the office and looked around at the functional room with its two desks and rows of filing cabinets, at Margaret's typewriter with its cover on, and the two telephones. The room looked stark, even with the long velvet drapes at the window and the beige carpet covering the floor.

Margaret had always brought flowers into the

253

room and there was the glass vase on the corner of her desk, but the waste paper baskets were empty and her swivel chair pushed tidily underneath her desk. For a moment he could see her there, her dark head turned to read the notes beside her machine, the way she smiled as she wished him good morning, and then his own desk with only the morning newspaper to show he had been into the room that day.

Leanne was standing near his desk gesturing towards the other half of the room.

'Darling, this room is far too large now that there's only you using it. I thought it would be a good idea if we halved it, keep this half as your study and the other half as a store room or even a small sitting room.'

'Why would we need a store room?'

'Well, I'm having stuff brought here, some we might keep, some we might sell. Then there'll be your stuff too.'

'My stuff?'

'Yes, darling. Didn't we say we'd change things, make this house our house? Most of it still belongs to Olivia.'

'And to me, Leanne.'

'No, darling, I suspect you just went along. Jules went along with many of the things I wanted to do, but then he was never really interested in the house, he didn't care for much outside the racetrack and the gaming tables.'

'Then why did you marry him?'

'Oh, he was amusing, and he took the place of my father. I wonder what she'd have done to this room?'

'Olivia hardly ever set foot in this room.'

'Not Olivia, darling, Miss Gates, your secretary.'

'She was quite happy with it as it was.'

'But that was when she was your secretary, Richard. Wasn't there a chance that one day she could have been something else?'

He stared at her, momentarily disconcerted, then looking away he said briskly, 'We were talking about the room, Leanne. I refuse to be drawn into your fantasies.'

'But are they so fanciful, darling? She's really quite attractive, she compared very favourably with any one of those other women, and she was here for some considerable time after you lost Olivia.'

'Like I said before, Leanne, shall we talk about the room, and any other part of the house you seem so determined to change? I can't imagine how you can possibly improve it.'

'I can't, but I intend to change it. I don't want Olivia's pictures staring at me every day.'

'They will belong to Vanessa one day, they are very valuable.'

'Why don't you ask her if she wants them?'

'Well, I don't suppose at the moment she has any room for them.'

'Then why don't you offer them to some art gallery? I'm sure they'd be delighted. Or sell them, Vanessa would be equally delighted with the money they'd bring in.'

He looked at her steadily. 'Leanne, I don't

want to talk about the pictures at the moment. I don't want to talk about any alterations to the house until the New Year at least. I certainly don't want us to quarrel about it.'

'Then let me have my way, Richard. I'm your wife, you want me to be happy here, don't you?'

'You know I do.'

'Then we won't talk about it until the New Year, then, darling, please trust me about the alterations, you'll be happy with them I promise.'

That was the moment Richard asked himself how much his wife's alterations would affect his bank balance.

Twenty-Three

Margaret Gates was relieved that Twelfth Night fell on a Saturday, particularly when she viewed the rather sad little Christmas tree on the table in the corner of the living room.

Her mother had bought her the tree, thrusting it into her hands, saying, 'You used to love decorating the house for Christmas but for years you've done nothing apart from a bunch of holly and some plant or other.'

'You always said you didn't like artificial trees and the real ones dropped their needles.'

'Well, I bought this at the church bazaar and I got the baubles to go with it. It'll cheer you up I hope.'

'What makes you think I need cheering up, Mother?'

'Well, after that party you'll need cheering up, it brought back too many memories, and not all of them happy.'

'You're paranoid, Mother. I enjoyed the party, met the new Mrs Lorival and my boss took me and brought me home.'

'I won't say another word,' her mother snapped. 'Do something with the tree and I'll see you on Christmas morning.'

Now the tree was coming down to be put on the top shelf of the kitchen cupboard complete with its baubles, to be resurrected next year and probably for a great many years to come.

In the days and weeks following Christmas huge builders' lorries, furniture vans and decorators' vans ploughed up the road outside the flats and stood outside the house. It became so congested that one morning Margaret was unable to get her car out of the garage. It was pouring with rain and she stood uncertainly at the garage door watching the front wheels of a large van spinning helplessly through the mud. It was then that Richard's car, slithering and sliding on the slippery road, came to a shaky stop outside the gates of the flats and Richard called to her through the car's open window.

'You'll never get your car out, Margaret, I'm

very sorry. Can I drive you to the station?'

Against the driving wind and rain she struggled to get into the front seat of his car and he said, 'You're going to the bank, Margaret?'

'Yes. If you don't mind dropping me at the station I'll be very grateful.'

'Unfortunately I'm not going into London this morning, I have a very urgent meeting in the hotel near the airport. I'm not sure when I'll be able to get away. Can you get home from the station later in the day?'

'Of course, I can get a taxi.'

They drove in silence but she knew him well enough to know that he was annoyed, not with her, but with the state of the road, the terrible morning and the lorries surrounding his house. It was only when they got to the station that he said, 'I'm afraid you're going to be inconvenienced for some time, Margaret. Why the alterations couldn't have waited until the spring I can't imagine.'

'We'll get used to them.'

'Probably, but you shouldn't have to. How long do you have to wait for your train?'

'About fifteen minutes, you did the journey quicker than I would have done.'

He smiled. 'You'll have time for a coffee.'

'Probably. Thank you for the lift.'

He got out of the car and came to open the door, which the tearing wind almost drove from his clasp, then with a brief smile she left him to run quickly across the path to the station entrance. She didn't look back, but she heard the sound of his car's engine as he drove away.

She was late arriving at the bank like quite a few other people that awful morning, and when Eric Davidson passed her desk he smiled, then at his door he turned to say, 'Oh to be in Egypt, or anywhere else for that matter now that January's here.'

'I do agree.'

'I'll have my mail as soon as you've gone through it, Miss Gates, I have a meeting at eleven.'

'Of course.'

The telephone rang just as she was about to take it in to him and she would have recognized the voice without any shadow of a doubt with its faint American accent, its low-pitched drawl, intimate and provocative.

'May I speak to Mr Davidson, please?'

'Who is speaking?'

'Mrs Richard Lorival.'

'Just a moment.'

After putting the call through she sat to wait until it had finished while she speculated on why Leanne Lorival should telephone Eric Davidson. Maybe to invite him to another evening party after the changes had been made to the house. She had the distinct feeling that Leanne could find a dozen reasons if she put her mind to it.

Immediately the call had finished she went into his office but businesslike as usual he displayed nothing unusual in his demeanour, neither amusement, artlessness or constraint, and yet he knew that she knew who his caller had been.

Without a word she placed his mail in front of him and he said evenly, 'I'll have my coffee at the meeting, Miss Gates, it's going to be one of those days.'

He left for his meeting just before eleven and she saw no more of him that day. She was glad to be going home, even if it was in a crowded railway compartment smelling of damp clothes and all those around her seemed sunk in gloom.

She hoped she wouldn't have long to wait for a taxi but as she joined the queue she found Richard suddenly beside her saying, 'The car's outside, Margaret, I was hoping I'd be in time to meet the train.'

She couldn't help the racing of her heart. Oh, why was he doing this? Why this sudden kindness when she wanted to hate him, to forget that she had ever loved him?

He took hold of her arm to battle through the wind and then she was sitting beside him in his car and they were nosing their way through the slow-moving evening traffic.

'Busy day?' he enquired evenly.

'Yes, the usual.' She was glad he didn't go on to ask her more. She didn't want him to ask her opinion of Eric Davidson as her boss, what she was doing with her life now was none of his business but Richard had always known the right things to say at the right moment.

'I feel very responsible for your predicament today, Margaret,' he was saying. 'I hoped I'd get to the station in time for your arrival, you'd have had a long wait for a taxi I'm afraid, and particularly in such awful weather.'

'It was very kind of you.'

'Not really, I'm glad to have been of some help.'

It was Margaret who broke the silence. 'How long are the alterations expected to take?' she asked.

'Heaven knows. They're certainly extensive.'

'Doesn't your wife like anything about the house?'

'Apparently very little.'

'I suppose there had to be changes.'

'Yes, that was inevitable, but it's my view it would have been easier to sell the place and find something else.'

'Would you have done that?'

'I don't know. There are many things I want to keep, things that are important for Vanessa to inherit. Vanessa will want nothing of the new place Leanne envisages.'

After that there was silence when they were both busy with their own thoughts and then they were driving up the road towards Margaret's flat and Richard said, 'Well, thank heavens the lorry got away. I hope tomorrow's going to be a different story.'

'Thank you once again for the lift.'

'I'm glad I was able to help. Stay there until the door is opened, this wind is dreadful.'

He stood with the open door pulling against his hands and Margaret ran up the path to struggle with the front door while the wind tore at her raincoat, then she heard Richard driving away.

There was no let up in the weeks that followed from the procession of vans and lorries that kept the road in a state of perpetual turmoil. Angry postmen and refuse collectors railed against the alterations that were going on, and Leanne usually made her escape for most of the day in her new high-powered Mercedes.

On the one day Margaret encountered the long-suffering housekeeper, Mrs Peterson merely shook her head dolefully saying, 'Don't ask me what's going on, I've been told not to discuss anything with anybody, that it's none of their business.'

'By whom?'

'Well, her of course. I'm tired of it all, my kitchen isn't my own any more and there's dust and grime everywhere.'

'I'm sorry, Mrs Peterson, perhaps it will all be sorted soon.'

'The house was beautiful, everybody said so, why is any of this necessary?'

Margaret smiled politely and moved away.

All she could see from her flat was that the garden was being laid out entirely differently. Gone was the rose garden Olivia had loved and the rockery with its banks of heather that had bloomed profusely at different times of the year. Now there was a parking area suitable for a dozen cars and other work going on behind the house.

How was Richard coping? she wondered. He seemed to be arriving home late in the evenings and at the weekends neither of their cars were there.

Richard could have told her that he spent most weekends in London with his daughter and his sister and her family, while Leanne told him it was a good opportunity for her to meet up with old school friends she had known in America and who now resided in England. Richard would never have admitted to being disenchant-, ed with his wife. He deserved her, he'd been a foolish man instead of a wise one and now he was paying the penalty.

Their time together was spent in a house that reeked of sawdust and paint. He hated those rooms that had been completed with Leanne's love of pale carpets and furniture and oriental pictures and ugly porcelain.

He'd stood in the centre of the newly designed drawing room looking around him with some dismay and she'd said, smiling, 'Darling, you do like it don't you? It's made the room look far more spacious and those pictures are priceless. She's becoming so well known and fashionable, in no time at all everybody will want to buy what she paints.' When he hadn't answered she said in her little girl, cajoling voice, 'Oh, I know Olivia's pictures were famous, darling, but aren't they all much of the same, the Lake District, the London parks and Italy? Think of orchids and pagodas, darling, so much more romantic.'

He was seeing the superficiality now behind her ingenuity, recognizing the speculation in her eyes hidden behind the kitten-soft expression on her face. He was no longer in love with her, he doubted if he ever had been.

His sister displayed her anxieties to her husband and son as they waited for Richard to join them for dinner. 'It's not working out,' she said quietly. 'He's upset about the house and all sorts of other things. He hasn't said anything, I just know.'

'And where is she every weekend?' Nigel said sharply. 'How many old friends is she supposed to have in this country – how do we know they even exist?'

'Where do you suppose she is then?'

He shrugged his shoulders, and Mina said quickly, 'She was at school in England for some time, she must know people here.'

'She married a Frenchman and spent years in the Far East, I'm sure you don't suddenly pick up with old friends you knew years before. They'd all have moved on.'

'Well, I still have friends I was at school with, even when they live miles away.'

'What's he going to do about Vanessa?' Alex asked sharply.

'Well, they seem quite happy together now, dear, more friendly than they've seemed for years.'

'I mean about the boyfriend and the marriage. Is it coming off or isn't it?'

'They're still together, dear, she hasn't mentioned marriage recently.'

'And she won't.'

'Why are you so sure?'

'Because one of the chaps asked him if marriage was on the carpet and he just laughed. Said he was fond of Vanessa, wasn't too happy with her old man and liked the stepmother. By that I assume he's met them and the meeting wasn't too amicable.'

'Oh, we all know about that dear, just before Christmas. They'd been drinking and Richard objected to him driving, it was months ago, I'm sure everything has been sorted. Vanessa seems happy enough.'

Alex exchanged a sharp glance with his father before saying, 'I think we should forget about Tim Hardcastle, I don't like him so I'm pre-judiced. I know some of the girls he's played around with, they're all of the same opinion.'

'Perhaps because he dumped them,' his father volunteered.

'No, Dad, I rather gather that in the end most of them dumped him. Oh, they all thought a lot of him at the beginning, then they got to know him and didn't like what they discovered. It's not just the girls, the chaps don't like him much either.'

'Well, if she's set her heart on him I don't think there's much we can do about it,' his mother said gently.

A few minutes later they greeted Richard with smiles and he said, 'I hope you haven't delayed dinner for me, the traffic was exceptionally busy this evening. I take it Vanessa isn't in for dinner?'

'No, dear, she's meeting friends.'

'Hardcastle I suppose,' Richard said frowning.

'She didn't say. She has made friends at the college, Richard.'

'How goes the alterations?' Nigel asked.

'I believe they're to be finished quite soon. Leanne said she intended to have a party to celebrate their completion, you'll all be able to pass your own judgement.'

'You mean we're invited?' Mina asked.

'Of course. I would think she's invited a host of people, I really don't know, I don't intend to have a hand in it.'

'Only pay for it,' Nigel volunteered.

'I expect so. I've already been stunned by most of the bills, when I questioned them she said she had enough money to pay for her more extravagant foibles.'

'Shall I like what's been done?' Mina asked doubtfully.

'Perhaps. Did you like it before?'

'Oh yes, I loved it, the colours, the warmth, the Englishness of it. I suppose I won't recognize it now.'

'I don't recognize it. I can stand at the window and think I'm standing in some villa on Victoria Peak. The trees always hid the village, but now I can visualize looking down on Victoria Harbour in Hong Kong, the cruise lines and the junks, the old railway grinding to a halt at the top and the pagodas of Kowloon in the distance.

She told me she was tired of the Far East, she wanted to return to the West, its timelessness and its stability, now all I'm reminded of every morning is my memory of the South China Sea and the clinking of rickshaws.'

'You wanted to go there, Richard.'

'I didn't know what I wanted. I thought I needed to get away. The thing is, when I got away other uncertainties were waiting for me that I hadn't bargained for.'

'I hoped you'd be happy,' Mina murmured.

Richard smiled grimly. 'Happiness, my dear, is an elusive commodity; impatience is a more dangerous one. I was impatient. I wanted to be happy again too quickly, I went on clutching at straws, a little bit here, a little bit there, and in the end the bits and pieces didn't fit and I had to go on looking for more.'

'And you thought you'd found them in Leanne?' Mina asked.

Richard's smile was reflective, then very quietly he said, 'Perhaps impatience is rearing its ugly head again, Mina. Perhaps once again I'm asking too much too soon.'

Twenty-Four

Once, a long time ago, Margaret had heard a friend of her father's say, 'It was so quiet I could hear the silence.' She'd thought it was nonsense, but then she'd been a child at the time, but now that the lorries and vans had long gone she could understand his words.

Obviously everything that had needed to be done had been done and she could only guess how the house must look inside; she had decided quite adamantly that there had been no improvement to the garden and the outside that she could see.

Her next door neighbour was of the same opinion.

'It's like some town hall,' Mary commented. 'So functional, and the garden was always beautiful. Surely you have to agree with me, Margaret?'

'I always liked the garden, Mary.'

'Well, I'll be waiting to hear what you think about the house next time you're invited.'

Of course she wouldn't be invited, why should she be? Last Christmas had been politeness, nothing more, but then Eric Davidson surprised her by asking, 'Would you like me to pick you

268

up on Saturday evening? Hardly worth getting your car out for such a short journey, Margaret.'

She stared at him in surprise before saying somewhat stupidly, 'Saturday night, Mr Davidson? I'm sorry, I don't understand.'

'The viewing of Lorival's house. Haven't you been invited?'

'No. Why would they invite me?'

'Well, they did at Christmas.'

'That was rather different. That was simply a polite gathering of people who had enjoyed his hospitality in other years.'

'Oh, is that what it was?'

'I haven't been invited, Mr Davidson. I hope you enjoy the function.'

There was a teasing amusement in his smile and she knew why. Leanne Lorival had telephoned him several times and he knew that she was aware of it. There was no need for him to explain anything to her, even if she put the worst construction on the calls. At the same time she was aware of his reputation, justified or not, but she told herself sternly that she must not feel any sympathy for Richard Lorival.

It was mid afternoon when Leanne was shown into her office and immediately Leanne was quick to explain. 'Why, Miss Gates, I'd forgotten you were Eric's secretary. How are you?'

'Very well, thank you, and you, Mrs Lorival?'

'Oh, very well now that I've got the house to my liking. I hope Mr Davidson is free to see me? I need his advice rather urgently.' When Margaret stared at her in some surprise she

269

laughed lightly. 'Never put all your eggs in one basket, my dear, my father taught me that a long time ago and he was very astute man. I suppose some of your loyalty to Richard still lives on.'

'My loyalty is to the bank, Mrs Lorival.'

'Well of course, my dear, I'm sure they have every reason to feel proud of you.'

Leanne had seated herself on one of the chairs near the window while Margaret informed her boss of her arrival.

'I do hope Eric isn't going to keep me waiting very long, we're having a dinner party tomorrow evening and lots of guests later on. You can imagine I have a great deal of preparation to do.'

She was very much at ease with the use of his name and Margaret said evenly, 'He's on the telephone at the moment, Mrs Lorival, he'll be free in a few minutes I'm sure.'

He came to the door to invite her in and across the room his amused smile was tantalizing.

She did not stay long, and after bidding goodbye to Margaret with a brief smile she was gone. Margaret knew well what tomorrow would entail: cars coming and going until the small hours. She wished she'd never bought her wretched flat because now every day she was too aware of the comings and goings at the big house.

She willed herself not to watch, but the longer days were an invitation to sit on her small balcony and from there she could see the gardeners at work, the comings and goings of Leanne, when she went out alone and when they went

270

out together.

She hated him for coming back. She told herself that she was glad if Leanne was having an affair with Eric Davidson, they deserved each other, but in the end she knew that she was the one being tortured.

Mina eyed her husband and son across the breakfast table with some asperity. In a short time they were due to leave for their weekend at her brother's house and neither of them wanted to go. When Vanessa joined them she seemed more concerned with the letter in her hand than any conversation going on around the table.

When Mina looked at her curiously she smiled, saying, 'It's from Sally Fielding, Aunt Mina, my old school friend. She's engaged and she's getting married next spring, she wants me to be her bridesmaid.'

'Oh, but that's wonderful, dear. Who is she marrying?'

'Some man she's known for ages, somebody who lives in the same town, an accountant I think.'

'You'll accept I hope?'

'I'll have to think about it.'

It was on her way to her father's house that Vanessa mentioned the invitation to Tim, who immediately said, 'Can't you make some excuse? Don't you hate those long, boring speeches where they're all congratulating each other, the best parents in the world, the most beautiful bride, the best son-in-law, even the bridesmaids get a mention.'

'You mean you wouldn't want any of that for your wedding?' Vanessa asked nervously.

He laughed. 'My dear girl, it wouldn't be for me – haven't I just said so?'

'You mean marriage, or the occasion?'

'At the moment, Vanessa, I mean both. We're having a wonderful time together, I just hope your old man doesn't feel it his duty to question me too closely.'

That was the moment Vanessa knew her future with Tim Hardcastle was a pipe dream, nothing more. They finished the rest of their journey in silence.

They were driving through the gates of her father's house when Tim said, 'It looks as though we're not the first, I'm glad about that.'

'That's Uncle Nigel's car, I don't see Alex's unless he's travelling with them.'

Her father embraced her and shook hands formally with Tim, while Leanne embraced them both avidly, saying, 'There are drinks in the drawing room, then you can both view the house before the rest of them arrive.'

'How many are you expecting?' Vanessa asked her father.

'Only the family for dinner, dear, the rest are friends and acquaintances joining us this evening.'

'Simply to view the house?'

'That is Leanne's idea.'

Vanessa stared around her in some dismay. It seemed to her that the house she had grown up in had somehow never been there. The colour scheme, the furniture, the pictures on the wall were all gone, and seeing her expression her father said, 'I know, dear, nothing is the same. Do you like it?'

'I don't know, it's too different.'

'I agree, it will take some getting used to.'

'Where are my mother's pictures, that one of Capri and the one she painted in Florence?'

'At the moment they're in the studio.'

'You mean the studio's still there?'

'Yes, and overflowing with unwanted furniture and carpets.'

'As well as Mother's pictures.'

He sensed her anger and a new maturity which might have pleased him at any other time, for now he only recognized her resentment and the reason for it.

By eight o'clock in the evening the rooms were beginning to get crowded, and whispering to her husband Mina said, 'I don't know any of them, do you?'

'No, I can't think why we were invited, although the fellow in the white tuxedo seems familiar.'

'Not to me he doesn't.'

Eric Davidson received special attention from Leanne, and Richard looked on with undisguised cynicism. Eric Davidson was handsome and charismatic, Richard knew something of his reputation, which hadn't prevented his rise to the top in banking circles, but Davidson was a playboy, he'd never aspired to be the marrying sort and he'd always been careful who he'd tangled with.

From a discreet corner in the conservatory Leanne was joining Davidson and another man while they talked business.

'You men are really too dreadful,' she carolled. 'I wanted this to be one evening when there was to be no talk about business and here you are isolating yourselves to talk about nothing else.'

'We're ready to circulate,' Eric's companion said.

'Then please do. Look around the house, tell me what you think of it.'

'From what I've seen of it, it's beautiful,' he replied.

'But you've only seen the conservatory, do look around.'

He smiled and left them and Eric said, 'I must have a word with Richard, Leanne. I don't want him thinking I know more than I should about things.'

'*My* things, Eric; nothing to do with Richard.'

'All the same, perhaps we should join him.'

'Will you need to see me one day next week at the bank?'

'Possibly.'

'I ask because I'm thinking of taking a few days' holiday, only a few days, but I feel I need to get away after all the turmoil of the last few months.'

'Where are you thinking of going?'

'Paris, Rome, I haven't decided.'

'Will Richard be going with you or is he too busy?'

'Far too busy. Don't you just love Paris at this time of the year? Why don't you treat yourself, Eric?'

He laughed. 'Now you really are inviting trouble.'

'But you get holidays, don't you, or are you so important the bank can't do without you?'

'Oh, they can do without me all right, I have plans for a holiday at the beginning of September, not quite finalized yet.'

'So there's to be no Paris or Rome?'

'Not for me I'm afraid.'

'You'll be sorry.'

He smiled, and looking up at him through narrowed eyes she said, 'You knew all about me the first moment we met, I knew it, I could see it in your eyes, so you know I can flirt, I like to flirt, particularly when the man I'm flirting with doesn't readily respond.'

Eric moved away, and Leanne watched him walking across the room to where Richard was speaking to John Gregson. He intrigued her but he exasperated her too. Richard hadn't been easy in those first few months, but Eric Davidson was not a grieving widower, he was a cynical beguiler.

Before he reached them Eric changed his mind. They were evidently talking business and he'd come to enjoy himself, so instead he wandered around the house.

A young woman stood in a doorway hesitating to come in further. She was tall and slender with dark auburn hair, eyeing with disdain the antics of Leanne and the dashing young man she was talking to. Intrigued, Davidson walked across the conservatory to speak to her.

'I'm wondering what you think about the alterations,' he began. 'You seem younger than most of the other women, I rather think your views will be different. I'm Eric Davidson.'

'I'm Vanessa Lorival.'

'Richard's daughter.'

'Yes.'

'You seem very interested in that young man's preoccupation with your stepmother.'

'I don't think of her as my stepmother and he isn't bothering me in the slightest. There's no accounting for taste, is there?'

Eric laughed. 'I'm not sure which taste you're referring to, hers or his?'

'Both, I think.'

'Might I suggest that quite recently you might have cared too much?'

'Perhaps I'm growing up – not before time, my father would say.'

He laughed. 'Well, it's nice when the young admit it,' he said evenly.

'Do you live in this area, Mr Davidson?'

'No, I live in Richmond. You might say I'm in the same business as your father.'

'A banker?'

'Yes. I work in the bank your father worked for before he went to Hong Kong, though we never worked together. He kindly invited me just before Christmas and tonight I'm here to view the alterations. What do you think of them?'

'What was wrong with it before?'

'I thought the house was lovely; evidently Leanne had other ideas.'

'Even down to the pictures.'

'The pictures?'

'Yes. My mother was an artist, her pictures were beautiful and much sought after, these are nothing in comparison.'

'Perhaps she thought they'd go with her furnishings. I've lived in the Far East, Hong Kong and Singapore, she hasn't left either of those places behind her.'

'I wouldn't know, I've never been there.'

'Not even when your father was there?'

'No. He wanted me to go, it was my fault I didn't.'

Richard too was circulating and Eric met him in the hallway. They shook hands and Eric said, 'I've just been talking to your daughter, Richard, charming girl.'

Richard smiled, saying, 'And no doubt she's been telling you what she thinks about the new decor.'

'Well, one would expect her to prefer the house as it used to be.'

'I never actually thought she was interested in that.'

'She's not too keen about the oriental atmosphere.'

'No, perhaps not. I find it a little overpowering.'

They talked pleasantries and Eric wondered if Richard knew anything at all about Leanne's visits to him at the bank. He was sure Richard would not concern himself with his wife's finances but as they went their separate ways he couldn't help thinking that there were many things lacking in this marriage.

A full moon was shedding its light across the expanse of patio and garden as Eric went for his car at the end of the evening, and it seemed that the car park was larger than he remembered it and the garden smaller. Part of the alterations he felt sure.

On his way home, on a whim he decided to stop at Margaret Gates's flat. No doubt she'd be intrigued to hear of the new Mrs Lorival's changes to the house, though she'd never admit to it.

Margaret was just thinking about going to bed when the ringing of her doorbell took her by surprise. Who could be calling at this late hour? Her surprise increased when she opened the door to find Eric Davidson looking rather sheepish, but she remembered her manners and invited him in, wondering if it was the right thing to do.

When Margaret had made coffee, Eric carried the laden tray into the living room and took a seat on the settee. Margaret poured the coffee, then went to sit in one of the easy chairs and he smiled mischievously, saying, 'The settee is far more comfortable, Margaret, but you please yourself. Now what do you want to know about the alterations?'

'I'm assuming you'll tell me but I'm not really all that interested.'

He smiled. 'Well, of course you are. You spent years at that place, now you wouldn't recognize it. Your office has gone. It now goes under the name of Richard's study with a desk, two easy chairs and all newly carpeted and curtained.'

'I guessed it would be.'

'It's very small.'

'Well, probably the half that was mine is now something else.'

'Oh yes. A sitting room from which you can see the garden – surprising, really, when there isn't too much garden left at the front of the house.'

'What about the pictures?'

'Not my cup of tea.'

Eric sank back against the cushions to drink his coffee and looking at him she felt that he seemed so at home in her tiny room. She speculated as to what might have happened if she'd joined him on the settee. Would one thing have led to another? After all, they were both unattached and fancy-free. She immediately discounted such notions. The girls at the bank all fancied him, they thought him decidedly dishy and the fact that he was a bachelor intrigued them and disconcerted them.

Why would he look at a woman in her thirties, reasonably attractive but that was the most one could say? And she wasn't a fool, there was no way she would get involved with the man she worked for again.

She realized that he was looking at her with a half-smile on his face, and quickly she said, 'More coffee?'

'No thank you, I should be going, but I couldn't pass your house without answering all those questions you were dying to ask.'

'I would never have asked you anything.'

'No, but you would have been left wondering and I couldn't have that. Tell me, what did you think of the first Mrs Lorival? I never met the lady.'

'She was charming and gracious. Very beautiful and talented, I can't tell you anything else.'

'Too perfect to be true. I met the daughter this evening, is she like her mother at all?'

'No, she's more like her father.'

'She seemed a little at variance with all that was going on there, particularly with her young man doing his utmost to captivate her stepmother.'

'That sounds like Vanessa.'

'Not a very happy household, too many undercurrents.'

'That was the opinion you reached in one short evening?'

'Two evenings, Margaret, have you forgotten the one before Christmas?'

'Well, that evening was different from the ones I remember but I didn't think there were any undercurrents.'

'Oh, but you did, Margaret. New wife trying hard to emulate her predecessor, all the women there intent on forming an opinion and a husband who was left wondering.'

'Wondering?'

'Perhaps not that evening, but that was the opinion I just formed after spending another evening there.'

'Perhaps it's an opinion you have formed after seeing more of Mrs Lorival.'

He threw back his head and laughed delightedly. 'That bothers you, Margaret, doesn't it? Who are you worrying about, Richard Lorival, me or the lady herself?'

'I'm not worried about any of you, didn't you say it was purely business?'

'I did, but did you believe me?'

'I'm not accustomed to answering riddles so late in the evening.'

'No, you're right, and perhaps it's time I wandered off home. Thanks for the coffee, my dear, I shall see you on Monday morning.'

She walked to the door with him and after shrugging his arms into his coat he turned to smile at her. 'Goodnight, Margaret, thanks again,' and he was gone.

From her window she watched him getting into his car and he drove off without looking up. He disconcerted her strangely. She felt she had known Richard Lorival well, as his secretary, as a friend, then as his lover, that was surely why his betrayal had hurt so much. She had the distinct impression that she would never truly

281

know Eric Davidson.

Later as Margaret lay in bed unable to sleep, aware of the sound of the cars leaving the Lorivals' house, she reflected on what might be happening there. How many guests would be staying on? Would Vanessa have made it up with her silly boyfriend and would Richard compliment his wife on the success of the evening?

Why did she have to think about them at all? she asked herself angrily. She had moved on, rebuilt her life, so why had he come back to ruffle the calm waters of her life, resurrecting the past she believed she had forgotten?

The anger she still felt for Richard Lorival kept her tossing and turning until the early sunlight illuminated her bedroom.

Twenty-Five

The following day, as he strolled through the rooms still suffering from the evening before, Richard knew for a certainty that he hated the house. When he gave Leanne his blessing to make changes he hadn't realized that she would change everything, and now all that remained of the old decor lay piled in Olivia's studio. Her pictures were covered with dust, some of them were torn and the few pieces of furniture that were left had been scratched. Ornaments that Olivia had valued were chipped and he did not think he was misjudging his wife when he believed she had done it deliberately.

He had wanted their marriage to work, he believed he had been in love with her; now he knew he had merely been stupid and lonely in a new world and in his stupidity he had discarded people who had really mattered to him, his daughter and, to his surprise, Margaret Gates.

He hadn't been in love with Margaret, it had been too soon, but if he hadn't run away things might have been different.

He was standing at the window of Olivia's studio, looking morosely out, when Leanne came to the doorway looking at him with un-disguised mockery in her eyes, and when he turned to look at her she smiled, saying, 'I thought I might find you here. You prefer these old treasures to my new ones.'

Joining her at the door he said, 'My sister and her husband had to leave, they told me to wish you goodbye and say how much they had en-joyed the evening.'

'How kind.'

'Alex left early.'

'Of course. Why don't you like Vanessa's boyfriend? I thought he was charming.'

'Too charming, perhaps.'

'Did you know his father has a yacht in the Med?'

'I didn't know, what of it?'

'He's invited me to join a party of them for a

283

few days in the autumn, you too if you're interested.'

'I'm not, Leanne, nor do I think he intended that I would be.'

'I told him I'd think about it. After all, I did say I wanted to get away for a short while, I was thinking of Paris or Rome, but this sounds far more adventurous.'

'And has Vanessa also been invited?'

'She's involved with her new job, I rather think their friendship, if you can call it that, is on the line.'

'That gives me some cause for satisfaction.'

She laughed. 'But you think your wife can take care of herself even when your daughter can't.'

'Are you saying you intend to accept his invitation?'

'I'm thinking very seriously about it. I wonder why Eric Davidson left so early, he called at one of the flats on the road there. Doesn't his secretary live in one of them?'

'Maybe they had business to discuss.'

'At some time after midnight on a weekend?'

'Well, how should I know why he decided to call to see her?'

'Why indeed. You knew her, why do you suppose her company might be infinitely preferable to what was going on here?'

'Since you've decided to ask his advice on financial subjects why don't you ask him, although I doubt if he'd tell you.'

She smiled to herself as she walked before him

down the stairs.

Of course Eric Davidson wouldn't tell her. If she even hinted that she'd known he was there she could visualize his handsome, cynical smile, the amusement in his narrowed eyes, and the indifference with which he would treat her probings.

She'd thought Richard the sort of man she could really love, a somewhat remote, grave man she had a certain amusement in bringing back into the land of the living, but Richard had fallen for her too soon, been a little too easy, that was why Eric Davidson was proving to be such a challenge. He was not suffering the loss of a loved one – it was doubtful if he'd ever been in love – but he was amusing, tantalizing and worth the effort, even when the results were hardly promising.

'What a mess the house is in,' she complained.

'I've told Mrs Peterson I'll get people in to put it to rights.'

'Oh well, I'm not sitting around here in all this, why don't we drive out somewhere?'

'If you like. We can call at that new place, see what it's like.'

It didn't take Leanne long to change into something entirely fashionable for what was to be an ordinary drive into the country, but as they passed the flats Richard was disconcerted to see an ambulance standing outside and he slowed down. Of course it could be any one of the people living in the flats, and Leanne was quick to say, 'I don't suppose it's anything to do with

285

her, Richard.'

At that moment a paramedic emerged, followed by Margaret, and Richard stopped the car and hurried towards her. She looked up with some surprise at his concerned face and he asked quickly, 'Is there something wrong, Margaret?'

She nodded, obviously distressed, answering, 'It's my mother, she was taken ill when she came for tea after church this morning and they're taking her to the hospital.'

'Oh, I'm so sorry, I hope it isn't serious?'

'Thank you. I'm going with her now.'

With a swift, bleak smile she left him to get into the ambulance and Richard returned to his wife impatiently fretting in the car.

'Well,' she asked, 'is it something serious?'

'Her mother. They're taking her to the hospital.'

'Do you know her mother?'

'Not very well.'

They drove in silence but he had visions of Mrs Gates's face on the few occasions he had met her, vaguely disapproving, suspicious of his relationship with her daughter, seeing Margaret's affection for a man who could not return it.

'Oh well,' Leanne said philosophically. 'She might find she has a shoulder to cry on in Eric Davidson. I'd be awfully careful not to bore him, though.'

Richard remained silent. More and more he was seeing the malicious streak in Leanne. What had once amused him now irritated him and he

286

found himself thinking about Olivia.

Looking at his face absorbed with his own thoughts Leanne was well aware that his thoughts were on a past she had no place in. Bitterly she asked herself why she had ever thought they could be happy together. Richard didn't love her; there were times when she felt he actively disliked her.

She had replaced the glamour of Hong Kong with rural England with its hunt balls and country shows, the class-conscious pursuits of people with money, bound by tradition and uncaring and disinterested in the things that had once been her life. She could tell from the questions they had posed they disapproved of her. Did she hunt? Did she intend to show her dog at the next show? And the garden party at Lady Jarveson's, everybody who was anybody would be attending that.

She had been keen to tell them about the nightlife in Hong Kong and Singapore, the islands in the South China Sea and the exotic lifestyles of people dripping with money, people with strange names and stranger faces. They hadn't been interested. Oh, they'd listened politely before moving away, and she'd been well aware of their amusement, thinking her pretentious and hardly one of them.

What was there to look forward to now that the house was finished, the party over, and every day no different from the one before it?

Making up her mind suddenly, she said, 'I do really feel we should get away for a few days at the very least. I'm tired after all those long months of building work going on, now it's finished surely we can enjoy ourselves a little.'

'I thought the alterations to the house were so that you could enjoy it more?' he said dryly.

'Well of course, and I shall enjoy it, Richard, but what is wrong with a week in Paris or Rome? Or perhaps we should take up Tim's invitation to sail on his yacht?'

'At the moment, Leanne, it isn't possible for me to get away, I daren't even think about it.'

'Then I shall go, you surely won't object?'

'Not at all, would it make any difference if I did?'

'You could be very bored on your own, Richard, unless you have thoughts that nice Miss Gates might take pity on you.'

'Why Miss Gates? She no longer works for me, she works for Davidson now.'

'In the same capacity, do you suppose?'

'As his secretary, that's how she worked for me.'

'Darling, there are secretaries and secretaries.'

'You're supposing too much about me, and perhaps even more about Davidson.'

'Perhaps you're right, dear. After all, she's nice enough but hardly Eric Davidson's material. I guess he'd go for glamour, sophistication, not small-town English conventionality.'

'I hope she has good news about her mother,' Richard said, biting down the instinct to defend Margaret. 'I don't know how close they were but I don't think she has any other relatives.'

He looked up at Margaret's flat on their way home but it was all in darkness and when he suggested calling to see if all was well Leanne said sharply, 'Why should you concern yourself, Richard? She no longer works for you, and if all is not well she'd probably much rather be left alone.'

'She worked for me many years, Leanne,' he replied.

'Well, she works for Davidson now, he should be more concerned.'

Richard could not say to his wife that in all probability Davidson's relationship was unlike the one they had shared. Perhaps in the morning he would telephone Davidson to see if he knew anything, and in the next breath Leanne said, 'Why don't you telephone the bank in the morning? If she isn't there her boss might enlighten you as to why.'

It was halfway through the morning the next day when he telephoned Eric Davidson at the bank. He had thought if Margaret was there she would have answered his telephone, but it was a strange female voice he spoke to and then he was speaking to Davidson.

He explained about the ambulance and Margaret's obvious distress the day before and immediately Eric said, 'She won't be in for several days, Richard, her mother died very suddenly yesterday, heart attack.'

'Oh dear, I am sorry. I met her a few times. Margaret will have taken it very badly I'm sure.'

'She won't be in until after the funeral.'

'No, I suppose not, I'll write to her.'

Their talk turned to business and Eric said, 'Richard, I know Leanne has told you that she's burdened me with her financial affairs, I'm sure you don't mind?'

'Not at all, in fact I prefer not to have a hand in them.'

'I need to see her within these next few days, one of her investments is giving me a headache.'

'She's intending to go to Europe for a short break, will it have to be before she goes?'

'I would prefer it.'

'Then I'll tell her to telephone you.'

As he put the telephone down Richard thought cynically that that was one meeting that would give Leanne pleasure. He had witnessed her behaviour the night of their party when it was very obvious she found Davidson more than attractive, even when faced with his less than reciprocal attitude.

Davidson was a high-flyer, a man to keep his affairs of the heart under wraps. If he ever married it would be circumspect, unburdened with meaningless dalliances.

With a worried frown he started to compose his letter to Margaret. It was not easy.

Twenty-Six

Two weeks after her mother's funeral Margaret thought it was time she made a start on clearing her mother's house. It did not surprise her that there was very little to do. Mrs Gates had always been both tidy and economical, only buying what she needed to buy and giving to charity what she felt she no longer needed.

She looked at the clothes in her wardrobe. Dresses she had had for years; even for holidays she'd said it was pointless buying clothes she didn't need. They went somewhere different so the dresses worn the year before had never been seen, why buy more?

There they all were in practical shades of beige and navy, three pairs of well-polished shoes to match and two good coats and a mack-intosh. In the drawers was clean, unglamorous underwear, the sort she probably wore as a girl and continued to wear; they'd been adequate and suitable so why change?

Her funeral had been well attended because she'd been a regular churchgoer, and the minister had spoken well of her devotion to the church and the help she was always prepared to give at whatever functions she attended, and the repast held in the church hall had been well attended and very much appreciated.

Now the house and the furniture was hers to do what she liked with and her mother's solicitor had informed her that her mother's money had been willed to her apart from a small legacy to the church.

Margaret was not really surprised that she was now richer by the sum of £15,000 even before the house had been sold.

The solicitor advised her to get her money well invested, even if it meant seeking the advice of people at her bank, and Margaret smiled at his insistence that it was indeed a fair-sized sum for the present time. She decided she would not involve the bank and consulted an accountant for advice instead. After all, she needed to be her own woman, for too long she'd been at the mercy of her mother's well-meant domination.

The house seemed so terribly empty. No rattle of teacups, no firelight shining on well-polished mahogany and no questions about how she spent her spare time and if her companions were suitable.

Her mother had asked many questions about the people at the bank, particularly her new boss, but she'd told her very little, except that he was a bachelor, which raised many interrogations, and since Richard Lorival's return her mother had constantly to reassure herself that all the feelings Margaret had had for him were now completely dead.

Finally satisfied that the house was in order, that dead flowers had been consigned to the dustbin and that she need not visit again for several days, Margaret decided to drive home.

She now had a house to sell and she was undecided what to do with her flat. People were advising her to move into her mother's house and she could see the logic of it. It was nearer to the station so that she didn't need to leave her car there every day. It was roomier than her flat, and worth more and she knew more people round about. Flats were for people who came and went, and there were no shops in the area, only that large house which she no longer went to.

It all sounded so reasonable, but she wasn't entirely sure that she wanted to be reasonable. If she was prepared to be honest with herself she knew that the best thing for her to do was leave the area, move nearer to London, and although property would be more expensive there she would no longer have to look up the road at Richard's house and the sight of his wife's sports car racing through the gates every evening and every weekend.

She had read Richard's letter with misted eyes. It was kind, solicitous and impersonal. Richard did not want her to think that once there had been something more. He was very sorry that she had lost her mother, but he had a new life now and although he might feel concern for her, that was all there was.

Foolishly she had tried to read more into it,

293

then she had tossed it in the drawer angrily. She needed her anger, anger had rescued her from melancholy, anger had been the saving of her.

The bank had been kind and generous but on Monday she was going back to her job there, back to hearing Leanne Lorival's voice on the telephone, seeing her smiling face tripping into his office, always fashionable, always gracious.

And Eric Davidson was gracious when he showed her out of the door, gracious and proper, and with that faint hint of amusement in his eyes when he turned to go back into his office.

She arrived home just as her neighbour was parking her car so taking some of her parcels from her she waited for Mary to join her. They were letting themselves into the flats when Leanne's car sped up the road and Mary said, 'She's never at home, wouldn't you think she'd stay in and enjoy the house now it's completed?'

Margaret smiled.

'One of our teachers said she heard her in the hairdresser's, that she was spending some time on the continent, Rome or Paris for preference, she said she needed a break after all the problems with the house. Have you ever been to Rome, Margaret?'

'No. I've been to Italy but not to Rome.'

'With your mother?'

'Gracious no, Mother wouldn't go further than the South Coast.'

'So you went with a friend?'

'I went with Mr Lorival, it was part of my job.'

'How wonderful. Just the two of you?'

Margaret laughed. 'Now you're reading something wildly romantic into it and it was anything but. Mrs Lorival was there painting, we were there to work.'

'Surely that doesn't mean you didn't see anything of Italy?'

'No. She gave us time off for good behaviour. Oh, I shouldn't have said that, she was very nice and I did see something of Italy, I saw Naples and the villages clustered on the hillsides, I would have liked to go back there one day.'

'Well, you can now, you no longer have your mother to worry about and I'm sure you'll have sufficient money.'

Handing the parcels to Mary, Margaret said, 'I can't believe that so much has changed in such a short time. Next week I'll be back at my desk and I'll have to think about where I want to live.'

'You're surely not thinking of leaving here?' Mary asked in some dismay.

'Well, there is Mother's house and it's nearer to the station. It's too big for me, but one or both of them will have to go.'

'I'd hate having to get used to new neighbours, I hope you decide to stay on here, Margaret.'

Somehow or other her words cheered Margaret up. At least somebody wanted her company. She had brought a bunch of flowers from her mother's house because there hadn't seemed any point in leaving them there, and as she arranged them in a vase in the window she saw Vanessa on her horse trotting up the road.

She felt a sense of surprise that she should be visiting her father, obviously for the weekend, since she'd shown little inclination to be there often since his return from the Far East. Mrs Peterson hadn't had much good to say about her boyfriend, she'd considered him cocky and something of a show-off.

It was precisely at that moment that she decided to get rid of the flat. If she stayed there it seemed to Margaret that she would spend her life watching the comings and goings at the big house. How often Vanessa came, if Leanne was at home, if they were away together. Angrily she told herself that it didn't matter, she no longer cared what happened in his life.

Vanessa looked up at Margaret's window, and seeing her standing there she raised her hand and smiled, in the next moment she had tied her horse to the railings and was ringing her bell.

Margaret's first thoughts as she opened the door was that she was very pretty, a tall, slender girl with auburn hair and a beautiful, smiling face.

'I hope you don't mind my calling but I saw you in the window, I hope Maxton will be all right tied to your railings.'

'I'm sure he will be. How long are you here for, Vanessa?'

'Until Sunday evening. I made up my mind suddenly, wanted to ride Maxton on such a lovely day.'

'Are you still living with your aunt in London?'

'No. I'm sharing a flat with two other girls, which means my life's my own.'

'Your boyfriend isn't with you?'

'No. Actually he isn't my boyfriend any more, we've decided to split.'

'Oh, I'm sorry.'

'No need to be, we weren't suited and my father's probably delighted, he didn't like him.'

'And there's nobody else?'

'Not for me, at least not at the moment. Tim's gone off to the Med, his father has a yacht somewhere there, I'm surprised you hadn't heard about that.'

'Why would I?'

'Well, he's shouted it from the rooftops loud enough. I don't know when or if I'll see him again.'

'Does he have a job?'

'He works for his father, they're very rich.'

'Does your father know you're visiting?'

'Well, he isn't home yet, it doesn't matter either way.'

'But Mrs Lorival is home?'

'No, actually she isn't. Mrs Peterson says she'll be away a couple of weeks probably, she's in Europe.'

'Would you like tea, coffee or a glass of something?'

'Anything that's convenient. Dad said you'd lost your mother, Margaret, I'm sorry.'

'Yes, it was very sudden, I never knew her ill,

perhaps it's a good way to go, but a shock for the people who are left.'

'I suppose so. Like Mother, that was a terrible shock.'

Deciding to change the subject Margaret said, 'So, what do you like doing in London? There's so much to choose from.'

'Now that I'm free of Tim I go out and about with the girls, like you said there's so much to do. Did you like the house now that it's changed so much?'

'I haven't seen it, but I liked it before it changed.'

'Tim said it reminded him of a Chinese brothel.'

'He's accustomed to visiting Chinese brothels, then?'

Vanessa laughed. 'No, but he's seen enough of them at the cinemas. It's very oriental, I'm surprised Dad let her get away with it.'

'New wife, new life.'

'I suppose so. Your boss was invited to the party, I thought he was awfully dishy – and so, may I add, did my stepmother.'

'Really?'

'Really, until he wandered off and Tim took over.'

'She was probably being welcoming to all her guests.'

'Dad always said you were the soul of discretion. Was it an awful shock when he decided to dispense with your services and go off to Hong Kong?'

'It was never permanent, Vanessa, changes are inevitable. Now that Mother's gone I am having to make changes.'

'You mean you're moving back to your mother's house?'

'I'm not sure yet what I'm doing, but it's either that or selling them both and moving nearer London.'

She excused herself to make the tea and she could hear Vanessa moving about the living room before she came to the kitchen door. 'Dad's just arrived home, Margaret. He'll have seen Maxton tied to the railings, perhaps I should go. Don't bother with tea, I'll call again if that's all right.'

'But of course, Vanessa. It's been nice having you.'

At the door Vanessa turned to say, 'My mother's pictures are piled up in the studio. I think he should give them away to art galleries, so many of them have paid a fortune for just one.'

'Don't they belong to you, Vanessa?'

'That's what he says, but what would I do with them? Where would I put them? I'd make more use of the money if he decided to sell them.'

'Doesn't it matter that your mother painted them?'

'Well of course. They're beautiful, but like you said life changes, we have to change with it.' With a brief smile she tripped lightly down the stairs and Margaret looked out of the window to see her mounting Maxton and riding him

299

up to the house.

Vanessa's visit had disturbed her strangely; she had sensed in her a certain mischievousness, as if she knew something apart from what they were talking about and she found herself remembering the child Vanessa with her sharp rejoinders and frequent indifference.

It had been her reference to Eric Davidson and her stepmother's obvious liking for him until Tim took over. Oh well, it was not her concern, soon now the comings and goings at Richard Lorival's house would be history to her.

Richard greeted Vanessa as she rode up the drive and decided to walk with her to the paddock.

'I saw him tied up at the flats, I take it you were visiting Miss Gates? I told you her mother had died.'

'Yes, I called to say I was sorry. I wasn't there long before I saw you coming home.'

'It's nice to have you, Vanessa, think about what you'd like to do.'

'I don't want to eat out, Dad. Can't we just talk and enjoy each other's company?'

He stared at her in some surprise, it had been so long since they'd enjoyed each other's company entirely on their own. He smiled, putting his arm round her shoulders with evident affection and saying, 'I shall look forward to that, dear.'

'I'm going to have a bath, I smell of horseflesh, then we'll have dinner. I spoke to Mrs Peterson earlier, she said you'd be coming home.'

Richard reflected somewhat sadly that there should have been so many evenings for just the two of them, like this. It would be different when Leanne came back, Vanessa would be a guest in the house she'd grown up in, and if they talked at all it would be about the present, not the past. Leanne would be gracious but unconcerned; Vanessa might be distant, over the years she'd been good at that.

Although she betrayed no hint of surprise that they had decided to eat at home, Mrs Peterson was inwardly pleased. Was this perhaps the start of normality, the calming of old wounds and the settling of differences?

Ever since the arrival of the second Mrs Lorival she'd felt troubled about her role in the house. In her heart she knew she was not what Mrs Lorival wanted, a middle-aged woman, a little dowdy, certainly a woman who could give little in the way of prestige to what Mrs Lorival might aspire to.

And she had the distinct feeling too that whatever Mr Lorival did there was no pleasing the new wife. One day she'd persuade him to sell the house and move to London. What would happen to Mrs Peterson then?

Twenty-Seven

Vanessa couldn't really remember when she had last sat down to a meal with her father, just the two of them alone, and she had to admit that she had found the experience entirely enjoyable. The meal was excellent, Mrs Peterson had seen to that, and her father had produced a bottle of her favourite wine and throughout the meal he had entertained her with the sort of stories and anecdotes any woman would have found entertaining. Her father had a charm she was only beginning to recognize now that she was grown up; as a child it had never registered.

There were things she had to ask, however, and neither his charm nor the wine must deter her from satisfying her curiosity.

Over coffee she asked, 'Have you heard from Leanne since she left for Rome?'

'I had a postcard from Rome, and another from Naples.'

'Naples! But isn't that some way from Rome?'

'She's decided to hire a car and do some touring around. I'm not surprised, she's never set foot in Italy before.'

'Have you any idea when she's expected home?'

'No.' He was staring at her in some surprise.

'I think I can tell you, Daddy. It won't be before the end of the month.'

'Why do you know and I don't?'

'Because I know where Tim is.'

'And what does that have to do with Leanne?'

'He's on his father's yacht in the Med and they're together.'

His astonishment gave her some amused satisfaction before he said somewhat angrily, 'Really, Vanessa, this is nonsense. She would have told me if that was her plan, and I would have had something to say about it.'

'Alex told me. He said Tim had bragged about it, possibly because it was over between us, and because he's such a braggart he couldn't keep it to himself.'

'Then there are probably a crowd of them. You're reading something sinister into it when probably it's all quite innocent and above board.'

'If that's the case why didn't she tell you? Two postcards, and no mention of it. Oh, Daddy. She was flirting with him at your dinner party, Aunt Mina was furious, but you were so busy talking business you didn't notice.'

'And you're saying all this because you were angry with him and probably with her.'

'I was angry with him because I'd just realized I didn't care two hoots about him or he for me. I hated her because of Mother's pictures and ornaments and what she'd done to the house,' she acknowledged.

'And because of that are you sure you haven't made all this up?'

'I haven't, but will you believe what she tells you? I'm sure you will.'

'You know, Vanessa, I was enjoying this evening, now it's spoilt. I suggest we change the subject.' But she had unsettled him, and with the knowledge of Tim's previous invitation, the truth was beginning to dawn on him.

The rest of the evening was a problem for both of them. Richard read his newspaper or watched television, Vanessa leafed through some of the magazines Leanne favoured and excused herself at just after ten saying she was tired.

After she had gone he sat staring gloomily into the fire, he had little interest in the television programme and he'd already read all that interested him in the newspaper some time before. He was aware that Vanessa had enjoyed telling him her news about Leanne, she had come to see him with that object in view, but how much truth was there in it?

Grimly he analyzed his own feelings. A young man, probably young enough to be her son, a man he hadn't liked, too much money and little substance. Leanne would care about the money and be unconcerned about the rest.

In the time he'd known her and the short duration of their marriage he had come to know what Leanne's priorities in life amounted to. For a brief period he had believed he loved her, but now he knew he had merely been blinded by her rare witchery in the exotic surroundings he had found himself in. Since their arrival in England he had given her all she wanted in an endeavour to prove himself wrong, now he was being forced to the conclusion that whatever enchantment she had had for him had gone.

Would she be honest about her stay in Italy, and how could he accuse her unless he was sure of his facts?

Two weeks later Leanne arrived home, suntanned and enthusiastic about Italy in general.

Over dinner that first evening she said somewhat reproachfully, 'Why did you sell that beautiful villa, Richard? What a ridiculous thing to have done. Oh, I know you connected it with tragedy, but you recovered from that yet let the villa go.'

'Would you keep something that had unhappy associations for you?'

'Yes, I would.'

'I had no intentions of doing so.'

'I walked up to it from the marina, there were a man and a woman sitting on the terrace, I spoke to them and told him who I was.'

'Was he the owner of the villa?'

'Yes, he remembered you.'

'You said you'd walked up there from the marina,' Richard said, suddenly registering the awful truth.

'Well yes, it's the main road along the bay. What of it?'

She was confused, rattled, and with some amusement Richard said, 'Why didn't you tell me you were with Tim Hardcastle on his father's yacht? Five postcards and no mention of it.'

'I spent a few days on it, there was nothing to it. Are you insinuating that there was?'

'I'm asking why you didn't tell me.'

'We bumped into each other in Sorrento, he invited me on to the boat, we had quite a party.'

'Really? Leanne, why don't I believe you? He boasted to Alex and some of his friends that you were sailing with him, Alex told Vanessa and she told me. Can you imagine how I felt, the husband of a woman who had gone off with a boy young enough to be her son on some yacht or other?'

'There was nothing to it.'

'Strangely enough, I don't really care whether there was anything to it or not, but I do care that you didn't feel you could be honest with me.'

She was staring at him now with angry, hostile eyes, before jumping to her feet and marching out of the room. He knew she would be back.

In only a few minutes he heard her feet running across the tiled hall before she flung the door open and stood angrily panting before she cried, 'Where are my pictures? What are those old ones doing on the wall above the stairs?'

'It is sacrilege to keep them gathering dust in the studio, Leanne, they were painted by my wife and they are valuable, far more valuable than the ones you replaced them with.'

'I'm your wife now, Richard, the new pictures were my choice, they matched the decor.'

'I agree with you, but when you were away I

had plenty of time to think about a great many things. Never once did you consult me about the alterations to my house, that doesn't really matter but Olivia's pictures do matter. They are going back on the walls, Leanne, whether you like it or not.'

'They look incongruous.'

'You like money, Leanne – I might say you were obsessed by it. Let us see which are the most valuable, your Chinese prints or Olivia's watercolours. I've asked Vanessa to take them, they belong to her, I can understand that she doesn't have room for them now but one day hopefully she will have.'

'So because she hasn't room for them I have to have them on the walls here. You're being vindictive, Richard, because you're angry. I knew you would be, that's why I didn't tell you about the yacht.'

'And wouldn't you have been angry if I'd played the same sort of trick on you?'

'Darling, you couldn't have, I'd have been with you. Surely you remember that you had the opportunity to come with me, you said you were too busy.'

'If I remember correctly the invitation was for Rome, not some yacht in the Med.'

'I don't want any of those pictures or Olivia's ornaments in the rooms I've changed. Doesn't your sister have room for them?'

'I have no intention of asking her, Leanne.'

Richard felt that he had won the first battle but had by no means won the war. He found himself remembering many things he had heard about Leanne in Hong Kong and conveniently forgotten. Men had found her amusing, good company but most of them had expressed doubts when he decided to marry her. None of them would be surprised if their marriage ended up on the rocks.

Leanne too sensed impending trouble. She'd been a fool. After her first marriage she'd told herself that she'd never marry again, divorces were messy things, particularly when there was money and property to be concerned about. She hadn't been in love with Richard, she'd never been in love with anybody, but he'd been the sort of man she'd admired, charming, educated and solvent. Now she felt an urgent need to get back to the Far East, she didn't need matrimony. As a beautiful woman, being separated from her husband would hardly be detrimental to her popularity.

Mrs Peterson sensed the coldness in the atmosphere between them, the silences and the distance. His aloofness and her petulance and although she kept her thoughts to herself she couldn't help wondering how long it would be before matters came to a head. She could never in a million years have visualized how dramatic would be the ending.

Richard had left the house early, and Leanne paused on the staircase to look up at the pictures she hated on the walls. Lonely lakes and misted hills held no beauty for her, streams bubbling under rustic bridges were mundane, forests of conifers were sombre, even sinister.

She needed to talk to somebody and her thoughts flew immediately to Eric Davidson. She pictured his dark, quizzical eyes, the amused smile on his clear-cut lips in a face that was too handsome.

Without a second's thought she rang his office and asked to speak to him. She recognized Margaret Gates's voice, businesslike, impersonal, and then she was speaking to Eric and asking when it would be possible for him to meet her.

He was consulting his appointment diary, then evenly he was saying, 'I'm afraid it will have to be Thursday morning, Leanne. Shall we say here at half past two if that's convenient.'

'Eric, I need to see you alone, not at the office. I have so many problems and not all of them financial. Please can we have lunch somewhere, somewhere where we can talk and not meet people we know?'

'It sounds very serious.'

'It is. I'm begging you to meet me.'

'Well, if it's as urgent as all that how can I refuse? Do you know Petronelli's in Chelsea? It's got a good reputation, if you like Italian food. I can meet you there at twelve thirty if that's convenient.'

On Thursday morning Mrs Peterson watched Leanne walking out to her car looking distinctly elegant in pale beige with the sheen of mink ties around her shoulders. It was evident she had an appointment which demanded she dress for it.

Eric Davidson was waiting for her at a discreet

table near the wall in a small alcove and he immediately rose to his feet and went forward to meet her. His first thoughts were that she was an attractive woman who had instantly captured the attention of other people dining there.

Over their lunch they talked pleasantries and it was only when their waiter had served them coffee that he said quietly, 'We can talk here, Leanne, or would you prefer to move on?'

'Oh no, this will do very well.'

'You're evidently very concerned about something, I hardly think your financial situation warrants your concern.'

'Eric, it's my marriage I'm concerned about. It's over, finished, or it will be very soon.'

Warning bells were beginning to ring in Eric's head, he had no wish to be involved in Leanne's marital problems. He'd been reluctant to act as adviser with her finances, anything of another nature was out of the question.

Leanne's woes and worries were tumbling out too quickly. Richard's unreasonable insistence about the pictures, the holiday and his annoyance, even when there'd been absolutely nothing in it. Her dislike of living in the country, his daughter's obvious dislike of her and oh, a thousand other things that were pulling them apart.

'I take it you're no longer in love with him?' Eric asked quietly.

'No, I'm sure I'm not, perhaps I never was.'

'Then you should talk to him, see a solicitor. I can't advise you on matrimonial problems,

Leanne, I'm a banker, you need a lawyer.'

She stared at him gloomily.

'Oh, I was so sure you'd at least be able to help me as a friend. You know how much I like you, I've no intention of telling Richard that I've asked you for help.'

'But what help can I give you, Leanne? Only you really know what you want out of this marriage, or if you want to end it.'

'He's being unreasonable. You've seen what I've done with the house, it's perfect, now he wants it back like before, and oh, it's just being here, I thought it would be so different.'

'How different?'

'I thought we'd be living in London, not in the country in a great big house with too many memories for him and a daughter who doesn't like me.'

'His daughter doesn't live with him though, you see her very seldom I'm sure.'

'I don't want to see her at all, she's a minx. She's obviously filled his mind with all sorts of things about Tim Hardcastle. He was her boyfriend, you know.'

'Was he still her boyfriend when you went off on the yacht?'

'No, they'd finished it on the night of the dinner party. I suspect it was still rankling.'

'How old is this Tim Hardcastle?'

'Oh Eric, you saw him, you know he's a lot younger than I am. He'd have liked there to be more but I assure you there wasn't. It was a fun time, I enjoyed the boat and the places we sailed to.'

Eric's expression was reflective as he sat back in his chair and she could not assess his thoughts, whether they were in sympathy or if he condemned her.

He consulted his watch, and she said irritably, 'I seem to have wasted your time, Eric, I'm sorry.'

'I wish I could be of more help, Leanne, I'm simply a shoulder to cry on, but as regards anything else I'm of little use I'm afraid. Do you have a solicitor here? I can give you the names of several well-respected firms.'

'Thank you, at least I'll be grateful for that.'

'I'm sorry, Leanne. I'm sorry that your marriage is falling apart. Perhaps I should advise you to think things over very carefully before you decide it has to be over.'

She rose to her feet and smiled, then without another word she left him.

He watched her walking down the road, her small, straight-backed figure walking quickly, and he could only guess at the disappointed anger in her eyes.

Twenty-Eight

Eric Davidson was well aware that his meeting with Leanne Lorival had not been what she'd expected. It had not taken him long to evaluate the sort of woman he was dealing with: the only daughter of rich parents, her widower father indulgent, doting, affording her everything she wanted and a husband who had been expendable when she tired of him. In an environment where she'd never been short of escorts. She was pretty, sophisticated and she hadn't needed their money. Now she found herself married to a man who was reluctant to play her game. All that she had envisaged was not coming true.

Was she really expecting that she could move on to him? If she did she was foolish, he didn't need her money, although he had no doubt it had tempted a great many others.

From the expression in her eyes he believed Leanne Lorival might prove a dangerous antagonist, not to him, but to Richard Lorival.

He lingered on in the restaurant after ordering another coffee so it was late when he arrived back at the bank, to be informed by Margaret that Mrs Lorival had been on the telephone and had requested him to ring her back.

Margaret had thought she seemed annoyed that he was not in his office and her first thoughts were that they had been together.

He frowned in some annoyance. Whatever game Leanne was playing he didn't want to be involved in it, and somewhat irritably he said, 'Very well, get her on the phone.'

Her voice was cajoling as he knew it would be.

'Eric, I'm sorry, I shouldn't have walked off in a temper but I really am very worried, I was so sure you would be able to help me or at least console me.'

'Leanne, as a friend I am capable of advising you on your accounts here at the bank but on matrimonial matters I am a non-starter. My advice was that you should get yourself a good lawyer, it was the best advice I could give you.'

'Oh, Eric, I know it was, but I was upset, I shouldn't be involving you in my troubles, but I needed a friend to talk to. I thought you might be he.'

'Then I'm sorry to have disappointed you.'

'Can't we meet another day, just a comfort lunch?'

'Well, I really am very busy at the moment. Leave it with me, I'll telephone you if I have any free time.'

'Promise?'

'Leave it with me, Leanne.'

He knew that she would be angry, frustrated, and he shuddered to think what sort of a mood Richard Lorival would find her in when he arrived home after a hectic day.

As he passed Margaret's desk later in the afternoon he said nonchalantly, 'If Mrs Lorival rings again, tell her I'm at a meeting. If she says it's urgent business make her an appointment.'

He gave nothing away from his manner but as their eyes met she was aware of an amused discernment in his eyes. Eric Davidson was well aware of her feelings for Richard Lorival; what he didn't know was that she had consigned them to history. He wouldn't believe it anyway, he would believe that any involvement between himself and Leanne Lorival would please her enormously.

Margaret was on the point of leaving her office when the telephone rang and immediately she recognized Leanne's voice, asking, 'May I speak to Mr Davidson, please?'

'I'm sorry, Mr Davidson has already left the office.'

'When will I be able to speak to him?'

'Well, he has several meetings in the morning. Perhaps I can ask him to telephone you.'

'No. I'll telephone him.'

She evidently did not trust him to ring her, and she had not given her name, quite evidently sure that Margaret knew who she was.

Sitting at Richard's desk in his office at the house Leanne sat back with a frown of annoyance on her face. Eric Davidson was avoiding her, but would he want to lose one of his bank's wealthiest customers? Maybe he'd find he wasn't as important as he thought he was.

Four telephone calls to the bank the next day procured no assistance and in the end Leanne snapped, 'Are you Miss Gates who used to work for my husband?'

Margaret admitted that she was.

'Well, surely you can instil into your boss some sense of urgency in this matter?'

'I can't interrupt his meetings, Mrs Lorival.'

'Perhaps I should speak to Mr Gregson.'

'I can put you through to his secretary, Mrs Lorival, but Mr Gregson is at the same meeting.'

'Oh, very well, I'll come into the bank.'

It was later in the afternoon when Margaret was able to tell Eric of his problems. He sat down rather wearily at his desk, before saying dryly, 'When you so kindly invited me in for coffee after that dinner party just before Christmas I outlined then what I thought about Mrs Lorival – flirtatious and worldly, decidedly ambitious. I should now be adding persistent. If you think there is something going on between us, Miss Gates, you are wrong. I haven't come this far only to have my wings singed by the likes of Mrs Richard Lorival. Surely you credit me with more sense.'

'It's none of my business, Mr Davidson, I haven't thought about it.'

'Oh, but you have, Miss Gates. Why would she invite me to a dinner party when I was never a colleague of her husband's? Why the telephone calls, the visits to the bank, and I might add the luncheon engagement I couldn't get out of?'

'Aren't you her financial adviser, Mr Davidson?'

'And that is all I am, Miss Gates. Don't be too reassured that this marriage is being helped to its conclusion by me.'

'Like I said before, Mr Davidson, it's none of my business, I really don't care.'

He got up from his desk and walked around to where she was standing uncertainly on her way to the door, and looking gravely into her eyes he said, 'I hope you don't care, I really do. Do you think I didn't know anything about your feelings for Lorival when you came to work for me? Gossip never loses anything and even if much of it was untrue the fact remains that you were very unhappy and extremely disbelieving that he'd abandoned you.'

'Abandoned me, Mr Davidson! I had a job here, I was never abandoned.'

'Oh, but you were. I'm not thinking about your job, I'm thinking about your hopes and I'm hoping that now you really don't care, it's over. If Mrs Lorival comes to the bank tomorrow I'm free from two until three thirty, after that I'm tied up.'

Bemused, she thought how quickly he could change the subject, one minute he was the kind, thoughtful friend, the next the crisp business-man better known to her.

'Shall I telephone her to make an appointment?' she asked him.

He nodded. 'Perhaps that would be best, make

sure to stress that I shall need to get away.'

Leanne breezed into his office the next day half an hour late, saying airily, 'I'm sorry, Eric, but it was the traffic, so awful at this time of day. Do forgive me.'

'Well, we'd better get started,' he said amiably. 'Now, which of your assets is particularly bothering you today?'

'None of my assets, Eric, my life.'

'I've made a short list of extremely good solicitors who are capable of handling all your matrimonial problems, here they are. Where your finances are concerned, like I said I will do everything I can to assist you, but in your marriage I'm afraid I can do nothing.'

'You can listen to my problems, be the sort of friend I imagined I'd found.'

'My dear lady, you're asking me to be the sort of friend you've known from childhood, a friend who's always been there, not some man you've only met on one or two occasions, either here or in your husband's house.'

'A friend is a friend however long one's known him.'

'I don't agree. Given time we might have become such friends but not yet. What do you know about me, what do I really know about you? Neither of us can advise the other on what to do with our lives, I certainly couldn't advise you on something as complicated as your marriage with Richard Lorival.'

'You don't know him very well either.'

'I'm aware of it. But I know about him, his

wife – or should I say his late wife – his job, his ambitions, his family and should I say his torments. I probably know more about him than he knows about me.'

'Oh, I think I know what he thinks about you, that you're the charming womanizer who's flying high and bewitching his wife.'

Eric looked at her with narrowed eyes before saying sternly, 'If that is how he thinks about me then perhaps we should decide it is time to end even this trivial relationship.'

'Trivial?'

'Why, yes. I'll ask John Gregson to take you under his wing, I'm sure he'll be delighted to.'

'You're playing with my custom, Eric, or does the bank value its rich customers so lightly?'

'I can assure you it doesn't but you must act as you think fit.'

'Perhaps after all I've not been very sensible in banking with you, maybe I should change.'

'That's entirely up to you. You've been with us a very short time, I think you'll find that we'll survive, Leanne, even without your custom.'

'Now you're angry.'

'No, I'm not angry, it's all a part of business, its ups and its downs. We'll be sorry to lose you, Leanne, and we'll wish you well.'

He rose to his feet to show her the meeting was at an end, and chagrined she said sharply, 'I'll let you know about Mr Gregson, expect to hear from me within the next few days.'

He smiled, extended his hand and then showed her to the door.

She did not look at Margaret Gates as she swept through her office so that Margaret could only surmise the meeting had hardly been congenial.

Richard was dining at his sister's house and Mina reflected that he seemed to be staying on in London more and more after he left the bank.

'Don't question him,' her husband warned her. 'If he wants to tell us anything leave it to him, obviously all's not well.'

She watched him pushing the food around his plate, evidently he had little appetite, and seeing her watching him he said quickly, 'I've had a bit of a stomach upset, Mina, I'm sorry I'm not very hungry.'

In spite of the warning glance from her husband Mina retorted, 'I don't think that's the only upset you're having, Richard. Why don't you tell me about it?'

'There's nothing to tell.'

'Then why are you here so often instead of at home, why do I find you staring into space and obsessed with your own thoughts?'

'I hadn't realized I was provoking so much interest.'

'Well obviously I'm worried, Richard, you're my brother. Surely if there's something wrong you can talk to me?'

In the long silence that followed they were all aware of the tension until at last Richard said, 'I'm sorry to be such a wet blanket but I am worried, I'm worried about a marriage that isn't working, neither of us are happy.'

'But why when you've given her carte blanche to do so much with the house and anything else she wanted to do? I can understand you worrying, the expense, the solitude when she was away, but what has she to be unhappy about?'

'I don't like the house, I should never have allowed it.'

'How could you have stopped it? Obviously she has different taste to Olivia.'

'It wasn't just that, she got rid of everything without even consulting me, one minute they were there, then new things came and they were stowed away in the studio. Then there was the holiday, supposedly to be spent in Rome, then it appears she spent it on board the yacht owned by Tim Hardcastle's father. Did you know?'

Mina and her husband stared at each other, then Nigel said glumly, 'Alex mentioned it, we didn't think it was true. Who told you?'

'Vanessa, quite deliberately. She couldn't keep it to herself.'

'I told her she mustn't tell you. So where does it go from here?'

'We have to talk, Mina, and the sooner the better, except that these days we're never in the same place together, either I'm missing or she is.'

'And where is she tonight while you're dining with us?'

'She said she was seeing Davidson at the bank, something to do with her finances, and later she was dining with friends at the Savoy.'

Richard smiled somewhat grimly and Nigel said, 'Couldn't she be dining with Davidson? She seemed to be finding his company very congenial at your dinner party...'

'Doesn't she trust you to advise her on financial matters?' Mina put in. 'Does she prefer to trust Eric Davidson?'

'It's her money, Mina, I prefer not to have any part in it and Davidson is a good man at his job.'

'How tolerant,' she murmured.

'Yes, well, but like I said Leanne and I have to talk, discover if there's anything left of our marriage or if we've reached the end of the road.'

'Not a very long road.'

'I agree. A road we should never have ventured along.'

'She's cost you a lot of money, Richard. Those alterations at the house must have cost a fortune, and you hate them don't you?'

'Yes, I do. I'm trying to introduce some of Olivia's pictures but she isn't happy with the idea, I didn't think she would be.'

'It is your house, Richard, and it's not as if they're photographs, they're worth more than the ones she replaced them with and where does Vanessa come into all this?'

'Something else we have to talk about, Mina.'

'Then the sooner the better. Doesn't Margaret Gates work for Davidson now?'

'She's his secretary at the bank.'

'I always thought she had a soft spot for you, Richard. Perhaps in time...'

'You always had a vivid imagination, Mina.'

'You ran away, Richard.'

'No, I simply got on with my life. I believe Margaret is quite happy with her job and Eric Davidson.'

Twenty-Nine

Leanne was not dining at the Savoy with friends. She had hoped Eric Davidson would invite her to eat dinner with him but her interview with him had left her frustrated and furious.

She'd always been able to attract the right sort of men. Richard Lorival hadn't been easy, but Eric Davidson had been ruthless in his rejection. She'd pushed things along because she needed him, it had been too soon, but he could have been more understanding, shown more tolerance, now she wasn't even sure how much he would tell John Gregson or how the state of her marriage would be discussed among people who knew Richard well.

She drove home, deciding to eat at a small country inn several miles from her destination. When eventually she drove through the gates she saw that Richard's car was parked in the drive and she trembled with agitation. Was this the night they would face whatever future they had?

As their eyes met across the room he said dryly, 'I didn't expect you home so soon, didn't you enjoy the meeting with your friends?'

'I decided not to meet them, I wasn't in the mood.'

'I'm sorry.'

She was walking about the room, nervously pausing to look at pictures, and eventually picking up an ornament from a small coffee table and looking at it closely, then putting it back so sharply she could have damaged it.

'You don't like it, Leanne?' he asked quietly.

'You know I don't, I suppose it's valuable?'

'Yes, it's Crown Derby.'

'When did you put it there?'

'I didn't. Vanessa put it there when she was last here, I'm surprised you haven't noticed it before. Try to understand how she feels, Leanne, she's my daughter, this is her home that you've changed beyond all recognition. In similar circumstances wouldn't you want to see some of the things you'd grown up with around you?'

'My father married three times. Each one of his wives changed things, I never knew what I would find. She hasn't brought them back because she can't live without them, it's because she resents me.'

'Can I get you a drink?' Richard asked, going over to the drinks cabinet.

'Dry martini. Did you dine with your sister and her husband?'

'Yes.'

'They're not too fond of me either. Oh, I hate

this house and this village.'

'Then we have to talk, Leanne. This is my home, my work is here, my life is here. What exactly do you want? I thought I'd done my best to satisfy your wants.'

'I thought so too, now I know you haven't. None of this is how I thought it would be. I thought we'd live in London, be in the centre of things, not hidden away in this rural setting with people I can't relate to.'

'Then what do you want?'

'I want to go back to the Far East. I have my own money, divorce me if you don't want to come with me.'

'Is that what you want?'

'Yes, if you won't do what I want. I'm not bothered whether you divorce me or not, being a woman separated from her husband has considerable advantages, particularly if she has enough money. The English courts are particularly biased in favour of the husband, or so I'm told.'

'So when do you propose to return to the Far East?'

'The sooner the better. The state of our marriage will cause a few raised eyebrows I'm sure. Are you going to be generous, Richard? After all, most of these things are mine.'

'Paid for by me.'

'But quite unwanted I'm sure. You'll be glad to see the back of me so that you can bring all the old things back to please both you and your daughter.'

She was looking at him over her glass, her amber eyes so much like a cat's, and far removed from that kitten-soft face she had used to captivate him.

Putting her glass down she said, 'I'm tired, it's been a busy day. I'm going to bed.'

'And where do we go from here?'

'I'm going up to London in the morning, I'll probably stay there for a few days to make arrangements at the bank, see about the journey back and you'll allow me to send for these things, Richard?'

'You mean after you've found somewhere to live there?'

'Yes, that won't be difficult. I know what I want, a house on Victoria Peak like the one I gave up when I married you, there's sure to be one. If we part amicably enough you could always visit me, Richard.'

With a brief smile she was gone, and refilling his whisky glass he sat down in front of the fire to think about his future. There were too many complications, he felt like a man drifting down a turbulent stream, bouncing off rocks that posed one problem after another and the horizon was too obscure and undefined.

He desperately wanted to talk to someone and for one brief moment he thought about Margaret Gates. He had seen the 'For Sale' signs outside her flat and he suspected that she had decided to move to her mother's house, but of course he couldn't talk to Margaret, she probably still hated him for the way he had treated her, and rightly so.

Instead he decided to telephone his sister.

After telling her briefly that they intended to divorce he waited several seconds before she said, 'But surely it can't have come to that, not so soon?'

'There's no going back now, Mina, I just thought I would let you know. Perhaps you'll tell Vanessa, I don't know when I'll see her.'

Eric Davidson received her news two days later without immediate comment. She'd appeared businesslike and adamant, concerned with the transferring of her account to the Bank of China in Hong Kong, and he had been equally businesslike, advising her that there would be no problems, that they were sorry to be losing her custom but obviously the transfer was essential.

It was only when he escorted her to the door that she said, 'Why don't you invite me to eat dinner with you, Eric? I'm in London until Saturday and London can be a lonely place. I'm no longer a threat to your cosy, singular world and it would be a gallant gesture.'

He smiled. 'Very well, Leanne. Now that I know you no longer want my advice on something I couldn't possibly have helped you with. Where are you staying?'

'At the Savoy.'

'Then I'll meet you there on Friday evening at eight o'clock.'

She smiled and walked through the door beyond Margaret's office. Margaret had heard their conversation and meeting Davidson's eyes she was well aware of the cynicism in them. He knew what she was thinking, that he was taking Leanne Lorival to dinner, that perhaps there was something going on after all and that it was all monstrously unfair to Richard.

Margaret thought that Richard deserved to be hurt – after all he'd done the hurting as far as she was concerned – but where would it all end? Was it simply an affair? She doubted if Davidson was in love with Leanne, she was an amusement, an assignation, he would make very sure that there would be no strings or comebacks, but how about her?

How much did she care, and how much did she care for Richard? She knew the sort of gossip that went on at the bank, borne out later in the afternoon when she left the building in the company of John Gregson's secretary. She liked Miss Jenkins, who was one of the old school, not given to gossip but obviously aware of it.

As they walked along the road together Miss Jenkins said, 'Has your flat been sold, Margaret?'

'Yes, I'm in the process of packing up, I'll be busy most of the weekend. They'll be moving in towards the end of next week.'

'And you're moving into your mother's house?'

'For the time being. I don't think I'll stay there.'

'I suppose the flat was very convenient when you worked for Richard Lorival.'

'Oh yes, just down the road from his house.'

'Do you see much of them?'

'No, only when they pass in their cars. They were kind enough to invite me to their Christmas dinner party.'

'Yes, I believe Mr Gregson told me. I've met Mrs Lorival once or twice when she's visited the bank to see Mr Davidson, does she have time for a chat?'

'No. She quickly comes and quickly goes.'

'There's been a bit of gossip, you know what it's like. I should think Eric Davidson's a match for anybody.'

'What exactly do you mean by that, Miss Jenkins?'

'Well, he's attractive. My boss is amused by it, he thinks she's smitten by him.'

'She is a customer.'

'Of course, but not all our customers are quite so purposeful. Come on, Margaret, having worked for Richard Lorival you must be a little puzzled, if nothing more.'

'I think Mr Davidson has her measure.'

'Well, of course. Hope you get sorted out with your packing, Margaret.'

On the way home Margaret spared a thought as to what Richard would be doing while his wife was being entertained by Eric Davidson.

She collected her car from the station car park and drove home in the usual rush of Friday evening traffic, and she had almost arrived there when she was overtaken by a small sports car and received a wave from Vanessa, who was driving it. She was obviously spending time with her father and perhaps that was why Leanne had decided to spend time in London. Maybe they didn't get on together, Vanessa could be fractious and perhaps Mrs Lorival had deemed it wiser to distance herself.

What a chore it was emptying drawers and cupboards, piling unwanted articles into cellophane bags, hesitating whether she should keep or discard until in the end she decided to ask her neighbour if there was anything she would like.

She knew that Mary was an avid reader and there were books she'd decided not to take with her, and one or two items of clothing that were far too good to throw away but which she didn't expect to wear again.

Two of them were dresses she'd worn at the Lorivals', still fashionable, and Mary went to several functions at the school and was always complaining that she never had enough changes.

She was delighted to take them, saying doubtfully, 'But if you move nearer to London, Margaret, won't you be wanting them?'

'No. Every time I wear them I can hear my mother say I'd been a fool to buy them.'

'But why, they're so elegant?'

'She thought I didn't need a new one every year for just one function.'

'Well, they're beautiful and I'll enjoy wearing them. I'm sorry you're leaving, getting used to new neighbours isn't easy.' Mary picked up the dresses hanging over the arm of a chair, saying, 'I'm so grateful for these, Margaret, I know when I shall wear this one.'

'Something special?'

'Well, we've got a new deputy head who doesn't know I'm alive, when he sees me in one of these he might revise his opinion.'

Margaret laughed. 'Not the man I've seen giving you a lift?'

'Oh no, that's Mr Robinson, very much married with three daughters.'

'And the new deputy isn't married?'

'No, apparently not.'

'Oh well, good luck with the dresses, Mary. Now I'd better get on with my clearing up. I'll see you before I leave, and you're very welcome to visit me any time, unless there's something better on the menu.'

They both laughed, and Margaret went back to her flat and the chaos.

Through the window she could see Richard's car parked alongside Vanessa's so it was evident they had decided to dine at home.

Later she made coffee and took it out on to the tiny balcony to drink it. The night was warm and as she sat there she visualized father and daughter spending the evening together. What would they talk about? She visualized Vanessa's face that was so pretty and yet could appear so remote and unfriendly.

Would they sit comfortably in that changed house surrounded by Oriental figurines and pictures, the pale carpets and paler walls, the gilt tables and silken drapes at the windows?

She could imagine the disdain on Vanessa's

face, the sarcasm she might use to show her father how much she hated it, and would he care? Then her thoughts turned to Leanne Lorival now dining in London with Eric Davidson.

He would have no difficulty in entertaining her with his conversation, his charm. She would find him interesting and sophisticated, able to converse on many subjects but what if she was looking for more?

Strangely troubled, she jumped to her feet and went back into the room, telling herself sternly that none of it was any of her business and it was time to get on with her packing.

Thirty

Driving out of London Leanne reflected that only twelve months ago she had been sending out invitations to Richard's friends and former colleagues to dinner when they would meet her for the first time. Twelve months, was that really all they'd had?

It was twelve months that had been filled with so many different things. The transformation of the house, the time spent in Italy and the knowledge that she no longer wanted her marriage or the way of life it promised her.

The Saturday morning traffic was light and as she left the city behind she became aware of the frost-laden morning and the sudden brightness of the pink-tinged sky. When she reached the house the gates were open and she contemplated the long, curving drive and the sight of Vanessa's white sports car standing outside the house. She hadn't expected that.

Vanessa didn't like her and she didn't like Vanessa. She'd wanted this morning to be just herself and Richard, now the girl was here and nothing would be the same. She let herself into the house and as she looked up at the curving staircase her first sight was of Vanessa standing on a short stepladder to hang a picture on the wall.

Vanessa stared at her. There was no warmth in their greeting, and then Leanne's eyes fell on a stack of her Oriental pictures pressed up against the wall while already they had been replaced by those painted by Richard's wife.

With some anger, she snapped, 'You could at least have waited until I'd left the premises.'

'I'm sorry, but I didn't know when you were coming. My father wasn't sure.'

Without speaking she went into the lounge and there too her pictures had been replaced and the ornaments she had discarded were back in place. It shouldn't have mattered. She was leaving anyway, but it did matter, that girl with her pretty face and cynical scepticism had infuriated her, and going back into the hall she said, 'Where is your father?'

'He had to take the car down to the garage, I don't expect he'll be long. Would you like coffee? I'll ask Mrs Peterson to make you some. I've finished in here now.'

'You think they're an improvement, do you?'

'They belonged to my mother.'

'I know, but did you like them?'

'Perhaps not when I was younger, perhaps I never really appreciated them, perhaps I was jealous of her talent because I never had any.'

Leanne looked at her searchingly. Some other woman might have felt a moment of compassion for the young and vulnerable Vanessa, but Leanne only felt her anger, and without another word she left her to go to the kitchen.

Mrs Peterson was engrossed in cleaning the silver, helped by Molly. They both looked up in surprise and Mrs Peterson said, 'I didn't know you were coming back today, Mrs Lorival. I'll make coffee. Have you had breakfast?'

'Just coffee, Mrs Peterson, in the morning room. How long has Miss Lorival been here?'

'She came yesterday, just for the weekend. Mr Lorival's gone with the car.'

'I know.'

There was no sign of Vanessa in the hall or the staircase and Leanne could only surmise that she'd gone up to her room. She waited for her coffee to arrive and then she wandered round the room looking at the pictures.

What was so captivating about lonely lakes and mountains, stone villages and daffodils on wind-swept shores, rustic bridges crossing mountain streams? And why were there none of Italy? At least she might have been willing to tolerate those.

Returning to the hall she looked at her Chinese paintings stacked against the wall. Richard would send them out to her but did she really want them? They would remind her of everything she wanted to forget and she could buy more. The artist was one of China's best and was making a name for herself not just in China but in all the Far East. She'd replace them with others when she returned to Hong Kong. Orchids and humming birds, bamboo and cherry blossom. In the next instant she had picked several of them up and was marching out of the house.

At that moment she wasn't sure what she was going to do with them so she laid them on the ground in the middle of the driveway before she went back for the others.

She made several journeys back to the house and Vanessa watched her curiously from the window of her bedroom. What was she doing with the pictures? And then she watched her hurrying back to the house, and in the next moment Mrs Peterson was knocking on her door, saying urgently, 'I think you should come down, Vanessa. She's gone mad, can't you hear her?'

'I've seen her with the pictures, what's she doing with them?'

'She's taking them all off the walls, all those your mother painted, the ornaments too, the Royal Worcester. Surely she can't be taking them back with her?'

Together they ran back to the staircase in time

to see Leanne removing the last picture from the wall in the hall before hurrying through the open door to place it on the heap on the drive.

They stared at each other in amazement and then Vanessa ran down the stairs and out into the cold morning air. Leanne stood overlooking the pile of pictures on the floor and she was busy pouring petrol over them followed by a lighted match.

Vanessa ran towards her, endeavouring to pull some of them clear, but Leanne was holding her back, and driving up the hill from the town Richard was suddenly aware of a cloud of smoke billowing into the sky and along the drive, and fear made him drive urgently towards the house.

The sight that met his eyes was unbelievable. The fire blazing on the drive, his daughter and his wife struggling together while Mrs Peterson was doing her utmost to separate them, and in the blazing pile the remnants of picture frames and what was left of canvases.

It was a nightmare he couldn't believe. Vanessa's tears, Leanne's frozen anger and then he was looking through the smoke at Margaret Gates's horror-filled eyes.

She had seen the fire from her flat, seen Richard's car speeding up the road, heard several screams and then suddenly she was running up the road in spite of every instinct that was telling her not to get involved.

After glaring at them balefully Leanne spun around and hurried back to the house, while

Richard said, 'Go back inside, Vanessa, there's nothing to be done out here, it's over.'

Mrs Peterson took the sobbing girl by the arm and dragged her towards the house, while Richard said quietly, 'I'm sorry you had to witness this, Margaret, I'd no idea she'd do anything so drastic.'

Margaret looked at the ashes on the drive and after a few minutes said, 'Why, why has she done this?'

'Anger, resentment, madness, I'm not sure. The marriage is over, she's going back to the Far East, but why she had to do this I really don't know. Do come inside the house, Margaret, it's freezing out here.'

'I'll get back now, Richard. I had to come, I was so afraid that something was wrong. I'm sorry the marriage didn't work out.'

He nodded wordlessly, then he turned and walked slowly back to the house.

As Margaret walked back to her flat she could still smell the smoke, the acrid scent of it on her coat, see their faces etched in anger, pain and disbelief and then later she reflected that a few years ago she'd have rejoiced in what she'd seen today, been glad that the marriage was over, gloried in his pain, felt that retribution had been done. So why didn't she feel that way now?

She was glad that on Monday morning she was moving into her mother's house. The flat was depressing with its preponderance of packed wooden boxes and bare tables and empty walls. Richard's house must be looking some-what similar, she reflected.

Richard surveyed his daughter's tear-stained face as she huddled in her chair sobbing quietly. At last she said, 'Daddy I can't stay here, I've got to get back to London, why don't you come with me to stay with Aunt Mina?'

'I have things to do here, dear, but I do understand your wanting to leave.'

'I'll go upstairs and pack my case, I don't want anything to eat, Mrs Peterson said she was making lunch.'

'If you're driving to London then you must eat something before you leave.'

'I'm not eating with her, Daddy, I don't want to look at her, I'll never speak to her again.'

'After today you'll never see her again, nor will I.'

'Daddy, I hate her. Why did she burn those pictures? They were my pictures, my mother's pictures, worth a lot of money.'

'Yes, I'm not exactly sure how the insurers will view their wanton destruction.'

'Can't you do anything about her? She destroyed them, she should be made to pay for them. Where is she now, what is she doing?'

'I don't know, but we'll soon find out. Now eat some lunch and get off to London.'

'I don't like leaving you on your own.'

'I'll survive, Vanessa. I've survived worse things.'

'Don't you love her any more? You must have

done once to marry her.'

'I don't love her, perhaps I never did.'

Mrs Peterson had produced sandwiches and coffee and they made a pretence of eating until Vanessa said, 'I'm really not hungry, Daddy. I'll pack my case and get away. I don't want to see her, I suppose she's in her room.'

He walked with her to the bottom of the staircase where they both stood silently staring upwards for several minutes. All they could hear was the occasional opening and closing of a door and Vanessa ran quickly up the stairs to escape into her own room.

Richard was about to return to the lounge when Leanne appeared at the top of the stairs. She was carrying a large holdall and her face was pale and hostile. She was trembling as she walked down the stairs and he stood watching, his expression cold, implacably remote.

For a long moment they stared at each other in silence, Leanne was the first to speak. 'I'm going, Richard, I've taken everything I want, I'm returning to Hong Kong next week.'

Without speaking he walked to the door and held it open for her. He was looking at her with that cool detachment she'd seen on Eric Davidson's face. Neither of them had in the end needed her, and without another word she turned and ran to her car.

Richard stood at the door until she drove swiftly away. She did not turn her head to look at him and he did not raise his hand in farewell. What better way, he thought, to end a marriage that should never have been.

Vanessa met him in the hall. 'Has she gone?' she asked.

'Yes. Did you see her upstairs?'

'No. I heard her come out of her room. I told you I didn't want to see her. Oh, Daddy, what about you? I'll ask Aunt Mina to come to see you, she will I know.'

'No, Vanessa, I'd prefer to be on my own right now. When things have settled down we'll all meet up again, by that time we might begin to feel some sort of amusement about the chaos.'

'What will you do with all that rubbish?' she asked him.

'I'll get the gardeners to clear it away in the morning. I never thought I'd hear your mother's paintings assessed as rubbish.'

'Oh, I didn't mean it like that. They were beautiful, now they're rubbish and it's Leanne's fault, she deserves to pay for it.'

He smiled and took her in his arms before watching her running towards her car. Then she was waving enthusiastically as she drove away. He suspected that in a few days she could be regaling her friends with all the trauma of the morning. She was young, the young forgot quickly and healed quickly and the world was a restless place with so many diversions.

In a few months Vanessa would have consigned Leanne's actions to history, something that happened to older people who made disastrous marriages and suffered for them. She'd tell her friends about Leanne, her sophisticated glamour, and probably turn her into some sort of theatrical wicked fairy.

Mrs Peterson was clearing the table when he returned to the house and as she left the room she said, 'Was that Miss Gates who came to the mess on the drive?'

'Yes, she'd seen the fire, she was concerned by it.'

'Aye, she would be. She's moving on Monday, back to the house in the town.'

'I saw the flat was for sale. When the gardeners arrive tomorrow or Monday morning will you ask them to get rid of the debris, Mrs Peterson? If it's Monday I shan't be here.'

'I'll see to it, Mr Lorival.'

From her window Margaret had seen first Leanne and then Vanessa driving away from the house, and now Richard was left alone to ponder on what was left. Did he still love Leanne? Would he decide to follow her and in the end would they agree that they'd been foolish? Would he be able to forgive her or would his anger be so intense he'd feel only hatred for her?

She found herself thinking of the evening Eric Davidson had spent with Richard's wife. Had it been meaningful, romantic or casual? She would never know.

When she returned to the bank on Tuesday morning things would be back to normal. No more telephone calls to her boss from Leanne, calls that had irritated and angered her, making her ask herself questions to which she didn't know the answers. Why should she care? Why, when for years she'd been telling herself it didn't matter what Richard Lorival did with his life?

She jumped nervously at the knock on her door, doubly resonant in the empty room.

Her neighbour stood at the door with a somewhat anxious look on her face, saying, 'I saw you running up to the house, Margaret. What was going on with all that smoke?'

'Oh, they were burning rubbish they'd cleared out of the house.'

'But on the driveway? Why not at the back of the house? I couldn't see through my window for smoke.'

'I know, it did seem silly.'

'Then I saw her going and the daughter. Do you think there's something going on? I mean Mr Lorival and his wife. She's hardly ever here, after all she's done at the house too. Honestly, Margaret, can you really think everything's as it should be?'

'I don't think about it, Mary, it's nothing to do with me.'

'But you worked for him a long time, you must have had some sort of feeling for him – respect, esteem, friendship.'

'Yes, that's what I had, respect and friendship. It doesn't mean I ask questions about the state of his marriage.'

'Well, I think I would, it's only natural. When I saw you running across the road I felt sure you were upset about the smoke.'

'Yes, I was, you're a little bit concerned yourself.'

'Yes, I am, but I didn't know any of them. I thought you'd know about things.'

'I don't, Mary. Simply rubbish burning in entirely the wrong place, I don't know who was responsible for that.'

Her eyes met Mary's blandly, and after a few moments Mary said, 'I can see you're all ready for the move on Monday morning. Do you need any help with anything?'

'No, you've been very good, Mary, I'm so grateful. I've got one or two things I'd like you to have, they're not much but you've been very kind.'

'But I don't expect anything, Margaret, really,' Mary demurred. 'You already gave me those beautiful dresses.' Margaret took her to a small table on which rested several potted plants and some china.

'But you can't give me these,' Mary said, picking up a figurine which she looked at admiringly.

'Well, that's something you always admired, I want you to have it.'

'But it's Royal Doulton!' Mary cried.

'That's right. You do like it, don't you, Mary?'

'Oh, I love it, but it's far too valuable to give away.'

'Mary, my father once told me that to give away something that has no value to the giver isn't a gift at all. I valued that, and I want you to have it and treasure it.'

'Oh, I will, indeed I will.'

Thirty-One

It was a Saturday afternoon in early March. The early morning sun had not fulfilled its potential and now the wind tore down the High Street and morning shoppers on their way home walked quickly with bent shoulders and quivering umbrellas. Margaret Gates viewed the rest of the day with little enthusiasm.

She had spent much of her adult life in this house but it didn't feel like home. It reminded her of her mother's strictures, the gossip of neighbours and dreams that had not materialized.

The neighbours, who had liked her mother, were suspicious of her. They had condemned her for leaving the house and her mother to live near some man they presumed she was having an affair with, largely, Margaret felt, because her mother had put her own suspicions into their heads.

She had already made up her mind that she would look for something else nearer to London but although she had feelers out nothing had really captured her attention.

She had not bothered to unpack many of her boxes, they remained stacked in her mother's bedroom with some of the smaller articles of furniture she had brought from the flat and which were not in keeping with her mother's more ponderous furniture.

There was a ring on her doorbell just after lunch and her heart sank at the thought of her mother's friend with the ambitious grand-daughter who was her most frequent visitor. So she was totally astounded to see Richard Lorival standing on her doorstep.

Heart pounding, she invited him into her living room, asking if he would like coffee or something else and receiving the reply that he was expecting his sister and her husband for the weekend and hadn't a great deal of time. They needed to talk.

She took the seat opposite, confused and unsure, but his smile was warm and friendly.

'I have a banking conference all next week. You know about it of course since Eric David-son will also be there. I had to see you today, I'm sorry it's all a bit of a rush.'

'You had to see me?'

'Yes. We go back a long way, Margaret, you know about my problems, particularly the more recent ones. I've decided to take up the oppor-tunity to work in Zurich, it's a seven-year con-tract and very lucrative. I've been thinking about it for some weeks now and have decided to accept it.'

'Why are you telling me?'

'Because I would like you to come with me. I would like my own secretary with me and we worked well together, didn't we? I couldn't ever

345

ask for a better secretary.'

She knew that she was staring at him in amazement and after a few moments he said, 'I'm sorry to have surprised you with this, Margaret, but think about it. Switzerland, Zurich. You've never been there, it will open all Europe up for you, new life, new friends, and I'll be there to look after you. Will you at least think about it?'

'I don't know what to say. It isn't something I ever envisaged and we haven't worked together for years.'

'I know. I was wrong about so many things, Margaret, but after Olivia died I couldn't even begin to think straight, I was tortured and vulnerable but that was then. Now I know where I'm going and I want you to come with me.'

'What about the second Mrs Lorival?'

'Leanne!'

'She wasn't happy here, could she be happy in Zurich?'

'Leanne and I are finished, surely you know that.'

'She's no longer your wife?'

'For the moment she is, we may decide to divorce, that is in the future. For now there are more important things to worry about. I've heard you've been thinking about moving nearer to London, but is that really what you want? Why not a completely new life in a new environment? Will you at least think about it?'

'When will you want to know?'

'Well, like I said, I'm away for a week. Can't

that be long enough, Margaret?'

He rose to his feet and pulled her up from her chair, and holding both her hands in a firm grip he looked down at her, serious and unsmiling. 'Promise you'll think about it, Margaret, a whole new world. Summer in Switzerland and the winter snows, the sort of advantages most women would die for.'

'I'll think about it, Richard.'

'And you do realize I must know your decision when I get back from the conference?'

'Yes.'

With a swift smile he put his arms around her and held her close for several minutes then he said, 'I'll let myself out, Margaret. I'll call next Saturday for your decision if that's all right.'

She nodded, then she went to stand at the window to see him wave to her from the door of his car.

She sank down into her chair but her mind was a blank. Think about it, he'd said, but her thoughts were a confused tangle of past and present. Oh, wasn't it just like a man to think he could change her entire life and have her accept it like a grateful puppy? It was true that six years ago she'd have been leaping about the room with delirious joy, but she was no longer the besotted little secretary with dreams of love everlasting.

As she passed the hall mirror on her way to the kitchen she stared at her reflection with customary honesty. She was a woman in her mid-thirties, not unattractive, with soft brown hair and hazel eyes, slender and average height and a dress sense that tended toward the genteel rather than the flamboyant.

How easy would it be to drift into what they had before, two people in a foreign land, one of them a man who women found attractive? It had been no problem for him in Hong Kong, it wouldn't be any problem in Zurich, and he was still married, still safe from predatory females on the lookout for romance.

He had given her a week to think about the rest of her life and it wasn't long enough. She could imagine how the people at the bank would react to her acceptance of his offer. The gossip among the girls, the cynical amusement with the men and Eric Davidson's less than convivial attitude. He would have no difficulty in replacing her, the women would fall over themselves in an attempt to capture his notice. Her acceptance of Richard's offer would not surprise him, but behind his amusement she would read his feelings that she was being stupid. He had known how Richard Lorival had hurt her and here she was asking for more of the same. The Eric Davidsons of this world had little time for women they would regard with utter disdain.

What would Richard's sister think of his decision, and how would she regard his invitation to his erstwhile secretary?

Margaret was thinking of Richard's sister just as she drove with her husband to see her brother. Nigel had already cautioned her to keep her thoughts to herself, offer no arguments and no interference, but Mina was not sure she could abide by his strictures.

As they sat down to lunch her eyes met Nigel's across the table, his full of caution which she felt she would be unable to emulate.

She had listened to Richard's enthusiastic account of all Zurich had to offer. Nigel had tried to change the subject but Mina would have none of it.

'But why Zurich, Richard?' she cried. 'You have a wonderful job here in London, a lovely home, or at least you had until she had a hand in it, and you can see more of Vanessa. Hong Kong was a disaster in many ways, don't you think Zurich could be another one?'

'Hong Kong wasn't a disaster, Mina, even if my marriage was,' he replied tersely.

'Well, who knows who you might meet in Zurich, some other woman looking for a rich husband and finding a man who is lonely and far away from home.'

'You make me sound easy meat, Mina.'

'I don't mean to, Richard, I'm your sister, I'm naturally concerned after seeing the other fiasco.'

'I can assure you, dear sister, I've no intention of making the same mistake twice. I've asked Margaret Gates to join me as my secretary, we worked well together for many years.'

'And will she accept, do you think?' Mina asked dryly.

'Well, I've asked her to think very carefully

about it. It would be a new life for her, an adventure, surely she'll see that for herself.'

'I'm not so sure. What about Vanessa, surely you've discussed this latest venture with her?'

'She thinks it's a great idea, has her eye on winter skiing and all that.'

The rest of the meal was eaten in silence and it was only when they were driving home that Mina said, 'I can't think that Margaret Gates will agree to work for him again. I always thought there was something going on between them after Olivia died, surely she won't give him the chance to hurt her again.'

'You don't know that for sure, Mina.'

'No, but I don't think I'd be far wrong. Oh, Nigel, I'm worried about all this. I don't want my brother to live in Switzerland, I don't want him getting entangled with some other woman we don't know, and if Margaret Gates decides to go back to him I feel I should have a chat to her first.'

'Gracious me, woman, why should you do that?'

'To ask her to keep an eye on him.'

Nigel stopped the car at the next lay-by, and viewing his wife with the utmost exasperation said, 'I should think that Margaret Gates is a woman with her feet planted firmly on the ground. She has a good job with the bank, she'll not have forgotten that Richard was hardly honest with her about Hong Kong, and personally I think if she goes off with him she's asking for trouble.'

'Trouble?'

'Yes. He's still married. He never mentions divorce, a fact that probably pleases them both. All Richard wants is a secretary who knows the score, knows all about the state of his private life including his marriage, and he's asking her to be content with a good salary, a different way of life and retirement at the end of it. If all she wants is a change of scenery, it shouldn't be enough.'

'You don't really like Richard, do you?'

'Of course I like him, that doesn't mean I have to agree with everything he says or does.'

'He's had a rotten time of late, surely even you can sympathize with that?'

'I do, but maybe he could have handled it better, maybe he let her get away with it, just like he let Olivia get away with things. You know that's true.'

She sat in silence and in the end he wondered if he had said too much. At last she turned to say, 'I'm sorry, Nigel, I shouldn't have interfered but Richard's my brother, my little brother who was always sweet-natured and easily bullied. I felt I had to say my piece, I promise I'll never interfere again.'

'Oh, but you will, Mina, you won't be able to help it, now let's get off home, forget Richard for an evening and try to rustle up some enthusiasm for a holiday – anywhere but Switzerland, my dear.'

Nigel knew full well that Mina's concerns would not go away but that in the end none of them would sway Richard from his future path. At the same time he spared a thought for Margaret Gates, who surely would need to think carefully about where life was leading her.

Richard, on the other hand, spent the evening planning what he would do in Zurich. Find somewhere to live, help Margaret find an apartment where she would be happy, meet new colleagues, build a new life. He had little doubt that Margaret would decide to join him. After all, what had she to lose? She'd be going to a new life entirely, and perhaps during the conference he could have a discreet word with Eric Davidson.

Her resignation would not trouble Davidson, there would be a queue of secretaries waiting to take her place, and he doubted if Davidson would care about her going.

Eric Davidson was a man concerned with his own career; the fate of his secretary was hardly likely to be a problem.

He'd wondered about Leanne and Davidson. He'd witnessed her flirting with him, seen her eyes light up whenever they'd met, and she'd been keen to put her financial affairs in his hands. All he knew about Davidson was that he was ambitious, a high-flyer and that he was unmarried. Obviously his career was the most important thing in his life, anything else was of secondary importance.

When Margaret Gates was going to work for him Richard had tried to find out as much as he could about Davidson's private life but without much success. He had numerous men friends, women liked him, they found him attractive and charming but whatever affairs he may have had had evidently been meaningless. There was no Mrs Davidson or long-standing liaison.

He had once hinted to Leanne that perhaps he was not really interested in women but she had said swiftly, 'That's nonsense, I should know.'

He hadn't elaborated on the subject and he'd surmised it had been wishful thinking on her part. Leanne believed that most men were captivated by her, she would not take kindly to the fact that one man in particular was not.

Personally he thought Davidson was brilliant in his chosen career and coldly calculating in everything else.

He felt sure that Margaret would be busily contemplating her new way of life and he knew he would have to reassure her that she had nothing to fear. That she would decide not to accept his offer never occurred to him. He was aware that she had loved him, their affair had been brief and at the wrong time but they had both moved on. It never entered his head that there might be some other man in her life. He'd never seen a strange car outside her flat, never seen a man visiting her or accompanying her in London, and he felt sure she'd have mentioned him if only briefly at one of the dinner parties he'd invited her to.

Richard retired to bed that Saturday night with a complacent belief in the unqualified success of his plans for the future.

Thirty-Two

A whole week had passed, a week when Margaret had slept badly, worried incessantly and reached no definite conclusion. Half of her wanted to go to Zurich, but the other half, the saner half, found one reason after the other why she should not go.

On Friday afternoon Richard would be returning from the conference and no doubt on Saturday morning he would call to see if she had made up her mind. He would expect her to jump at the idea, her doubts he would regard as silly and ridiculous, and yet the doubts persisted.

Suppose she went to Zurich with him, would she fall in love with him again? And how much would she expect from him? The telephone call she received from his sister didn't help.

Mina asked, 'Are you going to Zurich with my brother, Margaret? Are you sure it's what you want?'

'No, I'm not sure.'

'He seemed pretty confident that you would go.'

'I'm sure he did. Mina, it's one of the most important decisions I've ever been asked to make, it's so easy for him, it's a leap in the dark for me.'

'I know it is.'

'He'll expect me to tell him on Saturday and I'm still not sure. Have you any thoughts on the matter?'

'A great many. My husband says I shouldn't interfere but it seems to me that I haven't understood Richard for years. I never understood Leanne and sometimes I ask myself if he isn't still enthralled with the memory of Olivia.'

Those were the words that made Margaret decide what she should do, but Saturday morning found her weary after a sleepless night, and desperately anxious for the day to be over.

Richard arrived just before ten o'clock, greeting her with confident smiles as she opened the door. She had looked in the mirror that morning and been appalled at her lacklustre eyes and pallor. She had spent more time than usual with her make-up but she doubted if Richard would have noticed either her pallor or her attempts to hide it.

'Was the conference a success?' she asked him.

'Oh, the usual thing. We managed a game of golf, actually I played with Davidson, he managed to beat me.'

'Would you like coffee, Richard?'

'Not really, Margaret, Vanessa's coming to spend the weekend with me and I have a bit of shopping to do.'

'Doesn't Mrs Peterson do your shopping?'

'Most of it, but not everything. I hope you've managed to make your mind up, Margaret, I was sure you would have.'

'And what did you think my decision would be?'

For several seconds he stared at her uncertainly, then with a smile he said, 'You're an intelligent woman, Margaret, I'm sure you would see all the advantages. You have, haven't you?'

'Yes, I have, I've also seen the disadvantages.'

'Disadvantages! Surely there can't be any?'

'Not for you, Richard, a great many for me. I've been down this path before. I found it rocky and winding, to go down it again would be precarious. I have a home here, a good job, and a few good friends; in Zurich there would only be you and the commitment would be too much for both of us.'

'That's silly, Margaret. We're old friends, you'll have a better job in Switzerland and you'll make other friends. Surely you're not afraid of change?'

'Yes, I am, very afraid. I'm afraid of thinking my life is good only to find it isn't good at all. You've offered me a job, Richard, not a life. Here I have a life.'

'A life of sorts, Margaret. I can't believe I'm hearing all this. I can't believe you're thinking in this way.'

'I know. Years ago I'd have been ecstatic about it, I'd have thought I was the luckiest person in the world but this isn't the same me. I grew up, I stopped believing in fairy godmothers and Prince Charming. The world I found myself in was a much colder world but I've learned to live in it and appreciate its values.'

'So it's a definite no, Margaret?'

'Yes, Richard. I'm sorry. I do wish you well and hope that Zurich will be all you want it to be. No doubt I'll hear all about you through the grapevine.'

'I'm sure you will. I'm sure when you get around to thinking about things you'll realize you've made a big mistake.'

'Perhaps. I'll have to live with it, Richard.'

It had been easier than she'd thought. He hadn't tried to persuade her with promises of something more, a new togetherness, the ending of his marriage. No, he'd been the Richard she'd always really known, a man who would promise nothing, possessed by the past, perhaps still bewitched with a marriage that had ended on the tortuous road above the Bay of Salerno.

Later in the day Margaret telephoned Richard's sister to tell her that she would not be going to Zurich, and Mina said gently, 'I'm really not surprised, Margaret. Was Richard very sorry?'

'Yes. He told me I was foolish, he said he couldn't understand why I had turned it down, not even after he'd heard my side of the story. I wished him well.'

'So the torch has finally gone out, Margaret?'

'I thought it had gone out years ago, I just didn't want to relight it.'

'Well, there's still that attractive man you're

357

working for. He isn't married.'

Margaret laughed. 'Mina, he has a reputation more off-putting than Richard's. I'm happy to work for him, anything else would terrify me.'

Mina laughed. 'Well, good luck, Margaret. Thank you for letting me know.'

Now Margaret could look forward to the future. A new house nearer to London, perhaps, and her job on Monday. A new week, Richard finally out of her life and who knew what the future would bring?

It was the usual Monday morning. Mountains of mail and a boss who had greeted her with a cool smile and a formal good morning. The long list of people he needed to contact, and a hurried lunch with one or two of the girls who talked about what they'd done over the weekend, the bars and the boys, and who at the bank was interested in who. Margaret had heard it all before.

She could have opened their eyes wide with wonder if she'd told them about Zurich, a chance any one of them would have grasped with open arms. They would have all deemed her mad to have turned it down.

The rest of her lunchtimes that week she spent visiting estate agents and scanning their lists of properties which might interest her. Most of them were expensive and would make large inroads into her savings. The money her mother had left her had hardly been a fortune, but with the sale of the flat and eventually of her mother's house she would be able to afford something on offer.

She had little contact with Davidson during the next few days. He was constantly at some meeting or other, and yet once or twice when they did meet she thought he looked at her rather curiously until she wondered if Richard had said anything to him about Zurich. It didn't really matter, she wasn't going so she saw no point in telling him anything about it.

She was leaving his office on Friday afternoon when he said somewhat icily, 'Miss Gates, before you go might I ask when you are going to decide to tell me that I shall need to find a replacement to act as my secretary?'

She stared at him in some surprise before closing the door and returning to his desk where he indicated she should sit down.

'A replacement, Mr Davidson?' she enquired.

'That's what I said. It may have slipped your memory that I spent some time last week in the company of Richard Lorival when he was kind enough to inform me that he'd offered you your old job back, but this time in the more salubrious, or should I say romantic, environment of Zurich.'

'Did he tell you that I had decided to accept his offer?'

'Not in so many words, but he made it very clear that you would.'

'I declined the offer, Mr Davidson, I informed Mr Lorival last Saturday of my decision.'

His amazement was evident, to be quickly

followed by a brief smile before saying, 'I'm sorry, Miss Gates, perhaps I should have relied more on your integrity. Good afternoon.'

'You seem very surprised, Mr Davidson. You were so sure I would accept?'

He looked up, his expression bland, and in a voice tinged with satire he said, 'I think you would find that most people would be surprised at your turning down a chance to work in Zurich compared to what they would think of as mediocrity here.'

'Then perhaps I should be congratulated for being somewhat unusual. Good afternoon, Mr Davidson.'

All the way home she thought about her conversation with Eric Davidson. Of course Richard would think she would accept, she could imagine their conversation, Richard's certainty, Davidson's cynicism that once again she was rushing to his side like some hitherto abandoned puppy. Had it been so obvious when he'd dumped her six years before? Love and hatred merged into one, how they must all have pitied her. Well, this time Eric Davidson had been surprised, and hadn't there been a hint of admiration in his eyes?

Richard Lorival's latest manoeuvrings would be discussed among the men and their wives. He wouldn't care, he was shaking the dust of London off his shoes for seven years and if he decided to come back it would all be history.

How suddenly empty the house felt in spite of the bunch of spring daffodils she'd bought near the station. She lit the fire and made a cup of tea, deciding that she wasn't hungry, then she sat in front of the fire to watch the early evening news on the television.

It was the small television she had brought from the flat because her mother had always said she didn't want one. Perhaps when she got somewhere else to live she'd buy a larger one.

The heat of the room made her drowsy and it was the sudden ringing of the doorbell that brought her back to life. Her first thoughts were that it would be Richard hoping to get her to change her mind, and she was in two minds about opening the door. But then, why should she care? She'd said no once and she intended to abide by her decision, so squaring her shoulders she marched to the door, staring incredulously at the sight of Eric Davidson standing on the doorstep with a wry smile on his face.

'Well,' he said calmly, 'aren't you going to ask me in? It's awfully wet out here.'

'Oh, I'm sorry. Yes, please come in. May I take your coat?'

After hanging it up in the hall she said, 'Do come in, Mr Davidson, it's much warmer in here.'

She indicated a chair in front of the fire, then went to add more coal to it while he looked around appreciatively.

'It's certainly warmer in here,' he commented.

'Yes, Mr Davidson, I lit the fire as soon as I got home.'

'We're not in the office now, Margaret, can we

dispense with the mister?'

She stared at him helplessly before asking if he would like coffee or something stronger, and he said evenly, 'Coffee would be very nice. I had a brief snack in London, I wasn't very hungry.'

'No, I wasn't hungry either, please excuse me while I make coffee.'

While she busied herself in the kitchen she felt confused and troubled as to why he'd come, then he was standing behind her in the kitchen, taking the tray from her hands and carrying it into the living room. As their eyes met she said, 'I'm surprised to find you so domesticated, Eric.'

He smiled. 'Do we ever really know anybody else?' he said lightly.

'Perhaps not.'

Meeting her questioning gaze he said, 'You're surprised that I've come?'

'Very.'

'I don't like loose ends, particularly when the ends are so different from what I'd expected them to be. I was convinced you'd go to Zurich with Lorival.'

For a long moment she was silent, staring down into the fire, looking for answers she'd been afraid to ask herself before. At last she said softly, 'Six years ago I was desperately in love with him, I thought he'd turn to me after Olivia was killed and for a time he did. He was lonely and vulnerable and I was there, then he realized he wasn't ready for a real commitment and he had to get away. I hated him for the way he did it, that he didn't display more courage, and for six long years I told myself that I hated him, for what he did to me, for his marriage and his problems with Vanessa. When his marriage ended I told myself that I was delighted, it served him right, then I realized that it no longer mattered.

'When he asked me to go to Zurich with him in the first instance I was overjoyed, it was all coming right again, I'd waited a long time and it was going to be good again. Then I suddenly realized that like the last time all the good things were stacked on his side. He still had a wife, it suited them both, and more importantly I didn't love him at all, I didn't want the old times back, I wouldn't know what to do with them. That's when I decided I wasn't going to go to Zurich, I didn't want to go.'

'Was he very mortified?'

'Yes, I rather think he was. He'd been so sure I'd go with him. I've no doubt he'll find another Leanne, or some other woman totally unlike her if he's sensible.'

Eric laughed. 'Somebody different, hopefully. I had a surfeit of the second Mrs Lorival as you know. A very determined lady. I'd have been afraid to take her home to meet my mother.'

'Your mother?'

'Yes, I do have a mother. She lives in Winchester and tomorrow's her birthday so I've promised to spend the day with her. She lectures me on my lifestyle, my single state, my idiosyncrasies that don't always coincide with her own, but we'll spend a very happy day together and look forward to the next one. You'd like her.'

'My mother was unhappy about my feelings for Richard. I know that she was right, I was glad I was able to tell her so.'

'Yes, it helps to clear the air I think.'

'I really feel I should make something to eat. You have a fair journey back to London and you said you only had a snack.'

'Thank you, Margaret, but there's really no need. I have to get back now, I'm off early in the morning. I don't know what plans she's made, probably some party for her bridge friends and a chance for them to meet her less than perfect son.'

'I'm sure she doesn't think that.'

He smiled.

'Do you have brothers or sisters?' she asked.

'No. Just me to dote over and lecture.'

'Will you be staying overnight in Winchester?'

'No. We'll enjoy the party, then I'll leave them to their bridge evening. What do you do with yourself over the weekends?'

'Shop in the morning, visit the hairdresser, church on Sunday sometimes. When the weather's better I drive out into the country, perhaps spend a bit of time in my very small garden.'

'There's a very nice hotel not far from here, I once had dinner with John Gregson and his wife there. Avondale Hall, I think it was, do you know it?'

'I've heard of it but I've never been there.'

'Well, why don't I take you to lunch on Sunday? Call it my apology for believing you'd never be able to say no to Richard Lorival.'

'Well, you missed a very good chance of replacing me with perhaps somebody more efficient or glamorous, but there's really no need to offer me lunch as an apology.'

'When you know me better, my dear, you'll know that I really don't do things out of gratitude or as a sop for my conscience. I would like to take you out to lunch. I shall look forward to it.'

'Thank you, Eric.'

'I'll pick you up around eleven thirty.' He smiled and at the door he said, 'Until Sunday, then.'

She stood at the door, returning his wave, then waited until his car turned at the bend in the road.

Of course he'd invited her out to lunch because he thought she'd been courageous in turning Richard Lorival's offer down when he'd thought she'd have jumped at it because he didn't really believe she no longer cared for Richard, because she'd saved him the problem of replacing her in his office. Never because he suddenly found her in the least attractive or had any regard for her at all.

Upstairs in her bedroom she surveyed the clothes in the wardrobe. Evening dresses bought exclusively for Christmas dinners at the Lorivals', most of them years old. Business clothes for the office, the occasional afternoon dress for holidays she'd spent in discreet hotels with her mother.

She sat on the edge of her bed in disconsolate contemplation. Outside the office what did she really know about Eric Davidson? Most people said you got what you saw, in which case it was a handsome man with considerable charm, ambition and intelligence, but was there another Eric Davidson she hadn't really met?

In one brief evening he had surprised her with talk about his mother, a lady she hadn't known existed. What sort of feelings had made him take the trouble to drive to her home when he could have been doing so many other more interesting things?

Nothing in that wardrobe was suitable for lunch at Avondale Hall. She'd driven past it on several occasions, a beautiful hall surrounded by expensive cars owned by obviously affluent people.

On Sunday she'd be in the company of a rich man driving an expensive Jaguar, a man other men could respect and other women envy her for and tomorrow morning she'd shop for something she couldn't really afford in an endeavour not to let him down.

She could imagine the raised eyebrows if some of the executives from the bank were dining there. Once it had annoyed Richard; she doubted if Eric Davidson would be fazed by it, he was that sort of man.

How would she look back on it in future

years? As something incredibly special or something to feel grateful for and hopefully soon forgotten?

Thirty-Three

Margaret arrived at Marcello's on Saturday morning just as they were opening for the day. She had decided to get there early because she didn't want to encounter any of their usual customers like Mrs Turnbull or Mrs Eastman, who invariably shopped there on Saturday mornings.

The assistant greeted her with a smile, saying, 'We have a very good selection of new clothes, Miss Gates, the sort of things you like, business clothes and in your colours too.'

'Well, I am actually looking for something a little more dressy, I seem to have a surfeit of business clothes.'

'Really? Well, do sit down and I'll show you what we have. I'm sure there'll be something to suit you. What exactly are you thinking of?'

'A dress. Not my usual colour.'

'Well, you have always stated a preference for navy, beige or grey. What other colour do you have in mind?'

'I want something that goes with my camel coat.'

367

'Such a lovely coat, didn't you buy it from us?'

'Yes. So I think red is definitely out.'

'Yes, perhaps so. This blue dress is very nice, quite plain and classy, what do you think?'

She produced a dress in French navy which was elegant but somehow or other too much like the navy blues she'd worn so long and so often.

'Well, I was really thinking of a change. I know that dress is lighter than my usual blues but have you nothing else?'

From the corner of the room the owner's voice called out, 'That green dress, Miss Edison, wonderful for the lady's colouring and ideal to wear under camel.'

As soon as she saw it Margaret knew it was what she was looking for. In heavy sage green wool georgette it was discreetly plain, decidedly elegant, and by this time the owner as well as the assistant was enthusiastically telling her it was just right for her colouring and urging her to try it on.

As she surveyed herself in the mirror it seemed to Margaret that she was looking at another person, a slender woman with a figure entirely enhanced by the folds of the dress, a colour that emphasized her hazel eyes and the texture of her skin.

Common sense told her it would hang in the wardrobe alongside all those other extravagances she had worn only once or twice, and it was very expensive. Even as she wrote out her cheque she deplored her stupidity in buying it, but for one day she had to be special, to dine at Avondale Hall with a handsome, sophisticated man she barely knew, but a man she couldn't let down any more than she could let herself down.

As she left the shop carrying her exquisitely wrapped parcel Mrs Eastman was just stepping out of her husband's car at the kerb, and seeing Margaret leaving she said brightly, 'Shopping early, then? Did you find what you wanted?'

'I think so, Mrs Eastman.'

'For something very special?'

Margaret smiled. 'They have a very good selection this morning, Mrs Eastman, I hope you find something,' then with another smile she hurried away.

Margaret didn't hear the remark she passed to her husband. 'I wonder if she's dining with Richard Lorival and that's what makes it so special. Isn't he leaving for Switzerland soon?'

Her husband didn't bother to reply, he was only too familiar with his wife's sly comments.

Margaret's next call was at her hairdresser's, but this time she amazed him by saying, 'Something a bit different this morning, Jules, something not quite so severe.'

Jules beamed. 'I've been waiting for you to say that for years, Miss Gates. A softness to frame your face, and how about a little brightener? You have such pretty hair, what is wrong with a little highlighting?'

Margaret allowed him to do his worst, or best as it turned out to be, and as she surveyed the results she couldn't think why she'd never had

369

the courage to allow him to change her style before.

She spent some time looking in the shoe shops but decided that her shoes were adequate, indeed she was on the verge of moving away when a voice greeted her with the words, 'Margaret, I had to look at you twice. I thought it was you and then I thought no, it couldn't be. You've changed your hairstyle, you look absolutely beautiful.'

It was Mary Barrow, her neighbour at the flats, and in the next few minutes she was accepting coffee in a nearby café and listening to Mary saying, 'Why ever did you never have your hair done like that before, you look ten years younger and twice as beautiful.'

'I'm not beautiful at all, but I thought I needed a change.'

'But you are beautiful, Margaret, and you've been shopping at Marcello's, expensive. Some great occasion?'

'Not really. Lunch tomorrow with my boss.'

'Where?'

'At Avondale Hall.'

'Really? Your old boss or your new one?'

'He isn't new, Mary, I've worked for him for over six years, but there's nothing to it, simply a lunch date, probably to discuss business.'

'Don't men reserve lunch dates during business hours when they want to discuss business, not on a Sunday?'

'Well, I can assure you, Mary, this is a one-off. He called to see me the other evening, I hadn't been feeling well, I think he felt rather sorry for me.'

'Men don't ask women out because they feel sorry for them.'

'He thought I needed cheering up.'

'Was that anything to do with your old boss leaving the country?'

'How do you know about that?'

'Mrs Peterson told me, I doubt if she knows where she is these days.'

'No. It must be very difficult for her, but I can assure you, Mary, my luncheon date has nothing to do with the past. Like I said, it's a one-off. The new dress is for my holiday in the summer, it was time I had one.'

For some strange reason she didn't feel like spending the rest of the day on her own so she asked Mary if she would like to go back to the house with her but to her surprise Mary said, 'Any other time I'd have loved to, Margaret, but today we're taking some of the kids on a ramble. Some of their parents are coming and then we're having tea in some old farmhouse. I'm not sure it's a good idea in March but Mr Dowling dreamed it up and we all said we'd support him.'

'Mr Dowling seems to have become something of a live wire.'

She did not miss Mary's blushes as she said quickly, 'He's very good with the children and very enterprising. He's made a great difference to the school.'

'I'm glad, Mary. Well, I must get back, I've

done all my shopping and I'm not going out again today.'

'Well, do enjoy tomorrow, Margaret, it looks a beautiful place, I hope its all very worthy of the new dress and the hair.'

Margaret smiled. She couldn't explain the reservations she was feeling.

She stood in front of the long mirror in her bedroom on Sunday morning, surveying herself in her new dress and liking what she saw. She'd never been a fashion follower, she'd invariably dressed for the sort of life she lived and even on holidays she had never stood out from the crowd. This morning she was looking at a slender woman in a dress that flattered her figure and brought out the colour of her eyes and hair. The result was classical and elegant and as she walked into the living room she saw by the clock that she had an hour to wait.

She read the morning paper, did the crossword and surveyed the road, which was quiet. Most of her neighbours would have gone to church and the hands of the clock seemed to be moving so slowly.

The dress did look well with the camel coat, and not wishing to keep Eric waiting, she slipped it on and sat nervously leafing through a magazine.

He was late. Eleven thirty had come and gone and Margaret's insecurities piled up around her. He was not coming, he'd regretted asking her, tomorrow he'd be full of apologies and excuses and as the minutes increased so did her anxieties and her anger. She should have known after her experience with Richard Lorival that it could happen again. Now she could take off her coat, hang the dress at the back of the wardrobe and get into the things she normally wore on a Sunday afternoon.

She went one more time to the window, trembling, agitated, and then as she looked down the road she saw his car and the relief was so enormous she sank down on to the nearest chair.

The ringing of her doorbell sent her hurrying to the door and he stood smiling, saying, 'I'm sorry I'm late, Margaret, there was an accident on the road, bit of a hold-up.'

Was it really her voice saying, 'It doesn't matter, you're not very late.'

As she walked towards him across the foyer he thought he had never really seen her before. She had left her coat in the ladies' cloakroom and he was well aware that other eyes were looking at her with admiration. Looking down at her with a smile, he said, 'You're looking very elegant this morning, Margaret, you make me feel very privileged.'

She smiled. She knew she was going to enjoy the day, even if that was all there would ever be. They sat in the window of the lounge before lunch and as she sipped her martini she felt herself becoming more and more relaxed. This was the Eric Davidson who had climbed steadily in his chosen profession through his charm and his acumen, but Margaret was finding a sincerity in him, a truly genuine friendliness.

The lunch that followed was excellent, the music unobtrusive, the service quietly dignified, and as they drank their coffee later in the lounge Margaret's inhibitions left her. They chatted and laughed together and there seemed so much to talk about.

She asked him about his mother's birthday party, and with a laugh he said, 'It's exactly the same every year, her bridge friends and their chatter. I spent most of the afternoon looking at photographs of grandchildren, weddings and babies. I was careful to be duly flattering, interested and totally admiring and they were equally careful to congratulate my mother on having a caring and charming son.'

'I'm sure your mother agreed with them,' Margaret said.

'Oh, she did, it was only when we were on our own that she said she'd have preferred me to be visiting her with a nice wife and several children instead of living in solitary state and hobnobbing with some dubious girl or other.'

'And are you?'

'She tells herself I am, I think she would approve of you.'

'Older, staider, more ordinary.'

'You said that, Margaret, not I. My mother gives free range to her imagination. She has a son who lives in his bachelor pad in London, a son who keeps a harem of young, nubile beauties with great expectations and none of her values.'

'But she is very proud of you nonetheless.'

374

'I had good parents. My father was a banker, they gave me a good education, we lived well. They were both proud of my prowess at school and the success I made of my chosen profession. When the war came I went into the army, got a good commission and I don't really think either of them were too happy when I decided to work in Hong Kong and Singapore. I came back to England when my father died. My mother decided to move house and she's happy living in Winchester. She knows if she needs me I'll be there, but it doesn't stop her wishing I was the sort of son her friends lay claim to. Did you ever have problems with your mother, Margaret?'

'Yes, a great many. She didn't approve of my working at Richard's house and she was even more unhappy when I moved into my flat. She was happy when I went back to working at the bank in London.'

'Did she ask questions about me?'

'I'm afraid so. How old you were, if you had a wife, were you friendly or distant, were you the sort of man to erase Richard Lorival from my life.'

He laughed. 'And I'm sure you told her I was an unmarried, ambitious philanderer who was most unlikely ever to remove decent, upstanding Richard from your thoughts. Am I right?'

Margaret smiled.

'I know something of the gossip that goes on at the bank. How does the world view a bachelor in his forties, a man who surrounds himself with a coterie of women, perhaps even some married women? Or perhaps even a man who isn't interested in women? I rather think I fall into the earlier category.'

The lounge had filled up with people and when Eric smiled at somebody sitting across the room she turned her head to see Mr and Mrs Eastman sitting in the company of two other people.

She smiled uncertainly, the two women were intrigued, the men less so, and Eric said dryly, 'Does it bother you that they're here, Margaret?'

'Mrs Eastman is a bit of a gossip. I met her yesterday in town, she's not averse to asking questions.'

'Really? I've always found him agreeable, I don't know his wife.'

'But you met her at the Lorivals' Christmas party.'

'Did I? I can't honestly say I remember any of the wives, with my reputation you'd think I'd remember the wives and forget the husbands.'

'Honestly, Eric, your reputation is such that any one of those junior secretaries would give anything to change places with me.'

He smiled. 'Only last week I thought it likely I would have been promoting one of them to take your place. Every day I was getting more and more annoyed, wondering when you were going to tell me you were leaving, Lorival had seemed so sure that you would go with him. I think it was his confidence that jarred on me. The belief that you wouldn't be able to say no. When you told me you'd decided against it I

376

asked myself how much it had cost you to decline. Our conversation at the bank had been so bland, it hid too many undercurrents, I had to see you, and yet I couldn't understand why it was suddenly so important to me.'

'I think I can understand that. Richard said he didn't like change, he liked his life to flow like a peaceful river.'

'Well, he stirred a few muddy waters when he married Leanne.'

'I couldn't understand her putting her financial affairs in your hands when her husband was in the same profession. Why not in his?'

'Talk never loses anything, Margaret. I'd heard something about her when I was in Hong Kong, rich, floundering marriage, spoilt. She got Richard and it wasn't working. She was bored with her life in England, bored with a husband who had seemed exciting in Hong Kong and not come up to her expectations. I didn't want to handle her money even when business is business. I certainly didn't want an affair with Leanne, which is what she was hoping for.'

'Why are you so sure?'

'My dear girl, she was very obvious, and very angry when it didn't materialize. On that night I took her out to dinner I was unhappy with the situation. I knew what she wanted but without being downright pitiless how could I get out of it? Fortunately, fate came to my assistance in the shape of an American chap I knew and I was able to extricate myself from a very unsavoury predicament. I knew she was furious, but it had to be.'

Margaret could have told him at that moment exactly how that fury had erupted the next morning but she refrained. It was over, the hurts and the anger, time for all of them to move on.

Looking through the window towards the distant hills, Eric watched a pale, watery sun endeavour to climb through the clouds and then said, 'The day's improving. What do you say we drive around for a while, find some cosy little cottage where we can have afternoon tea before the day changes yet again?'

'I'm not sure I could eat another thing.'

'Oh well, we'll drive on anyway. You know this area better than I do so you can direct me.'

They drove mostly in silence, but it was a comfortable silence between two mature people who had no need for small talk. They never found the cosy tearoom Eric had envisaged but for a while they parked on the banks of the river and sat watching the men fishing along its banks.

'My father used to take me fishing when I was a little girl,' Margaret confided. 'He said I chatted too much and frightened the fish away. What sort of things did you do?'

'I went away to school, but in the summer my father had a boat moored in the Solent. One of these days I keep thinking I'll buy a boat and catch up on old times.'

As they sat in silence she was reflecting on their different lifestyles. A public schoolboy from a rich family background and a girl from a respectable, ordinary family with no particular acumen.

She'd felt it with Richard Lorival and she'd been fool enough to think it didn't matter to him. Now, sadder and wiser, she knew it mattered all too much.

As they drove back Eric said, 'The clouds are darkening, it's beginning to look like a storm.'

'Yes, I thought so too. What a shame, the day started out so beautifully.'

Indeed, long before they reached Margaret's house the rain was coming down in torrents and he struggled with a golf umbrella he found in the car and they ran laughing to the front door.

She didn't invite him in, instead she stood with an outstretched hand, saying, 'I'm sorry you're going to have such a wretched journey home, Eric, but it has been a wonderful day, thank you so much.'

He smiled down at her. 'Yes, I've enjoyed it too, Margaret, and tomorrow it's the bank as usual. I'll telephone you when I get back just to end what's left of the day.'

The house felt cold so she put a match to the fire and went into the kitchen to make herself a cup of tea. All the way home she'd agonized about whether she should invite him in, but in the end she'd decided against it. They'd spent a lovely day together, she didn't want him to think she expected more, but she couldn't help feeling disappointed.

As she slipped into a sweater and a pair of

slacks she viewed her dress with some misgiving. It was beautiful. When would she next have the opportunity to wear it?

She could hear the rain beating against the windows, see the swaying trees along the road and she was glad to draw the curtains and put on the lamps. She thought about him driving back to London in the storm and hoped the ending wouldn't make him wish he'd never bothered about her.

It was nearly twelve o'clock when the telephone rang and his first words were, 'I hope you hadn't gone to bed, Margaret. If so, I'm sorry that I couldn't call earlier, I had hold-ups this morning and another on the way home.'

'I wasn't in bed, Eric, I'm glad you arrived home safely.'

'My mother rang up in a panic. Apparently she's been trying to get me all afternoon. I explained how I'd spent my day and with whom.'

'I hope you told her that I've worked for you for over six years, am in my mid-thirties and not one of the glamorous girls she always associates you with.'

'I told her who you were, I also told her that you were pretty and extremely nice. I know the next move she'll make.'

Margaret laughed, secretly flattered. 'And what will that be?'

'That I should take you down there, just to reassure her that I'm telling the truth.'

'Oh, surely not!'

'You don't know my mother, Margaret. You'd

380

like her.'

'Well, I doubt I shall ever meet her, so we'll just have to hope you managed to put her mind at rest.' She tried to sound casual, but she felt anything but.

There was a long pause before he finally spoke. 'Margaret, I know that we work together, and that you're probably very cautious after what happened with Lorival – once bitten twice shy and all that – but I had hoped we could see each other again ... What I mean to say is ... Well, I thought...'

Her heart began to beat rapidly. All this time she had stopped herself from thinking of him as anything but her boss, had allowed herself to believe that the gossips were right and he was a confirmed bachelor. Now she found herself hoping against hope that – that what, exactly? She didn't know, hadn't allowed herself even the glimmer of a hope that happiness could be hers. She sank heavily into a chair.

'Oh!'

'Margaret, are you all right? I'm sorry, I've shocked you, offended you—'

'No, no it isn't that!' Anything but that! 'It's just so sudden. I had no idea...'

'Well, to tell you the truth, neither did I, until today. But when I saw you looking so beautiful and realized how at ease I was in your company I finally admitted to myself that you are more – much more – than just a secretary to me. For years I've told myself that I was too busy to feel lonely, that my life was meant to take a different course, but now...'

His voice trailed away, leaving her head spinning.

'But work, the gossip—'

'None of it matters. All that matters is how I feel about you. For the first time in my life I feel ready to open myself up to another person, and that person is you.'

And suddenly it was all too much for her. All the tears she'd held back over the years, all the hope she'd buried deep down inside herself came bubbling to the surface and she found herself sobbing uncontrollably.

'Margaret, dear Margaret, please don't cry. I'm so sorry I've upset you. It was too soon, I should have realized that.'

'No, no, it isn't too soon.' She heard the words come tumbling out of her mouth but had no control over them.

'So you're saying ... that I can hope?'

'Oh, Eric, there's no need to hope, can't you see that?'

'I can't do this over the telephone. I need to see you. I'm coming to you!'

'But Eric, it's the middle of the night!'

'No, Margaret, it's the first day of the rest of our lives together.'